SHADOW OF THE WITCH

KIRSTEN WEISS

misterio press

COPYRIGHT

Visit the author website to sign up for updates on upcoming books and fun, free stuff: KirstenWeiss.com

ABOUT SHADOW OF THE WITCH

WILL FORTUNE FAVOR THE brave, or the grave?

In the shadow of tragedy, Brandy embarks on a quest for answers that leads to a mobster's mansion in Lake Tahoe. But what she finds within the Dragon House's walls is more than she bargained for: a murdered man and a medieval scroll on the alchemy of luck.

Digging deeper into the mystical world of luck and chance, Brandy becomes trapped in a web of magic and deception that threatens to unravel her reality. Brandy must race against time to solve the murder and decipher the text. And if she can't confront her deepest fears, she may lose everything.

Will fortune favor the brave, or will the grave claim her?

A mystery for readers who appreciate the teachings of Paolo Coelho and believe spiritual transformation doesn't mean chasing a destiny that leaves the world behind. *Shadow of the Witch* is an interactive, metaphysical mystery from the Mystery School Series that will leave readers spellbound.

Featuring Riga Hayworth!

The cover of Shadow of the Witch *hides a secret only YOU can unlock! Scan the QR code inside to watch the cover come to life in augmented reality. Dive into the mystery!*

INTRODUCING THE UNTAROT APP: STEP INTO THE ENCHANTMENT OF KIRSTEN WEISS'S MYSTERY SCHOOL SERIES!

EMBARK ON A JOURNEY that intertwines fiction and reality as you dive into the captivating world of Kirsten Weiss's upcoming Mystery School series. With the UnTarot app, you can wield the very cards the characters from the books utilize, tapping into a wellspring of ancient wisdom and boundless magic.

Imagine harnessing the power of the UnTarot cards to unlock hidden insights and unravel the threads of fate. With the UnTarot app, you gain access to a treasure trove of captivating readings and interpretations. As you explore this mystical experience, you'll be drawn into a world where the boundaries between fiction and reality blur.

- **Authentic Connection:** Immerse yourself in the enchanting ambiance of the Mystery School series. The UnTarot app faithfully captures the essence of the books, allowing you to connect with the characters and their adventures on a whole new level.

- **Ancient Wisdom, Modern Convenience:** The UnTarot app marries centuries-old divination techniques with cutting-edge technology, creating an accessible experience for both seasoned practitioners and curious novices.

- **Free Exploration**: Yes, you read that right! The UnTarot app is entirely FREE, ensuring that everyone can join in the magical journey of self-discovery, insight, and revelation.

Ready to embark on a journey that defies the boundaries of time and space? The UnTarot app beckons you to step into the wondrous world of Kirsten Weiss's Mystery School series. Download the UnTarot app and let the magic unfold before your very eyes!

Download the UnTarot app for FREE today and embrace the enchantment that awaits!

CONTENTS

To Karen
Extraordinary

A NOTE TO THE READER

THIS WORK OF METAPHYSICAL fiction includes supplementary emails from the Mystery School, including worksheets. You can skip them, skim them, or work through them. It's your book and your choice! Have fun with it!

If you do play with the worksheets, I'd love to invite you to post photos of your completed exercise sheets (feel free to color them in), quotes, and/or insights related to *Legacy of the Witch* and the UnTarot on social media using the hashtag #MysterySchool, #UnTarot, or #KirstenWeiss so I can see and then repost yours on my page! If you'd like weekly mystery school inspiration, I invite you to join the school's email newsletter at https://bit.ly/mystery-awaits

This book and the exercises in it can be read on your own, with a friend, or as part of a book club. You can also create your own Mystery School: a group of people who gather together to discuss the book, the UnTarot concepts, and the exercises. See the book club questions at the back of this book for some ideas of things to discuss.

THE COVER HOLDS A SECRET

SCAN THIS QR CODE to bring *Shadow of the Witch* to life in augmented reality. Watch as the mysteries of the cover unravel in a breathtaking video experience.

Scan me

THE AD

Have you been feeling lost?

Is there a hollowness in your heart of loss, of unfulfilled purpose, of unfulfilled destiny?

We know how that feels.

It's a painful place to live.

Are you ready to fill your heart and find the community, the family, and the collective that is committed to the same mission?

The mission of serving and healing the world by sharing your magic, by opening your heart, by transforming into your best self?

We're called the Mystery School.

We're a global collective of thousands of people, all committed to serving the universe by sharing our magic with the world.

There is no greater feeling than figuring out how to share your light, your energy, your voice and making a meaningful difference in the lives of others.

So, if you want to finally feel like you are home, like you have community, like you have a mission in your life, and you want to serve the collective in a deep way, join us in the Mystery School.

The transformation you'll experience is a feeling you can't imagine. You'll get all the support you need on this path. You're not alone anymore.

https://bit.ly/mystery-awaits

CHAPTER I

SHE DIED AT 3:58 AM on a Nevada highway. It was February 2nd—neither a particularly lucky or unlucky day. But it was the day my sister was killed, which makes the date unlucky for me, unluckier for her.

The accident was random. A driver swerved onto the shoulder, over corrected, and plowed head-on into my sister's pickup.

My sister Sarah always drove the speed limit. *Exactly* the speed limit. I'd teased her about it.

And I couldn't stop wondering if she'd gone a mile per hour faster or slower that morning, if she'd spent an extra moment to chat with someone at the gas station, if she'd stopped an extra second at a light, if the accident might have been avoided or not been so deadly.

But none of that happened. Instead, chance took her out with the precision of a trained hitman.

Chance.

Fate.

Luck.

It had become close to an obsession in the months since, and it had brought me here—to a Lake Tahoe highway. I eased up, braking, my SUV following too close behind a slow-moving Cadillac. I was more sensitive to accidents now.

The sapphire lake winked between pines. Distance gathered between the Caddy and my car on the rolling, winding road, and I glanced at the dash clock. I'd be late if the guy in front of me didn't start hitting the speed limit.

My knuckles whitened on the wheel. If chance could maneuver two people into a single deadly moment, was it possible I could maneuver chance into something good? Something to make up for the awful? Didn't chance owe me that?

I couldn't let the idea go.

I'd attended lectures. I'd pored over books by occultists and fringe scientists. I acquired translations of ancient texts. But even the ancients seemed to believe Fortuna was uncontrollable, unbiddable.

I'd even consulted AI. It had returned a bland, unsatisfying response. But I suspected AI would be taking over my Silicon Valley job soon, so maybe I was prejudiced.

Was luck something we created? Was it mere chaos?

I liked the first answer, feared the second, and suspected there was a third I hadn't yet grasped.

I'd hired a specialist in old books to find out-of-print texts for me. I'd dipped into online occult chatrooms. I'd even succumbed to an ad on social media and joined an email mystery school.

The Caddy's brake lights flared, and it turned down a road toward the lake. I stepped on the gas and rolled my window down. Though autumn chilled the morning, I wanted to breathe the Tahoe air.

The world had changed, and I hated it. I couldn't go back, couldn't tell my baby sister not to get in that pickup, couldn't say goodbye.

I'd tried to return to my normal routine—the routine before Sarah's accident. Routines are supposed to be healing.

Routine felt like a betrayal.

I couldn't stop thinking of things I'd known we'd do together as a matter of course. Trips we'd planned to take. Wine we'd planned to drink. And now, we wouldn't.

I gave up on rebuilding my routine. The routine was gone. My work had fallen apart—though my company hadn't realized it. My workaholism had given way to a new obsession: luck. I quit my job before they could find out.

And then I discovered the luck text.

To be accurate, the expert I'd hired discovered it for me—a fragment of scroll that shouldn't exist. But it did, and another fragment lived in the hands of a collector at Lake Tahoe.

The fragment cost most of what was left of my savings. My grip on the steering wheel tightened. I still wasn't sure if the scroll was worth it. I hoped I'd soon find out.

A panther slunk along the earthen roadside. I blinked, and it vanished. But my attention had been caught, and I sucked in a breath. An orange kitten trotted ahead, oblivious to the cars roaring past.

I slammed on my brakes and pulled over. Belatedly, I glanced in my rearview mirror, catching a glimpse of my silvering hair, hazel eyes, and a minivan. The minivan swerved and barreled past.

I cursed, stomach tightening, and edged over until my bumper nearly brushed a pine. My SUV tilted on the sloping shoulder. I waited for a pickup to pass, then opened my door.

The door was heavy at this angle. It took me longer than it should have to drag my fifty-something form from the car. My fitness routine had fallen by the wayside, and I'd put on ten pounds of grief.

The afternoon air was chill, the sun lowering between the trees. Blindly, I reached inside and drew out a furry vest.

My heart clenched. *My sister's vest.* Fake fur, of course. Sarah may have had the soul of a poet, but she'd been a genius with her money.

Grimacing, I slipped into it. The vest had a hippy vibe, wasn't my style, and didn't go with my button-up blouse and khaki slacks. But that didn't matter on a cat rescue mission.

I hurried to the other side of the SUV. The kitten was gone.

I adjusted my vest and scanned the pines. I'd imagined a panther. If I'd imagined the kitten too, I was really...

The kitten crawled through a stand of manzanita, its belly low to the ground. I exhaled shakily.

"Here kitty." I moved slowly toward it. Was it feral? I swiped my hand over my bobbed hair. If it was wild, my odds of retrieving the animal were low.

The kitten turned its head and blinked gold-brown eyes.

My heart tightened. They were the same eyes as our childhood cat, Danger. Sarah and I had found him on our doormat at the cabin our family rented every year at Flathead Lake. It had taken a full day of begging, but our parents had let us keep him.

The kitten trotted toward me and bumped the pointy toe of my alligator boots. I squatted to run my finger along his spine.

The cat let me pet him, and I picked him up. He curled against my vest and purred. Not wild then, but there was no collar.

"All right then." I ran a finger along the top of his striped head. There were bits of dirt and bracken in his fur, but he looked healthy. "I'll figure out what to do with you later."

Returning with the kitten to my SUV, I settled him on my lap. His claws dug into my slacks. I winced and started the car. He looked so much like Danger it was uncanny. But the resemblance was a coincidence, no more.

Ten minutes later I drew up to the iron gates of a stone-walled estate. An impersonal electronic eye studied me while I rolled down the window and reached for the intercom.

The gates swung open before I could press the black button. Swallowing down my erratically beating heart, I drove inside.

The driveway was long, sloping, and graveled. Stones pinged off my car's undercarriage, and I wondered if the gravel was part of the estate's defenses, an audible warning of intruders. A curving, wooden roofline emerged above the pines.

I stopped a good twenty yards from the house and gaped.

Lake Tahoe has a famous Scandinavian castle called Vikingsholm, built of stone and wood. This house topped it.

Varnished red logs stacked three stories high and shaped into pitched roofs with curving dragons slinking along the eaves. Turrets and towers topped with onion domes and spires. Balustrades and fretwork painted a deep yellow. And the lake spread like a cold, glittering gem behind the mansion.

I'd stepped into a fairytale. An alternate dimension.

The kitten dug his claws deeper into my khakis, bringing me back to myself. I'd read about Wingate Weald and his Scandinavian *dragenstil* house. But seeing it in person was a very different level of understanding.

Someone rapped on my window. I jumped in my seat.

A man with curling salt and pepper hair and a matching, neatly trimmed beard scowled. Despite his graying hair, he had a young vibe, his tanned face smooth except for the lines spoking from the corners of his brown eyes.

I rolled down the window. "Hi, are—?"

His frown deepened. "Didn't you hear me honking? You're blocking me in." He jerked his chin toward a white Honda Accord, pockmarked from hail damage.

My face heated. "Sorry. I was just so..." I motioned toward the house.

"Stop gawking and move your..." His gaze raked me. "...car."

"Right. Sorry." I pulled forward and touched my straight, silvery hair.

Insecurity wriggled in my chest, and I was too damn old for insecurity. But my ten extra pounds of grief weight weren't exactly confidence-building.

Not that I cared what *he* thought. I hadn't been blocking him in *that* long.

The man stalked to his battered Honda, the movements of his lean figure smooth beneath his parka and baggy jeans. Getting into his Honda, he roared up the drive, scattering gravel in his wake.

I pulled up behind a sleek black Lincoln and a blue Subaru SUV, and I detached the kitten from my slacks. "Don't do anything I wouldn't do." I set him on the passenger seat.

The kitten yawned, curled into a tighter ball, and closed his eyes.

I hesitated. I didn't like leaving animals in cars. The morning was nippy, clouds piled against the snow-topped, eastern Sierras. But I couldn't exactly bring him inside. According to my research, my host hated cats.

I grabbed my satchel and closed the door carefully so as not to wake the kitten. Then I tugged down the hem of my sister's furry vest and walked up the mansion's reddish wooden steps. I looked for a doorbell, couldn't find it, and raised my hand to knock.

The door opened before I got a chance.

The man inside was well over six-feet tall. Beneath his green Henley, he had the build of a basketball player. He smiled, his teeth white against his dark skin, the skin around his pale-brown eyes crinkling. "Brandy Bounds?"

"That's me."

"He's expecting you." The man stepped aside.

I stepped over the threshold, my eyes adjusting to the dim light, and I inhaled the ghosts of cut pines. But the scent was just another phantom—another hallucination. The house had been built in the 1930s.

I imagined there *would* be spirits here—of the original owner, of pets, and perhaps of the odd guest. But imagination was all I had.

I'd been expecting blue-beamed ceilings and more dragon carvings inside. But the mansion's foyer was Scandinavian modern. Charcoal walls decorated with bleak modern art. Parquet floors and blond wood furniture with beige cushions.

I faced the man. "And you are...?"

"Tobin, the estate manager. Tobin Washington."

I smiled. "Nice to meet you."

He turned and walked down the spacious hall. The tips of my ears heated. So far, I was oh-for-two when it came to polite introductions. But what had I expected?

Tobin stopped beside a wide, open doorway. He motioned me inside.

I walked into a chocolate-colored room with floor-to-ceiling windows overlooking the lake and Sierras. In the center of the room, a fire burned in a metal, bowl-shaped firepit atop a granite slab. The firepit must have been gas, because the flames leapt between glass stones the color of charcoal. A rounded near-black hood hovered above the fire.

Four rounded beige chairs bracketed a lower granite table beside it. Three of the occupants rose—two men about my age, in their forties or fifties—and a fit, muscular man in his mid-sixties. I would have pegged him for fifty as well if I hadn't already studied photos of him: Wingate Weald, ostensible investment manager.

The fourth, an auburn-haired woman of indeterminate age, tilted her head. She looked oddly familiar, but I couldn't place her. The woman's eyes seemed to gleam purple in the flickering firelight, and then they were brown again.

A silence fell that stripped me bare. I stared back at the four, but didn't really take in what I was seeing, only getting distorted impressions. The woman a witch. One of the men a funeral director. The youngish blond man had an air of unreality about him. And the older man...

My heartbeat raced, seeking escape. I couldn't do this.

I had to do this.

"Brandy." The name, spoken in a rich baritone, broke the spell that held me.

Wingate strode forward, broad hand extended. His thick white hair was slicked back against his head. He pumped my hand enthusiastically, and I smothered a wince at his grip strength. "Glad you could make it."

Uneasily, I glanced at the others. Was I the only one who saw something feral in Wingate's green eyes? His civilized charcoal suit, his pristine white shirt open at the throat to expose a gold four-leaf-clover charm, did nothing to bely this impression.

"I didn't know you had guests," I managed to say. I'd counted on us being alone. I'd dreaded it, too.

"Everyone, this is Brandy Bounds. She's the ex-Chief Operating Officer *and* Chief Financial Officer for a rather impressive Silicon Valley tech company." Wingate met my gaze. "I heard they had to hire two people to replace you, which either makes her a savant or a workaholic. And she did it all as a single mother. I hear he's a Stanford grad?"

Heat flared at the front of my skull. *Don't talk about my son.* I smiled. "I enjoy my work," I said, heart pumping. I stopped myself from wiping my palms on my slacks.

"And yet you quit your career. But fortune favors the bold, as they say." Wingate motioned toward a narrow, gray-haired man in a frayed black suit. "This is Ezra Blackthorn, my specialist on occult texts."

The funeral director. I extended my hand toward the man.

Instead of taking it, he looked down his hooked nose at me. His dark, hooded gaze glowed with intensity. "It's nice to meet you," he said in a measured tone.

I dropped my hand. "You have your own occult text specialist?" I asked my host.

Wingate smiled. "I don't stint on things that matter. And this is Riga Hayworth."

I started. *That* was who she looked like, that old silver screen actress, Rita Hayworth. But had he said her name was Riga? Was she a celebrity impersonator?

In a liquid motion, the woman rose. Though she looked like Rita, her clothing was more Katherine Hepburn: wide-legged slacks, a blouse, a brown silk scarf knotted around her slender neck. "I'm a detective of sorts."

"What sort?" I asked.

"Metaphysical." Her arms hung loose at her sides.

"I see." But I didn't see at all. It didn't surprise me Wingate had brought in someone like her. But what *was* a metaphysical detective?

Wingate threw back his silvered head and laughed. "The look on your face, Brandy. Don't worry, she's a real private eye. And with her experience with the occult, I thought she might come in handy."

"In case I'm a fraud?" I asked, mouth dry.

"Exactly," he purred. "Now, did you bring it?"

I opened my bag and drew out a folded sheet of paper. Wingate snatched it from my hand and opened it. His lined hands trembled.

I looked a question at the third man. He was real all right. How had I thought otherwise, if only for a moment?

"Family," the young man said briefly. "Name's Devin."

"My nephew assists with my private investment firm." Wingate didn't bother to look up from the sheet of paper. A muscle jumped in Devin's jaw.

Devin's blond hair was thick and close-cropped. His neck was thick and his shoulders broad. What did he *really* do at Wingate's "investment" firm, so small and elite that those two were the sole managers and employees?

I glanced toward the door. Tobin had vanished. I suspected he hadn't gone far.

Wingate looked up and handed the page to Ezra. "This is all of it?"

"Of course not," I said, "just a copy of the first inch." My gaze flicked to Ezra. The occult specialist's fleshy lips moved silently, mouthing the words in the text.

"Where's the rest?" Wingate demanded.

I shifted my weight, my back suddenly sticky. "Somewhere safe," I said coolly.

"And the scroll's condition?"

"Excellent."

Wingate stared. His square jaw tightened.

This was it. I held my breath. Had I gone too far? Not far enough?

Wingate threw back his head and barked a laugh. "Touché. I presume this is a cash-on-delivery transaction?" He plucked the sheet from Ezra's long fingers.

"That," I said, "and, as I mentioned on the phone, I'd like to study your portion of scroll."

He dropped my sheet of paper into the firepit. The flames leapt to devour it, then retreated, satisfied.

"Do you have your portion on you?" Wingate asked.

Ezra's long nose twitched. He leaned forward.

"No," I lied. "Like I said, it's somewhere safe."

"Can you get it tomorrow?"

I nodded.

"Then why don't you spend the night here?" Wingate asked. "I have plenty of room."

Riga's expression flickered. "That might not be such a good idea."

For whom?

Wingate was a notorious game player, and he wasn't inviting me out of generosity. He was up to something. That was only one of many excellent reasons to decline his invitation, foremost being that my host was probably a killer.

But it was that *probably*, that sliver of doubt, that swayed me. That, and my sister. Because I was playing a game too. If I was in the house, it would be easier to win it. "That's a generous offer," I told the old mobster, my mouth dry.

The mob connection was only a rumor, after all. Though the security at the estate and the suspiciously well-muscled "estate manager," Tobin, made the rumor seem more believable.

My face tightened. But maybe Wingate was just security conscious.

"I accept," I said. And then I remembered the kitten in my car. *Dammit.* What would I do with him?

There was a faint sigh. I thought it might have come from the Rita Hayworth clone.

"Tobin will show you to your room," Wingate said. "Dinner's at six sharp."

Tobin silently materialized beside me. I trailed his tall form into the hallway.

"COO and CFO, huh?" he asked.

He *had* been listening at the door. I nodded.

"How many hours a week did you work?" Tobin continued.

"Nearly all of them."

He snorted. "I know the feeling. Got any bags?"

"In the car." I followed him outside. "Er, how does Mr. Weald feel about cats?" I fumbled the hooks on my vest, snapping it closed. Maybe I'd heard wrong about his anti-cat stance.

"Hates 'em."

Terrific. Wingate really *did* think cats were unlucky. I aimed my key fob at the SUV and opened the hatch.

Tobin retrieved my oversized, lipstick-pink suitcase from the back. I tucked the kitten inside my furry vest and buttoned its clasps. The orange cat purred against my stomach.

Tobin carried my suitcase inside. "Third floor." He led me up a grand, elaborately carved staircase that wound around itself four times. Pale light filtered through its stained-glass ceiling.

"Wow." I studied the painted portraits on the staircase walls. They stared back, disapproving.

"The fire department wanted Wingate to take the staircase out," he said. "They said it forms a chimney if there's a fire. But the house is historic, so it stays."

On the third floor, he led me into a modern Scandinavian-style room overlooking the driveway. I guessed I didn't rate a lake view. But I wasn't a real guest, and I wasn't on vacation.

After Tobin departed, I settled the kitten on a fluffy white pillow, set up my electronic notebook on the sleek, narrow desk, and opened my suitcase on the stand for that purpose.

I did not hang my things in the blond-wood wardrobe, the faces in its grain mocking. Tobin would no doubt want to rummage through my suitcase while I was at dinner.

I didn't know how the estate manager—bodyguard?—would react to the cat, but I'd worry about that later. If Wingate threw me out on my ear, I'd move to a hotel. If I could afford one. Tahoe was no longer the middle-class vacation haven it used to be.

Too paranoid to extract the actual scroll from its hiding place, I studied my sketch of it in my electronic notebook. Re-reading the text didn't kill much time. Playing with the kitten made a better distraction.

At six sharp, I washed up, brushed the cat hairs off my blouse, and descended the stairs. Firetrap or no, the staircase was gorgeous. A weak beam of silvery light shone through the stained-glass ceiling. The moon?

I was unsurprised to find Riga, Ezra, and Devin were dining with us in the black-walled dining room. I *was* surprised when Riga dominated the conversation with a dissertation on the connection between ancient Greek philosophy and the New Age movement.

Ezra disputed Riga over the role of beauty in society. Even when arguing hotly, he looked like a mortician. It wasn't just the worn black suit. The man had an aura of decay.

Facing the picture windows overlooking the unblinking lake, Wingate smiled in his throne-like chair from the end of the blocky wood table. He quizzed his blond-haired nephew, Devin, about a recent meeting with one of their investment clients.

Devin shoveled food into his mouth and gave one-word replies. He glanced repeatedly at the door, as if expecting someone who never arrived.

When Wingate did speak to me, it was to boast about his acquisitions. Wingate, I was soon to learn, liked the best. He also had a passion for *feng shui*, explaining the placement of the dining table and "flow" of the room, while the metaphysical detective nodded.

"Maybe I should ask *you* to manage my investments," Ezra said across the table to Wingate.

"Eh?" Wingate asked.

"I was just complaining about the state of the stock market," Ezra motioned to Riga. "Perhaps my money would be better in your hands."

"You couldn't afford my services." Wingate adjusted the cuff of his charcoal suit jacket.

"You couldn't stomach the risk," Devin muttered, and Wingate shot him a sharp glance.

We lingered over port and a rich chocolate cake. When I figured Tobin had had enough time to satisfy himself that the luck scroll wasn't in my suitcase, I yawned and retreated to my room.

My suitcase appeared untouched, but I'd used the old hair-in-an-obscure-place trick. The hair had been moved.

The orange kitten had moved as well, to a low, sand-colored couch. An open, half-empty tin of tuna sat on the wood floor beside it.

Tobin. Smiling, I went to the window.

The headlights of two vehicles—Ezra's and Riga's, I guessed—glided down the driveway and vanished. I rubbed my damp palms on my khakis. *Alone at last, and in a mobster's house.*

Propping a chair beneath the doorknob, I went to bed. I didn't expect the chair would stop anyone, but it might give me a warning.

I set my alarm, but I didn't need it. Sleep was impossible, despite the luxury sheets and down-filled duvet.

I stared at the beamed ceiling, checking the phone on the bed stand every thirty minutes. On my final check, I nearly knocked over the water carafe.

But it was three—the witching hour for us over-forties. It was time.

I threw off the duvet and changed in the dark from my nightgown into a pair of sweats. I didn't put my shoes on.

If I was caught, being barefoot would make it appear more likely I'd just come down for some warm milk. It would have to be milk or a snack, since someone had thoughtfully left that full water carafe.

Shifting the chair beneath the doorknob, I slipped into the hallway. I paused, listening. A clock ticked from somewhere inside the house.

My eyes adjusted to the gloom, but I took my time feeling my way down the wide stairs. Wood creaked, and I froze at the base of the staircase. Silence met my ears—silence and the throbbing of my heart.

I exhaled. The sound must have been the house settling. I moved forward.

Ten years earlier, a home decor magazine had done a photo spread of Dragon House. From its pages, I knew Wingate's library faced the lake and was on the first floor. Its shelves had been filled with rare texts—only in the best condition, of course. I hoped this was where his portion of the luck text would be.

But I wasn't to find it.

Not that morning at least. Not when my bare toes caught soft cloth wrapped around a hard mass. Not when I went crashing to the floor. Not when I sat up, looking around wildly to see if anyone had heard.

Not when I felt the body.

THE OUROBOROS

Behold thy serpent, wings spread wyde
A cercle wrought, by every syde
In its grene coils, Fortuna's flou
Needs revolve for thine to growe
In days of wo, in moments bryght
The serpents turn, both day and nyght
Seek ye the path of Fortuna's embrace
If thy heart be opened with gentle grace
Customes simple, rites of the wys
Come to naught if in thy mynde
Thou be not in soule and hande
True to thy heart and to thy lande
And in thy thoughts thou do refrain
From ungentile acts, and ye shal gain
Graynes of erthe and drops of dew
Blessyngs in their essence trewe

Thus seek ye Fortuna's tyde
In ebb and flood, wyth Her abyde
For if ye walk wyth heart unbarred
Hennes fynd fortune in every part
Unto all beneath the firmament
Fortune favours the fortunate

So fortunate let thou be
In lyfe's perfect harmony.
Embrace the cercle, hold it neer,
In joy and sorow, love and fer.
For in the serpent's wynged dance,
Lyes the secret of lyfe's chance.

CHAPTER 2

SOME THINGS YOU CAN only learn the hard way. I'd thought I was the type of woman who stayed cool under pressure. But I learned I was *not* the type who remained calm under finding-a-dead-body-kind-of-pressure.

Gulping short breaths, I stumbled to my feet, pulled my phone from the pocket of my sweats, and turned on its flashlight. The light bounced unevenly across the charcoal wall, the parquet floor, Devin.

Devin. In its wavering beam, the dead man seemed to vibrate.

For the first weeks after my sister's death, I'd lived in an in-between world, another dimension where the landscape wasn't quite what I'd remembered. I'd caught glimpses of things from the corners of my eyes—terrible things—giant cats and shadow people and strange, oceanic creatures with tentacles like black ribbons, hovering in the air.

I'd always had vivid dreams. I didn't like that they were bleeding into the daylight hours. But when the world grew recognizable again, I resented it.

Devin's lifeless body was no dream. This was real.

I switched to a two-handed grip before I could drop the phone. The blond man stared at the high, beamed ceiling. His blue eyes were open and blank, his expression slack. Purplish bruises bloomed on the front of his neck—two thumbprints.

I blinked rapidly, but the dead man didn't go away. He was real, not a phantom, not a hallucination. Still, my brain scrambled, stuck on the fact that he was dead.

I'd had *dinner* with Devin last night, and he'd been alive. He'd explained he was Wingate's nephew, was a lawyer, and he lived with his wife at Dragon House, working as Wingate's assistant.

And now Devin was dead. It didn't seem possible. He'd hogged the mashed potatoes. That had irritated me, because I loved mashed potatoes, and Wingate's had been excellent.

And why the hell was I thinking about mashed potatoes? I returned to my one-handed phone clutching and dialed 9-2-2 on my first attempt.

"What the hell?" a man shouted.

I jumped. The phone clattered to the floor, landing flashlight-side down. Its light streamed faintly from beneath it, illuminating the phone's rectangular shape.

A light switched on overhead, and I winced. Tobin, in gray sweats that nearly matched my own, gaped first at Devin's body, then at me. He shook himself. "What did you do?"

"I just found him there," I blurted and bent to pick up my phone.

"Don't touch anything," he said.

"It's my phone. You saw me drop it."

His skin darkened. "Right. Don't move." Tobin turned and strode down the hall, up the winding staircase.

"Shouldn't we...?" Call 9-1-1? I hesitated.

Oh, the hell with it. I dialed, identified myself, and spoke with a dispatcher.

There was an odd hesitation. "The Dragon House?" she asked.

"Yes." Impatient, I repeated the address.

"Deputies are on their way," she said, tone again brisk. "Don't touch anything."

Tobin and Wingate hurried down the wide staircase.

"What are you doing with that phone?" Wingate barked, his black silk robe flapping around the knees of his matching pajamas.

I clutched it to my chest. "It's mine."

"I know it's yours." He reached the bottom of the stairs and strode toward me. "What are you doing with it?" The gold, four-leaf-clover charm winked against his bare chest.

I edged away from him. "I called 9-1-1."

Wingate cursed. He stopped beside me and studied his nephew. Then he stepped over the body, opened the door behind it, and vanished inside the dark room beyond.

A click, and the light switched on. The door drifted wider, coming to a rest against Devin's body. I shuddered and looked away.

Tobin met my gaze. "What were you doing down here?"

"I was hungry."

His dark brows lifted.

"Devin ate all the mashed potatoes," I said a little wildly, and my face heated. *Mashed potatoes again? Why was I stuck on the damn things?*

Wingate emerged from the room, lifting his ebony robe as he stepped over his nephew's body. "The glass in the door is broken, but nothing appears to have been taken. Devin must have surprised a burglar."

The two men turned to me.

"I didn't hear anything," I said. "I was looking for the kitchen."

"Devin was strangled," Tobin said. "Look at his neck. She couldn't have done it."

Wingate grunted. "His wife's going to have a fit."

"A fit?" I gurgled. My sister had died in an accident, and I still hadn't recovered from the shock. I couldn't imagine losing a loved one to murder.

"She'll get over it," Wingate said.

My eyes narrowed with anger. "What the—?" I clamped my jaw shut. I'd *known* the type of people I'd be dealing with here—the type who counted life cheap. But Devin's wife would be pitching more than a *fit*.

"Should we tell her?" Tobin asked his employer in a low voice.

Wingate shook his head. "I need to make a call." He walked a bit down the hallway, pulled a cell phone from the pocket of his silk robe, and pressed it to his ear.

My brain did another hiccup before realization set in. Devin lived *here*. Which meant... "Devin's wife. Is she...?" I glanced up the twisting staircase.

Tobin nodded.

"She wasn't at dinner," I said.

"Fortuna has an active social life," he said coolly.

Suddenly I realized I wasn't wearing a bra. I crossed my arms over my chest. "I'm going to go up and..."

Before Tobin could object, I turned and jogged up the stairs to my room. The kitten rolled atop my pillow. He ignored me as I slipped on a bra and pulled my sweatshirt back over my head.

"I'm glad *someone's* having a good time," I muttered, yanking on my tennis shoes.

Red and blue lights flickered across my pale beige ceiling. I looked out a window. The police had arrived.

Closing my bedroom door behind me, I returned downstairs.

"Where's the woman who made the call?" A bearlike man with a grizzled jaw asked. He held his broad-brimmed hat loose at his side. His jacket was so green that it was nearly black. A gold badge gleamed on his chest.

"That would be Ms. Bounds, Sheriff." Wingate glanced at me.

The sheriff nodded to a tall, weedy-looking deputy. "Take Ms. Bounds's statement."

The deputy led me down the hall, through the entryway, and outside. Lights from half a dozen sheriff's cars flashed across the wide lawn and strobed through the pines.

"Am I being taken to the station?" I asked, alarmed.

"No." The tall man smiled faintly. His badge read *Linnel*, and I stiffened. "I wanted to take your statement away from the others," he said. "That way it won't contaminate what the others have to say."

I'd read that was standard police procedure. But something in his expression told me his explanation wasn't the entire truth.

I told him the same lie I'd told the others about looking for the kitchen and stumbling across Devin's body. That the last time I'd seen Devin alive had been at dinner. Then I told him all about that dinner, and who had been there, and why I was here.

I did not mention the mashed potatoes.

"A luck scroll?" the deputy asked, showing the first sign of real curiosity.

"Possibly by George Ripley," I said. "Circa 1475. He was an English artist and alchemist. The scroll is illustrated..."

Headlights swept the wooden steps, and a black SUV stopped behind a sheriff's car. Riga Hayworth, in a suede safari jacket, stepped out. She hurried up the steps and inside the mansion without sparing us a word or a glance.

I frowned, surprised the deputy hadn't tried to stop her.

"She's a detective," the deputy said. "Kind of. The sheriff..." He shook his head. "He'll deal with her."

Huh. I glanced at the mansion's arched, open door. Just what sort of relationship did a metaphysical detective have with a sheriff's department? Though Wingate *had* said she was a "real" PI.

A woman's shriek echoed inside the house, and I started.

The deputy grasped my arm. "Don't move."

"But someone—"

"The sheriff will take care of it. What's your interest in this luck scroll?"

My throat tightened. It had been a long night. If I told him the whole truth—about my sister—I might start blubbering.

"The study of luck is a hobby of mine," I said. "I intend to sell Wingate my section of scroll, in exchange for taking a look at his and for a fat check."

"How fat of a check?"

I named a figure, and he whistled. "I guess it's true there's a sucker born every minute."

I folded my arms. "The historical value alone makes my piece of the scroll worth it. And put together with Wingate's section of scroll, the value will double."

"Right. Sorry. None of my business. Where are you staying?"

"Here, for now. Third floor, driveway view."

He lifted a brow. "You couldn't pay me to stay in that firetrap. Have you heard about the stairs?"

I huffed a breath. Who cared? "They form a chimney, yes."

He asked more questions, took my contact info, and let me go.

The hallway where Devin's body lay was now blocked with police tape. I backtracked, searching for a new way back to my room. The main staircase *couldn't* be the only way upstairs.

In a side hallway, I walked past the sheriff interviewing the man whom I'd blocked in the driveway yesterday.

"Notice anything strange or unusual?" the sheriff was asking.

A narrow doorway opened onto a dimly lit set of stairs. A servant's passage?

The man shrugged. "Wingate fired the entire housekeeping staff yesterday morning. I think he's using a caterer for the meals now."

Slowly, I made my way up the stairs.

"Why'd he fire them?" the sheriff asked below me.

"Because thirteen people showed up," the man said, his voice a rumble deep in my belly.

"Why was thirteen a problem? Was he being overcharged?"

"I doubt it. It was something about the number thirteen." The man's voice grew distant. "Wingate's got a thing about luck."

My stomach lurched.

Luck.

Fate.

Or had it been perverseness that had put Wingate on that highway the morning my sister died?

Had it all been a game to him, testing his luck? Standing in the middle of the highway, in the dark? Whatever the reason, he'd caused the accident that had killed my sister.

I swallowed. Staying here was paying off. I'd already learned more about Wingate, and I'd learn the whole truth of my sister's death. I'd learn the why.

But staying here was also dangerous. A man had died tonight.

Eventually, I found my way through the tight, twisting servants' hallways to my room. I didn't have to remove the kitten from my pillow—he'd returned to the couch.

Something else lay on the white pillow though, a dark, oversized card. I blinked rapidly, lightheaded.

Someone had been in my room.

THE GAME

SEEKER:

The witch understands that every action she takes involves multiple levels of gameplay. There are the mundane tasks: washing the dishes, spending time with friends and loved ones. And then there are the magical and spiritual energies we bring to those tasks. Do we cook mindfully, infusing our food with love and magic? Do we bring presence to our work and relationships, thereby doing deeper work on ourselves?

And how do we deal with the external energies at work in our lives? Do we believe life is happening *to* us or *for* us?

The witch can align herself with nature's energies—such as the moon phases, the seasons, and the solar cycles. But there's a greater, universal energy: the flow of life. Once we're in that flow, our desires manifest more easily, luck flows *to* rather than *away* from us, and love blossoms in the greatest and highest good.

And how does the witch get into this flow? Through regularly practicing gratitude and generosity. Through creating rituals such as meditation and visualization that help align us with these energies. And by lightening up and treating life as a game—not because life is unserious, but because when we're *too* serious, we bog down our own energies and get out of flow.

Download the attached exercise and *play* with it.

SCAN ME

The Game

A focus on what matters. Attention to higher levels. Spirituality.

What if we thought of life as a game? Not in the sense that life's unimportant, but a game in the sense that there are rules and strategies for success? That every challenge—big and small—is an opportunity to try a new play, to test our skills, and to treat others in the spirit of good sportsmanship? And what if there were different levels of games—the practical games of playing house and work, and the higher-level games of spiritual transformation, truth, love, and beauty?

Note: it's possible to play multiple levels at once.

The symbols:

A game board makes up an ocean shore. But which game is being played? Higher-level chess? Or checkers? The checker is being tossed by the waves, but the chess pieces remain on shore.

The questions:

If this situation was a game, what are the rules and strategies for success? Which game are you playing?

The Flow of the Game:

Every action involves multiple levels of gameplay. There are the mundane tasks: washing the dishes, spending time with friends and loved ones. And then there are the magical and spiritual energies we bring to those tasks. Do we cook mindfully, infusing our food with love and magic? Do we bring presence to our work and relationships, thereby doing deeper work on ourselves?

4 things I do mindlessly:

I can level up my gameplay for each by:

1: _____

2: _____

3: _____

4: _____

CHAPTER 3

I SANK BACK IN the curving, wooden desk chair, the kitten coiled in my lap, and I frowned at the mystery school email. I'd been getting them roughly once a week, so the arrival of this one was no surprise.

But the UnTarot card... I plucked the card from the blond-wood desk and studied it. *The Game.* The cards usually came in my mailbox. My free hand fisted. Who had put this in my bedroom?

Was Wingate part of the school? The old mobster was infamously superstitious. Maybe he'd joined it. Maybe he *was* the school. Maybe those emails had always been a way to manipulate me—

I jerked my head in a brief negation. No. There'd been nothing in those emails to set me on the hunt for the Luck Scroll. Nothing to connect me to Wingate. This was the first I'd received that had mentioned luck at all.

How had the card followed me here? My teeth clenched back a yawn. With all Wingate's security, it *must* have been someone inside the house.

"You're an initiate," Riga said.

Starting in my chair, I turned toward the open bedroom door. I was certain I'd closed it behind me. My voice hardened. "And you're a snoop."

She knew about the school. *Calling me an initiate...* That's what they called newbies at the Mystery School.

Riga's full lips quirked. She crossed her arms and braced one shoulder against the door frame, rumpling the sleeve of her suede safari jacket. The ends of its belt dangled. "I'm a detective. That makes me a snoop by definition. And you left the door unlocked."

"That's no excuse for walking into my private bedroom."

"In Wingate's home. Do you think *he* cares about such fine distinctions?"

My mouth flattened. "Did you put this card on my bed?" I brandished the card.

Riga walked into the room and took the card from my loose fingers. "No. It doesn't work that way." She frowned. "Unfortunately."

Ha. "Then you *are* part of the school. That card didn't get here by itself."

"Didn't it?"

I rolled my eyes and slouched deeper in the hard, wooden chair. "What do you want?"

"I *wanted* to know what you'd seen when you found Devin. Now I want to know why you joined the Mystery School."

My neck tightened, and I gave a short, negating shake to loosen it. "I didn't see anything until I stumbled over Devin's dead body. And I joined the school because it was free, and the cards were pretty. Are you an initiate too?"

"No."

"But you knew I was."

"I saw you holding that UnTarot card. Only members have access to them. That's an interesting card, under the circumstances."

I glanced past her, into the hallway, but couldn't see much. Whoever had laid the card on my pillow must have known or suspected I wasn't what I'd claimed.

"I don't know what game you're playing." Riga returned the card to the desk. "But it's a dangerous one. This house is no place for a tech company COO."

"*And* CFO."

One corner of Riga's mouth lifted. "You're proud of your work, yet you abandoned it two months ago. What really brought you here?"

"I'm just researching a scroll," I lied.

"That's quite a departure from spreadsheets and financial statements."

I leaned back in my chair and swiveled to face her, my hands resting on its arms. "So, I'm a Renaissance woman."

She rubbed the back of her neck. "Whatever you're after here, it's not worth it. Don't let his pocket squares and luck obsession fool you. Wingate's a dangerous man."

"I thought luck was only a harmless superstition."

She shot me a sharp look, and once again, I thought I caught a gleam of violet in her brown eyes. "Don't discount the power of superstition. Go home, Brandy. One man's already dead." She walked from the room, closing the door silently behind her.

I rose from the desk chair. She was wrong. Sarah *was* worth it, and Devin's death had nothing to do with me.

Did his murder have something to do with my sister though? Uneasy, I shook my head. I needed to keep playing. In the morning, I'd demand to see the rest of Wingate's scroll.

I returned to bed and fell into an uneasy sleep. Until Sarah's death, I'd been able to become aware inside my dreams and control them. But no longer.

I almost managed it that night though. I flew through the air above a tropical island. When I realized I was dreaming, I changed the scene to dark woods.

Smoke coiled from a chimney. I dropped to the ground in front of our parents' old cabin by the lake and told myself Sarah would be inside.

But when I opened the door, someone else waited by the stone fireplace, an ivory-haired woman. She wore an old-fashioned Slavic dress with white billowy sleeves and an embroidered vest.

I scowled. "You're not my sister. Sarah?" I called, focusing on memories of my sister. I imagined her walking into the cabin. *Sarah. Bring me Sarah.*

"You can't find her here," the woman said. "Not yet."

The door to our childhood vacation bedroom was to the right of the fireplace. I strode to it, yanked it open—

And woke up. I scrubbed my face with my hands and my thumb brushed fur.

The kitten had filled the space between my neck and shoulders with his body. I stroked him lightly with one finger, and tried, unsuccessfully, to return to my dreams.

When I stumbled down the stairs that morning, the library door was crossed with yellow police tape. Low voices murmured behind the closed door.

A cat growled behind me, and I twitched guiltily. Had I accidentally let the kitten out? I looked around the wide hallway, but it was empty. I jogged up the winding staircase to my room.

I opened the door. The kitten rolled in a patch of sunlight.

My stomach fluttered. That growl... It had been much deeper than anything I'd heard the kitten produce.

But I'd *swear* I'd heard it. And Wingate disliked cats...

The kitten stopped his play. His brown-gold eyes fixed on mine, and he mewled, high and light.

I shook my head. I must have imagined the growl. Maybe my guilty conscience had turned the sound of the house settling into something more. *Or you're going crazy.*

Unsettled, I returned down the stairs. Tobin and a young man I didn't recognize passed me in the wide, charcoal-painted hallway.

"You report to me," Tobin said. "Not Wingate."

The newcomer was about my height and muscled like a bodybuilder. Something gleamed cold white around his wrist, and then vanished. His wrist was bare—another trick of the eyes. "But I just—"

Tobin jabbed his chest with his thumb. "To *me*."

"Sorry. Right."

"And your new AI security wasn't predictive after all."

"I told you how it worked." The other man nudged his thick, black-framed glasses higher on his nose. They matched the color of his hair.

"It's learning," the young stranger continued. "We caught the guy on video and know how he got in. This will improve the AI's predictive capacity." The two men turned a corner, and the rest of his words were lost.

I found my way to the dining room with its strange, near-black walls. The man whose Honda I'd blocked in yesterday shoveled the final remnants of scrambled eggs into his mouth. He was dressed simply in baggy jeans and a wrinkled blue, button-up shirt.

"...out of luck." Wingate chortled from his highbacked chair overlooking the sparkling lake. "Get it? It's a pun. Luck." He brushed a fleck of scone from his cravat. It landed on his navy dinner jacket. He scowled and swiped harder at it, knocking it to the white tablecloth.

I scowled too. I'd worn a stretchy navy jacket and slacks with a white blouse. Wingate and I were matching.

The man with the salt-and-pepper hair scraped back his chair from the long table and stood. "I've got better things to do." Without a glance, he strode past me and out the door.

"Good morning." I wandered to the sideboard. Enticing smells emanated from its silver warming trays.

Wingate grinned. "Is it? I'd have thought you'd be dining in your room after what happened last night."

"Is in-room dining an option?"

He threw back his silvery head and laughed. "There's more to you than meets the eye."

My insides tightened. "Not really. I told you what I want."

"Yes, but not why you want to read the rest of that scroll so badly." He slathered lemon curd on a fresh scone. "You're not an academic."

"Is that what he is?" I inclined my head toward the doorway. "An academic?"

"Sam, you mean?" Wingate motioned negligently toward the door behind him. "Right, he wasn't at dinner last night. You two haven't been introduced. Yes, he's an archaeomythologist, which sounds made-up to me, but my AI assures me it's an actual profession."

"You have your own AI?"

"Built on the back of an existing platform, of course. I like to have my own things. Only the best, you know."

I knew. I piled eggs and bacon on my plate. Lifting the lid on a silver tray, I snagged a scone that smelled of cinnamon and apples.

"The burglary hasn't scared you off?" Wingate persisted.

"The murder unnerved me. But no, it hasn't scared me off." I took a miniature jar of clotted cream from the sideboard and set it on my plate. I didn't bother with the usual "sorry for your loss." Wingate obviously wasn't sorry at all.

"I wonder..." He tapped his chin, his four-leaf clover ring flashing gold. "Could you have had something to do with Devin's death?"

I forced myself to turn and face him. "How?"

"You *did* find my nephew's body. The person who finds the body is always a suspect. At least that's what my AI told me."

"Yes," I said dryly. "You wouldn't have acquired that knowledge from anything as prosaic as a TV drama."

He grinned. "Successful people don't have time for television."

"The secret to my mediocre career."

"Hardly mediocre. I know who you worked with. And for. And that you clawed your way up from a lowly financial analyst position to CFO, all without having completed your bachelor's degree."

I stilled. He knew that? Not even my ex-employer knew that. "I got the final credits."

"Three years ago, *after* you'd become CFO." He shifted in his seat. "I'm glad you decided to stay at Dragon House. I want you where I can keep an eye on you."

An icicle slivered down my back. Maybe staying at Dragon House wasn't such a great idea after all.

CHAPTER 4

MAKING 'EM WAIT IS an old trick, designed both to aggravate and to apply time pressure to the person waiting. When you want a deal done and time is short, you're more likely to cave on the finer points of a negotiation.

Except Wingate and I had already agreed on our deal. So when he told me he'd be spending the rest of the day away from Dragon House, I had to assume he really *was* too busy to view my portion of scroll. Or to let me view his.

It was aggravating.

After breakfast, I took the kitten out to play and do his business. He acted more like a dog than a kitten—sniffing the bracken beneath the pines and exploring his surroundings.

I scanned for cameras. It took me fifteen minutes to find the first. Once I knew what to look for, the others came more easily. They were well hidden in the pines.

I phoned my son, Joe. Predictably, it went to voicemail. This didn't bother me. These days, twenty-somethings didn't use phones for talking, and he liked sleeping late. But worry quavered in my stomach.

Joe'd been convinced a fight between Sarah and her husband had sent her to Tahoe. He and Sarah had been close, and he was looking to blame someone for her death. A part of him blamed me. And he hadn't approved of my luck obsession.

But what *had* my sister been doing here? Not come to see Wingate. Not at that hour. Aside from her death, there'd been no connection between the two that I could find.

I shook my head and sent Joe a text. The kitten came to lay beside me. I scooped him up and drove him to a shelter.

The plump young woman at the counter studied him from behind thick black spectacles. "It's only, we have an *awful* lot of cats."

"You can't fit in one more?" I wheedled and set the kitten on the high counter. He gave me a grumpy side-eye then licked an orange paw.

"We *can*," she said, drawing out the final word.

"Then what's the problem?"

"We're not a no-kill shelter. And when we've got as many cats as we do now, odds are they won't get adopted out."

"What?" I snatched the kitten off the counter. No way I was leaving him here. "Never mind. Where's the nearest no-kill shelter?"

She winced. "Reno. Are you *sure* you don't want to keep the cat?"

An hour and two-hundred dollars later and muttering about highway robbery, I left the shelter with an inoculated and microchipped kitten. I opened the rear hatch door. "No good deed goes unpunished," I grumped.

I strapped my new, "gently used" cat carrier into the backseat. "And this is only temporary," I assured the kitten.

We drove to the nearest pet store. It was in a wood-timber strip mall along the highway. I bought food, litter box and litter, a flea collar, and toys. *Only temporary.*

On the far side of the lot, a man had set up a photo stand with a live mountain lion. I piled my acquisitions in the back of the SUV. The kitten hunched in the cage and watched the big cat through the SUV's open hatch.

"Eat your kibble and maybe someday *you'll* get that big," I joked. The kitten shot me a sour look.

How was I going to sneak all this past Wingate? Tobin was the real one to watch out for though, and he didn't seem to mind about the kitten.

Movement caught my eye on the other side of the highway. A man on a bicycle, naked despite the chill, flew along the bike path. I blinked and watched him sweep around a curve. He was definitely, unfortunately real.

In the parking lot behind him, a woman in wide-legged trousers stepped from a black SUV. She shook her head and walked toward a two-story wooden office building. Her auburn hair glinted in the sunlight.

I wrinkled my forehead. *Rita—?* I mentally corrected myself. *Riga Hayworth?*

Taking the cat carrier, I shut my SUV and walked across the highway to the wood and stone office building. At the base of sheltered wooden steps was a sign listing the occupants. *Riga Hayworth, Metaphysical Detective,* was on the second floor.

I climbed the stairs and found her office at the end of the open hallway. I knocked, tried the knob, stepped inside. The antechamber was small, with space only for a chair, end table, and lamp. A crash came from a room off to the side.

"Hello?" I called.

Riga stuck her head from an open door. "Oh. It's you. Good. Go on in." She motioned toward a closed, wood-paneled door. "I'll be there in a minute." She ducked back inside the room.

Judging by the scent of coffee, I assumed it was a kitchen. My mouth pinched. She'd sounded like she'd been expecting me here. I hadn't been expecting me here.

I tried the other door and walked inside the corner office. The wood floors were unfinished, the Edison lights and leather chairs luxurious. Picture windows overlooked Lake Tahoe. Gas flames flickered in a fireplace made of river stones. A brass clock ticked on the mantel.

I sat, setting the cat in his carrier in the chair beside mine.

"Now." Riga walked into the office and shut the door behind her. "What can I do for you?"

"I'm not looking to hire a metaphysical detective, if that's what you're asking. What *is* a metaphysical detective?"

She sat in the executive chair behind her desk and sighed. "Metaphysical is the study of the supernatural, or the use of speculative or abstract reasoning, which is frequently the only way to study the immaterial. I look for first causes."

"I'd say it sounds like mumbo-jumbo, but I'm peddling part of a 15th-century luck scroll, so..." I shrugged.

She grinned. "How *did* you find that scroll?"

"It was luck, really."

"Luck or synchronicity?"

I shifted in the leather chair. It must have been good leather, because it didn't squeak beneath my navy slacks. "I suppose both imply supernatural intervention, though synchronicities don't have to be lucky—simply meaningful."

"And your finding the scroll was both?"

Her guess was too close for comfort. I looked past her, out the picture window, at the lake. For a weird moment, I had the sense it was looking back, cold and disinterested.

Uneasily, I tore my gaze from the window. "Are you investigating Devin's death?"

"His murder," Riga corrected. "And no. I'd need a client in order to investigate, and so far, I don't have one. Unless you'd like to hire me?"

"No," I said. I'd no idea what metaphysical detectives charged, but it had to be out of my price range now. "What happened was terrible, but I'm not involved."

"Aren't you? What's your modality?"

Modality of what? "Sorry?"

"What magic do you practice? Shamanism?"

I lifted a brow. "I don't practice magic."

"But you joined the Mystery School," she said.

"Do you have to be a witch or shaman to join?"

"No, of course not. But... do you *see* things?"

My fingers twitched, digging into the chair's leather arm. The hallucinations... No. That had been grief.

I leaned forward in my chair and changed the subject. "Have you worked with the sheriff before?"

If my change of topic annoyed her, she didn't show it. Her strange, brown-violet eyes didn't flicker. "Yes. He's a good man, smart and dedicated."

"And there are video cameras all over the estate," I said. "They must have caught an image of the intruder," I said, fishing.

"One would assume."

"You haven't seen the videos?"

"No."

"And the sheriff didn't tell you anything?"

"He's not in the habit of sharing evidence." Riga's tone was laced with irony. "Not with a metaphysical detective."

Dissatisfied, I sat back against the soft leather. She'd come running to the house after Devin's death, and the sheriff had let her inside. She had to know *something*.

"Besides," she continued. "I was at Dragon House that night. He can't rule me out as a suspect. Or you, for that matter."

"The killer came from outside the house. That doesn't point to me." Though it did to her. She'd left Dragon House *before* the murder.

Unless... Devin's death couldn't be connected to Sarah's. Could it? The only connecting factor to the two was Wingate though, not me.

"Are you sure?" Riga cocked her head.

Dammit. "The video would tell us for certain."

"Would it?"

Augh. Answering questions with questions was maddening, and a game I wouldn't play, especially since I was unsure of the answers. I rose and picked up the cat carrier. "Well, it was nice seeing you again."

"I don't think our first meeting was a coincidence," she said. "Not with you being in the mystery school."

I stopped. "*Did* you put that card on my bed?"

"As I said before, no. The right cards find their way to the members who need them, when they need them. The question is, was the card you received a warning or an invitation?"

"Maybe neither. Maybe the card choice was random."

She braced her elbows on the desk, her chin on her laced fingers. "You're peddling a Luck Scroll. I don't think you believe in random."

No. I did not. I turned and left.

❦

At Wingate's long dinner table, I scanned the others. Sam, the man I'd blocked into the driveway, sat beside me and shoveled red potatoes into his mouth.

He smelled like he'd recently showered. Sam rubbed his jaw, his hands making scratching sounds against his salt-and-pepper beard.

Wingate sat at the end facing the windows. Our host had changed into an expensive-looking suit the color of a reef shark cutting through the Pacific.

Ezra, still looking like an embittered mortician, had returned. The occult text specialist sat opposite me. He stared down his hooked nose, nostrils quivering, and dissected a piece of trout with his fork.

I gripped my butter knife more tightly. Was one of them a murderer?

Ezra hadn't spent the night at Dragon House. If he'd wanted his own crack at the luck scroll, had snuck in, been surprised...

But why? He'd been invited by Wingate to examine my section of the scroll. Why try to steal a look at Wingate's copy when no one else was around?

I cleared my throat and turned to Sam. "I'm Brandy, by the way."

He looked up from his decimated plate. "Sam."

"What brings you to Dragon House?" I asked.

"Research."

I flicked my gaze toward the beamed ceiling. He was as bad as Riga Hayworth. At least Sam replied with answers instead of more questions, even if his answers were only one word. "What kind of research?" I asked.

Wingate laughed shortly. "You shouldn't have done that. Sam's as obsessed with his work as you are with yours. Brandy was the Chief Operating officer *and* Chief Financial Officer for a tech company."

My spine stiffened. It had been true, and I'd been proud of how I'd climbed that ladder. It had taken two decades to get where I'd been. Why was it so irritating coming from Wingate's mouth?

Ignoring him, Sam turned to me. "My interest is the 13th-century Livonian Crusade, and the defeat of the Estonian pagan tribes by the German Order of the Sword Brethren in 1217 AD."

"Not CE?"

"AD," he said firmly. "That's what the crusaders called it, and I'm old-school."

And I bet it drove his colleagues nuts. I glanced down at his hands, loose on the white tablecloth. They were scarred, weathered. Sam was more than an academic. I imagined the rough feel of his hands on my skin and quickly bent my head to my plate.

"Wingate has letters from one of the crusaders describing that crusade and the tribes they conquered," Sam finished.

"What do the Estonian—or Livonian crusades have to do with luck?" I asked.

"Nothing," Sam said. "Why would they?"

Wingate's mouth curved, and he adjusted his cufflinks—a pair of gold dice. "Sam is one of those scholars too focused on his subject to notice much around him. The texts came to me in the chest along with the Luck Scroll. You're aware of the story of the chest?"

I was aware, and I nodded.

Wingate continued anyway. "I was attending an auction of Norwegian ceramics. A box came up for auction, contents unknown. The auctioneer was whimsical. She thought it would be amusing to have people bid on a lot box. I was feeling lucky."

"You won the box," I said, "and it was *not* worthless."

"Indeed no, though I had to pay a pretty penny for it." Wingate smoothed his gray silk pocket square. "The scroll was inside it, along with other random documents. I decided to hold on to the rest, just in case."

"Did the police turn up anything more in Devin's death?" Ezra asked.

Wingate's nostrils flared. "If they have, they haven't told me. We gave them the security video."

"What was on it?" I asked.

"A man walking up my back patio and breaking into my library."

I nodded. Someone *had* come from outside. The patio faced the lake. Lakeshore access would be simpler than trying to climb over those glass-studded stone walls. All it would take was a small boat.

"Alas, the camera didn't capture the killer's face. He was smart enough to keep it covered."

A thirty-something woman strode into the dining room. All the men but Wingate leapt to their feet. She was slender and red-headed, her ivory skin darkened with freckles. Her slim-fitting black dress could have come off a fashion runway.

Ezra bowed respectfully. "Fortuna. My condolences on your loss."

"Your condolences?" she asked, shrill. She whirled on Wingate. "You blamed him for everything, didn't you? *You* got my husband killed."

"Please," Wingate drawled. "No drama tonight."

"Drama?" She slapped a slender hand to her chest. "My husband is *dead.*"

"Which is very exciting, no doubt," Wingate said. "But we're trying to enjoy our meal."

Fortuna and I sucked in sharp breaths—she, I expected, to shout. I was shocked by Wingate's callousness.

Tobin stepped into the room's open doorway. "Is there anything else you need tonight, Mr. Weald?"

"Like removing Fortuna to her room?" Wingate asked archly. "No, Tobin. You can take the rest of the evening off from listening at keyholes."

The muscular estate manager nodded. "Tomorrow then." Tobin turned and left.

Fortuna's chest heaved. "If you think—"

"I think you should consider your next words very carefully," Wingate said.

Her crimson lips pressed together. She turned on her high heels and followed Tobin out the door.

"Now." Wingate raised the bottle by his plate. "Would anyone like more wine?"

I declined. Drinking the wine would have been a waste. I wouldn't be able to taste it after that ugly scene.

Sam finished before me, pushing his chair back and muttering good nights. I hastily followed in time to see him jog up the stairs.

Of course, Sam was staying at the mansion too. I scraped my teeth across my bottom lip. He'd been here when Devin was killed. I'd seen him afterward talking to a deputy.

More slowly, I made my way up the stairs and to my room. I checked my phone. My son hadn't returned my text, and my heart fell.

I couldn't blame him if he were avoiding me. Sarah had been a surrogate mother to Joe. The fun mother who didn't worry about bills. I pocketed the phone.

Joe was hurting as much as I was. I just wished we could figure out a way to move through our grief together.

The kitten growled from his perch on the windowsill. The noise should have been comical coming from such a small body, but my scalp prickled.

"What's out there?" I went to the window and peered out. But all I could see was my own haunted face, a pale and phantomlike reflection in the night-blackened glass.

CHAPTER 5

BREAKFAST IS MY FAVORITE meal of the day, so I had no qualms about taking advantage of Wingate's spread. He might be a killer, but there was no point to wasting food. That would just be wrong.

The caterers had provided a hotel-style buffet. Silver warming trays gleamed on a sideboard in the dark-walled dining room overlooking the lake.

Plate laden with food, I turned from the long, narrow table. My plate jammed into Sam's midsection. Scrambled eggs skidded across it, splashed the academic's blue, button-down shirt, and dropped to the parquet floor.

Aghast, I studied the mess.

Sam lifted a brow. "At least they're not green."

"Sorry." Setting the plate on the sideboard, I grabbed a cloth napkin and scooped the stuff off the floor.

"That's your first move? The floor?" Sam asked, expression outraged. "This is my only good shirt." He motioned toward the eggs on his broad chest.

I sucked in my cheeks. "But as you say, at least the eggs aren't green. And you're not exactly helpless."

Though it was a very nice shirt and a very nice chest. Neither deserved to be stained with eggs. And I had no business ogling Sam. Sarah'd often joked about our bad taste in men.

We'd both had terrible judgment when it came to romance. I wished I'd figured out sooner I was better off alone.

Sam grabbed a clean napkin, dunked it in a nearby water carafe, and swiped at the front of his shirt. "I've been reading Dr. Seuss to my nieces and nephews."

"I caught the reference," I said, straightening.

"Kids of your own?"

"Grown." After my husband's desertion, Sarah had done most of the reading to Joe. Dullness settled in my chest. I hadn't been there enough. That was on me. Now, Joe treated me more like an aunt than his mother—fondly but thoughtlessly.

Wingate strolled into the dining room, plucked a sliced bagel from a silver-lidded warming tray, and smeared cream cheese on it. "Good morning."

Sam grunted a greeting to our host.

"I'd like to look at the scroll today," I said.

Wingate dropped the bagel on a plate and ambled to his high-backed chair at the end of the long table. "I'm sure you would."

"And I thought you wanted to examine my portion."

"I want Ezra to examine it." He sat, whipped a white napkin from the tablecloth and unfolded it on his lap. "And Ezra can't be here today."

"Do you want the scroll or not? Because there are other interested buyers," I lied.

Wingate's gaze turned sly. "But they can't show you what *you* want—my portion of the scroll."

"Can *you*?" I asked.

Sam huffed a laugh. He poured a mug of coffee from the sideboard.

Wingate reached inside his navy blazer and extracted a folded sheet of paper. "One rotten photocopy deserves another." He extended it to me.

I snatched it from his hand and unfolded it. One line of calligraphy curved around the bottom of a wooden wheel. I swallowed. *Fortune's wheel.*

I spread the photocopy on the white-clothed dining table. Pulling my own copy from my pocket, I unfolded it and laid it beside Wingate's. The text appeared to be in the same hand, but I was no expert.

"I'd like to see the rest of this," I said in a strangled voice.

"You're making it too easy for him." Sam strolled with his coffee from the dining room.

"He's right, honey," Fortuna said from behind me.

I started. When had she gotten here?

But Fortuna and Sam weren't wrong. I *was* letting Wingate bait me.

And I needed to see the rest of the scroll. If luck could be controlled, maybe I could make things better. No *more family tragedies.* My throat compressed. I couldn't lose any more people I loved. I couldn't lose Joe.

"When?" I asked him.

Fortuna poured a glass of orange juice. She sipped it delicately. Frowning, she brushed her hand on her dress, leaving a faint, white smear on the ebony fabric.

"Tomorrow." Wingate patted his mouth with his napkin. His gold clover ring glinted in the light from the window, but it wasn't half as dazzling as the lake. "Ezra will be here tomorrow at nine AM sharp. We can show each other our scroll sections then."

"Fine," I ground out. "Tomorrow." I folded both copies and tucked them into the rear pocket of my blue slacks.

Fortuna followed me up the stairs toward my room, her high heels rapping on the wide staircase. "Wingate's a master manipulator," she said. "But maybe your tactic *is* best. If you keep making it so easy, he'll get bored and quit."

I stopped outside my bedroom door. "I'm very sorry about your husband."

The younger woman exhaled and blinked rapidly. She studied her black pumps. "I always wondered if a sudden death would be easier than knowing it was coming and waiting and dreading the end." She met my gaze. "It isn't."

My heart clenched. "No." It wasn't. I opened my bedroom door.

The striped kitten trotted past me and into the hallway before I could stop him. Fortuna picked him up.

"How on earth?" Fortuna smiled. "You *do* know Wingate hates cats? Which is good enough reason for me to keep your secret."

Stroking the kitten's head, she walked into my room and looked around. "I see you *haven't* made yourself comfortable."

Fortuna nodded to my open, pink suitcase. "Though you brought enough clothing for a long visit. Maybe this extended stay hasn't been such a surprise?"

I reached for the suitcase lid to close it and paused. Someone had rummaged through my clothing again this morning. When I'd left for breakfast, my blue silk blouse had been in a packing cube. Now it lay on top of one.

"Fortuna's a lovely name," I said.

"The Roman goddess of fortune." She walked to the window, angled the wide, wooden blinds, and peered out at the driveway. "But you being a luck scholar, I'm sure you already knew that."

"I'm not exactly a scholar."

She faced me and set the kitten on the floor. "Neither is Wingate, but he knows what the name means. Why do you think he keeps me around?"

"Because you're—were—Devin's wife?"

"Hm." She paused beside my writing tablet and ran her finger along the desk. "It's a little dusty in here, but I don't suppose you want the room cleaned with the cat inside."

Returning to the window, she unlocked and opened it. Cool, mountain air flowed into the room. "Best to air this place out so no one knows. Take the cat for a walk, and I'll send someone in while you're away."

I rubbed the bridge of my nose. "I don't think you can walk a..." *Never mind.* "Thanks. I'll do that."

"What's your interest in luck?" she asked.

I shut my suitcase. "It's hard to explain."

"Try." She braced one shoulder against the panels in the blond-wood wall.

I smothered my irritation. If I played along, maybe she'd tell me something useful. "Do you think it's possible that luck really could be... a force? Something tangible and not just randomness or coincidence?"

"Oh," she said wisely. "You're one of those."

"One of what?"

"You're like Wingate. You think there's a way to control luck." She shook her head. "If luck was a force, do you really think you could manipulate it?"

My neck muscles tightened. I was nothing like Wingate. "I don't know. Maybe... I could get on its side."

"Propitiate the goddess?" She laughed. "Good luck with that. Maybe what we call good luck and bad luck are just things that are meant to happen."

"So... fate then?"

"Aren't luck and fate the same?" Fortuna shifted off the wall and clacked out of the room before I could answer.

I frowned. Someone had been in my room again. I didn't think it was Tobin. He'd already taken his shot. Wingate? Fortuna? They'd both arrived for breakfast after me. Sam had been in the dining room when I'd arrived, but he'd left before me.

I herded the kitten into his carrier and grabbed my writing tablet. The kitten probably did need fresh air, and I wasn't going to hang around the mansion all day.

I found a lakeside coffeeshop with a patio overlooking the water. The sense of the lake's watchful disinterest was gone, but I didn't want to turn my back on it. *Ridiculous.*

Unbuttoning my sister's furry vest, I found a table inside and took a chair facing away from the lake. The back of my neck crawled. I shifted on the metal chair.

I turned on my writing tablet and typed in Ezra's name. He had a simple website advertising his services as an expert of and trader in rare occult texts. No social media.

Fortuna provided a richer vein of online intel. Society pages, scandals with married men, and finally an announcement of her marriage to Devin. Lots of social accounts, but no hint of extracurricular activities since.

I didn't research Wingate. That research had been done. There were rumors of mob connections, though he'd never been charged with a crime. His money had purportedly come from his investment company.

Riga Hayworth was another matter—married to a wealthy casino own-er, in and out of the news for various occult and not-so-occult murder investigations. Her website, however, was a simple black screen with a contact button and the text:

RIGA HAYWORTH

METAPHYSICAL DETECTIVE

At least Ezra's website included a business address. I packed up my writing tablet and picked up the cat carrier. Sipping the remains of my extra-large coffee, I drove to the occult bookshop.

Ezra's shop was at the back of another wood-timbered mini mall. I parked and walked to the door.

EZRA BLACKTHORN

SPECIALIST, OCCULT TEXTS

A *Closed* sign hung beside it in a narrow window, so dusty it was impos-sible to see more inside than certain suggestive silhouettes. I knocked, feeling foolish.

Crawling heat swept the spot between my shoulder blades. I turned from the door, certain there would be someone in the trees, watching me.

No one was there. Wind scattered golden aspen leaves across the parking lot and rivered through the pines. Their slender trunks bent, needles whispering in indistinct voices.

I shivered. Fumbling my key fob, I hurried to my SUV, and returned to Dragon House.

That night, I awoke again at three. I cursed softly. I'd been in the dream cabin again. And again, I'd awakened before I could reach Sarah.

Something scratched, tentative, at my bedroom door.

I sat up, expecting to scold the kitten for sharpening his claws on our host's furniture. But he sat silhouetted in the moonlight at the window.

The kitten growled, that strange, deep sound that prickled my scalp. The scratching at my door stopped.

I threw off the thick duvet. Glancing from the door to the kitten, I crept to the window.

The shadow of an enormous cat slunk across the driveway and vanished into the pines. The kitten hissed.

The skin on the back of my neck twitched. I trotted to the thick bedroom door and tested the lock. And then I backed toward the bed, and I did not go back to sleep.

CHAPTER 6

THE PAT-DOWN TOBIN GAVE me outside Wingate's private library was impersonal, professional, efficient. His expression when he found my section of scroll was amused. He studied my electronic sketchbook and set it aside.

"What exactly are you looking for?" I asked.

"Anything you can take a picture with." He stepped aside, pocketed my phone, returned my satchel, sketchbook, and scroll case, and nodded toward the thick wooden door. "The others are in there."

"Others?" *Plural?* Tucking the metal case beneath my forest-green blazer, I opened the library door. I walked inside a library thick with the scent of aged paper and leather bindings.

Built-in bookshelves lined the near-black walls. In one corner was a comfy reading setup with two pale leather wingchairs. Wingate, in a navy suit and cravat, lounged in one of them.

In another corner stood an incongruous metal barstool and a small, high table stacked with leather-bound books. A long, dark-wood table stretched down the center of the rectangular room.

Riga, in a white blouse and wide-legged khaki slacks, braced one shoulder against a bookcase. She didn't look up when I entered, her gaze fixed on a picture frame which lay on the long table.

Ezra paced in front of the French doors overlooking Lake Tahoe and massaged his bony hand. The broken window in the door had been repaired. Money might not buy happiness, but it bought efficiency.

In the wingchair, Wingate crossed his legs. "And so it begins."

My chest heated. No. It had begun last February with my sister's death. "The scroll?"

Wingate nodded toward the central table. I moved closer. The narrow picture frame's glass seemed to absorb the morning sunlight. Beneath the raised glass was the scroll, its vellum blazing with medieval paint.

"Ah, ah." Wingate waggled his index finger. "Show me yours first."

Cocking my head, lips pressed flat, I edged aside my blazer. I drew the metal scroll case from the waistband of my jeans.

Wingate barked a laugh. "Have you been carrying that on you the whole time?"

I had. At my back, at my side, wherever my clothing would allow. It had been damned uncomfortable. But at least two people had searched my room since I'd arrived at Dragon House, so my precautions hadn't been unreasonable.

I unstopped the end of the scroll case.

Ezra hissed and hurried forward. "It shouldn't be handled by amateurs." He whipped a pair of white cotton gloves from the pocket of his funereal sports jacket.

I let him take the case. Wingate rose, fingers twitching. Riga straightened off the bookcase. They walked to the table and watched Ezra carefully unroll the scroll.

Brilliant colors leapt from the vellum, and Ezra released a slow breath. "It's in excellent condition."

Since I'd practically memorized my segment, I edged away to study Wingate's section on the table. The scroll was four feet long and beneath what appeared to be non-reflective glass.

Like mine, it was covered in rich images and text. Unlike mine, several sections had been torn clean across the vellum, and water stains dimmed the text. I frowned.

"Of course," Ezra said, "the Ripley Scroll is only associated with George Ripley because it includes his alchemical poetry. We don't really know who painted it. But these do appear to be in the same hand as that of the Ripley scroll. And of each other. At least at first glance."

"First glance?" Wingate asked.

"I'd have to conduct some tests, in a lab. Her fragment shouldn't be exposed to oxygen," Ezra fretted. "It's damaging." He jerked his head toward the framed scroll on the table.

"The frame for my scroll was specially constructed," Wingate explained to me. "It's hermetically sealed with inert argon pumped inside. Don't ask me why. I don't know exactly."

"To maintain the atmospheric pressure," Ezra muttered.

Riga leaned closer to the scroll. "They're by the same hand," she said in a low voice.

Ezra's gaze flicked to the library's beamed ceiling. "Is that your *professional* opinion?"

She slipped her hands into the pockets of her khakis and shrugged. "It's what Wingate's paying me for."

But I wasn't paying her, and I narrowed my eyes. If Wingate wanted to cheat me, he'd ensure she told me that mine was *not* a missing piece of Wingate's Luck Scroll and, therefore, worthless.

Wingate caught my gaze. "Don't worry. Riga can't cheat me. It's against the rules."

Riga blinked. She looked away, toward the French doors. Behind them, a trio of Canada geese waddled along the lakeshore. "And your nephew's death?" She met Wingate's gaze. "Was that against the rules?"

"Devin's death was a tragedy," he said.

"It was murder," she said. "And I intend to get at the truth of it."

"Oh, truth." Wingate gestured dismissively. "What is truth? There is no truth."

Riga's mouth twisted. "What a pathetic excuse for bad behavior."

Wingate smoothed the front of his elegant navy suit. "I don't see how—"

"If there's no truth," she said, "there are no lies. No good or evil, no beauty or ugliness. Everything is permissible. There's only power—which works in your favor since it's all you've got. Your moral relativism is a stinking corpse, and it rots everyone it touches."

"And yet you're here," he said.

"You can't touch me." Her voice was cool, but one hand was fisted in the pocket of her wide-legged trousers. "And I don't think you'll like the result of your philosophy when you're the weaker party."

"Is that a threat?" Wingate asked.

"It's the truth."

I realized I was holding my breath, and I released it. Riga's antagonism toward Wingate was scorching, and my face and chest heated.

Wingate stared at her a long moment then laughed. "Well?" He turned to me. "You said you wanted to copy it. As a gesture of goodwill, go ahead. I trust you to sell me your portion of the scroll."

"Hers may not be legitimate," Ezra warned, his gaze flicking uneasily to Riga. "Look at the condition it's in. It's suspiciously well preserved."

Wingate cocked a mercury eyebrow. "You know quite well that the damage to my section of scroll could have occurred after it had been separated from hers."

I pulled my electronic notebook and stylus from my bag. "I *would* like to copy your section now."

"Have at it." Wingate motioned negligently toward the non-reflective glass.

Bending over the table, I began the painstaking task of copying the text. The damage to it slowed my hand. So did *ye olde English* and the calligraphic hand.

I did not attempt to mimic the latter in my copying. The words were what mattered, not the format.

It took over three hours for me to transcribe his scroll, Wingate wandering in and out to check on my progress. Riga and Ezra watched me the entire time.

I set down my stylus, and my jaw hardened. I met Riga's gaze. Or I tried to. Her brows drawn downward, she glanced from my portion of scroll to Wingate's. Did she realize as well that there was a third piece missing?

The "sample" Wingate had shown me included the image of the bottom of a wooden wheel that had run nearly the width of the paper. It could only have been a Wheel of Fortune—a classic symbol of the ups and downs of luck found in nearly every Tarot deck.

There was no Wheel of Fortune on Wingate's scroll. The only other wheel on the framed vellum was too small, a part of the Sun and the Moon drawing. Neither included the line of text he'd shown me.

The top of my head heated. It was a sloppy omission if he'd planned to cheat me. So sloppy it had to have been intentional.

But why? I rubbed the back of my neck, my gaze clouding. Why tease me with the knowledge that he hadn't shown me the whole scroll? Why would Wingate let me know that he was holding out on me?

THE SUN AND THE MOON

Of the sunne and of the mone
Take ye both, they both trowe
Of diligent endeavor be
And wyth candor thou shal see
Knightly Sol we humbly begg
Illumyne this mundane egge
Wyth bold purpos charge to thy aim
In dignity to fortune's clayme

Luna, reflective orb so bryght
Dancing through dredefull depthes of nyght
Observe the world through knowing gaze
Surrender to thy sylver wayes
For the ballance must be founde
Between heavens and the grounde
From the wedding of mone and sunne
Wyll fortune be in conjunccioun.

CHAPTER 7

MY NAILS BIT MY palms. "Where's the rest of it?" The afternoon sun turned the lake to molten gold. It warmed the library's wood floors and high bookshelves.

"The rest?" Wingate dropped into his leather wingchair in the corner.

"The Wheel of Fortune," I said, tone sharp. "The portion from the image you showed me."

Riga edged closer. She studied Wingate's fragment of scroll and frowned. "She's right. A piece is missing. A piece you have, Wingate. Why?"

Ezra shook his head and made a clucking noise in his throat. He walked to a built-in bookcase and pretended to study the shelves.

Wingate laced his fingers over his stomach and stretched out his well-shod legs, crossing them at the ankles. "I don't know what you're talking about."

My neck corded. Crocodile grins are a thing. The length and sharpness of a crocodile's teeth are a warning to other crocs. Wingate's grin made me wonder if crocodiles had their own version of smug. If so, his had just won the world championship. *The bastard.*

Riga's strange eyes narrowed. "I won't be part of a cheat."

Wingate laughed. "Don't look so dire. That section is being restored. Isn't it, Ezra?"

Beneath his funereal suit jacket, Ezra's narrow shoulders twitched. "Yes," the antiquarian croaked.

"The deal was I would see the entire scroll." My voice was unpleasantly shrill, and I bit back a wince.

"And so you shall," Wingate said smoothly. "But not today. And isn't this enough to start with? Surely copying the images will keep you occupied for the rest of the day? It isn't as if you have anywhere else to be."

Annoyed, I pursed my lips. That was true. I *didn't* have anywhere else to be. But I didn't like that Wingate knew it.

The library door opened. Sam ambled into the room, a backpack slung over one shoulder of his blue, button-up shirt.

Wordlessly, the academic dropped it on the high corner table where a stack of leather-covered, loosely bound books lay. He sat on the stool beside it, flipped on a desk lamp, and rummaged in his worn pack.

I gritted my teeth. "Our deal was—"

"Yes, yes." Wingate raised his hands negligently. "And you'll see the other piece soon. If you think the main piece is a challenge to read, it's nothing compared to the section I'm having restored. You'll thank me when it's done. In the meantime, enjoy."

He walked to the door, placed his hand on the knob, and turned. "I'm sure you'll find a way to keep yourself occupied until the fragment returns from the restorer."

Wingate strode from the room. Ducking his head, Ezra scuttled after him.

Riga's lips compressed, and she exhaled heavily through her nose. "He's lying."

My laugh was mirthless. "You think?" Carefully, I rerolled my portion of scroll and slid it into its metal case. But why? A deal was a deal, and he wasn't getting his hands on my scroll unless he showed me all of his.

I stilled. But maybe he didn't *want* to buy mine? Maybe seeing mine had been enough?

Throat dry, I swallowed. Had I overplayed my hand? If Wingate had everything he wanted, there was no need...

I shook my head. No. First, Wingate liked to possess things and only the best things. He'd want to own the complete scroll. Second, my main goal wasn't to sell my part of the scroll. This delay might work in my favor.

"You should leave," Riga said in a low voice. "Don't play his game."

"Yes," I said through clenched teeth. "I *should* leave. But I won't."

A soft sigh escaped her lips. "I was afraid you'd say that."

"Wingate playing games again?" Sam hunched over his table, his back to us. "Shocking," he said, sarcastic.

"*Again?*" I asked.

Sam turned to us and scratched his graying beard. "He put me off for months before he finally agreed to let us see these letters. By that time, my research assistant was ready to have her baby, and she couldn't come out here."

"So, you got stuck with the lowly copying work?" I asked.

He grunted an affirmation. Riga eyed me.

Ignoring them both, I opened my notebook, and the screen background of an Oregon beach. I'd gone to that beach with Sarah years ago. A local artist made a labyrinth in the sand every Sunday. By the afternoon, the rising tide washed it away. Sarah and I had been the first ones through the completed labyrinth that morning.

It had been magical—not just the smooth sands and towering rock formations spotted with purple starfish, abandoned by the water. But the ephemeral nature of it all, the impermanence. The knowing that the labyrinth would soon vanish never to be seen again. My throat thickened.

I swiped my notebook to find a blank page. But I swiped too far, and one of my earlier sketches appeared on the screen—of Dragon House and the lake.

"You're an artist?" Riga asked.

"I wasn't formally trained."

"Does Wingate know how good you are?"

"We didn't discuss it."

"Hm." The corners of her mouth tilted upward.

I walked around the long, wooden table with my gear and studied the top of the scroll. Then I sat and relaxed my gaze.

Nodding, I began to sketch upside down. After the outline of the sun and moon was done to my satisfaction, I added the details with my stylus.

"Not formally trained?" One corner of Riga's mouth lifted.

I moved the text I'd copied beside the sun and moon. "High school art class doesn't count." I tackled their faces and the folds of their clothing.

"It's interesting," Riga said. "Ripley was an alchemist. I expected to see alchemical symbolism like the sun and moon." She pointed at the king and queen.

"But?" I asked, not lifting my head.

"But the artists of the medieval period tended to think of Fortune—or luck—as something uncontrollable. Were the alchemists able to somehow influence it? And if so, what of fate? Because the medieval worldview was heavily influenced by the idea that your fate was your fate. You couldn't change it."

"Do you believe that?" I asked her.

"I believe there are forces bigger and more powerful than us, and they act on our lives. But I also believe we have free will. Few people exercise that free will—"

I snorted. "That's cynical."

"But true," she said. "Most of us operate on autopilot, according to our unconscious programming. We react the same way to the same stimuli. We don't question our assumptions. And when we're not in the habit of asking questions, of exercising our free will, it becomes easier to be manipulated."

"And luck?" I asked, interested despite myself.

"I guess the real question is how random and chaotic is the universe? Does it only *seem* random? Or is one of those forces—call her Fortuna—throwing sand in the gears? I'm curious as to what the remainder of Wingate's scroll will say."

I spent the rest of the afternoon in that library beneath Riga's watchful gaze. An occasional grunt emerged from Sam's corner.

When I finished, Tobin was waiting outside the door. The estate manager swiped through my digital sketchbook and returned it to me, along with the phone he'd confiscated.

I jammed both in my satchel while he patted Riga down. Tobin returned her phone to her as well and glanced at the closed door. "Sam?"

I shrugged. Sam hadn't said more than two words to us once I'd gotten to copying the scroll's images. He'd still been at his books when I'd finished.

But Sam *did* turn up for dinner. He ignored me there as well. Riga stayed to dine and lectured us on alchemy.

Ezra and Wingate didn't make an appearance—Tobin informed us they'd gone to Sparks on business. He didn't tell us where the widow, Fortuna, was.

I made my excuses as soon as I could and escaped to my bedroom. The orange kitten seemed indifferent to my arrival.

I paced the room. I didn't believe for a second that Wingate was restoring a section of scroll. If it were true, he could have told me about it earlier.

Wingate was hiding it somewhere—somewhere he could no doubt gloat over it. His bedroom? His office? A hidden room?

I walked to the windows. The taillights of Riga's SUV glided away from Dragon House.

I drummed my fingers on the sill. If Wingate was still in Sparks, this might be my best chance to look for the scroll.

The kitten meowed. It sounded like a warning.

"But you're a cat." I ran the back of my finger along his soft fur. "And I don't believe in omens," I lied.

Besides, this bit of snooping would be easy. I wiped my palm on my jeans. From my earlier explorations of the house, I'd already located Wingate's private office—a luxuriously appointed room on the second floor overlooking the lake.

I made my way down the wide, twisting stairs. Portraits of men in antique dress stared disapprovingly down at me.

On the second floor, I walked to the office's carved wooden door and knocked lightly. No one answered. I glanced up and down the corridor, throw rugs lending muted color to its wood floors, and slipped inside.

Closing the door behind me, I let my eyes adjust to the darkness. A three-quarter moon illuminated high-backed chairs, bookshelves, a desk.

I glided to the desk and tried a drawer. *Locked.* My stomach jittered. I glanced at the closed door behind me.

The scroll fragment wouldn't be in a desk. It would be kept protected, inside a glass case. Though if it were small enough, it might fit in one of the drawers...

I shook my head and walked to a bookcase, banging my knee on a low table in the process. Smothering a curse, I rubbed my knee. *Ow, ow, ow.*

The overhead light flicked on, and my heart stopped. I swallowed, straightened, and turned.

Sam leaned in the open doorway. He folded his arms over his button-up shirt. His jeans hung loosely on his slim hips. "Looking for that last piece of scroll?"

Chagrined, I straightened. But the best defense, etc., etc... "Why not?"

"Because Wingate isn't the kind of guy you want to mess with. It isn't worth playing against someone like him."

No risk, no reward. But some people never learned that. I guessed Sam was one of those people. "I'm not you."

His bearded face tightened, and he stepped away from the door frame. "Be thankful I'm not Wingate. He wouldn't find your little exploration entertaining."

I smiled bitterly. "How much longer will your work keep you here?" I asked sweetly.

"Another week."

Great. Wordlessly, I strode past him and up the stairs to my bedroom.

The kitten trotted to me when I walked in the door. I'd like to think he'd been worried, but he turned and hurried to his bowl, mewling piteously.

I glanced inside the metal bowl and frowned. "There's still plenty of food in there." What was his problem?

He pawed at the bare spot at the bottom.

Whatever. "Fine." I added more food to the bowl, and the kitten buried his pink nose in it.

I went to bed with a paperback I'd brought—a mystery romance set in Regency England. The kitten curled beside me and fell asleep, purring like a backhoe.

Despite the noise, I fell asleep too. I walked into the dream cabin. *Sarah. Come through the door.* The old woman looked up from her knitting by the fire and wagged a finger. "You're not ready."

WHACK. The sound of my book hitting the floor startled me awake and off my pillow. I blinked in the darkened bedroom. *Damn it.* I'd been so close...

The reading lamp's narrow cone of light was the room's only illumination. Its light warped in the water carafe by my bedside. I reached to turn off the lamp and noticed the kitten was no longer on the pillow beside mine.

My hands fisted in the duvet cover. "Kitten?" I whispered.

I grimaced. Why was I whispering? The windows were closed, the door locked. The kitten had no doubt found a better place to sleep and would reemerge in the morning.

I clicked off the light. Moonlight slipped through the blinds, making prison bars on the wood floor. The air seemed somehow thicker, closer, oppressive. I gasped, drawing in slow breaths that didn't fill quite my lungs.

Throwing off the heavy duvet, I padded to the windows and reached for one of the wooden blinds. A current of dread raised the hair on the back of my neck. My hand froze, inches from the glass.

Someone was watching me. And not someone outside. Someone *inside* the room. And in that watching was a thick malevolence.

I forced myself to turn. A sphinxlike silhouette detached itself from the shadows beneath the desk. I laughed shakily. *The kitten.*

Its shadow grew, elongating.

"Are you ready to come to—"

The words died in my throat. The blackness deepened. From it burned two ancient yellow eyes, feral and cruel. The shadow spread, its darkness rippling across the wood floor.

That wasn't the kitten. It wasn't anything real or natural or good.

It was a monster.

THE PHILOSOPHER'S STONE

Lo, take ye now the quintessence
And transmute that to its essence
Elixir of lyfe yet ye distille
Obedient to Fortuna's wille
Lest lyke the mage of olden tyme
Who sought Fortuna's gentler clyme
Wyth offerings blyssed and customs dere
Began his quest, released his feare
And Fortuna's favor he dyd knowe
Until in arrogance he dyd showe
His pryde ryvall wyth humylite
And his gred wrestle wyth charyte
Losing favor in fortune's syght
Did he feele ful destiny's blyght
And lo beneath Fortuna's whele
Did he receive the losse of wele

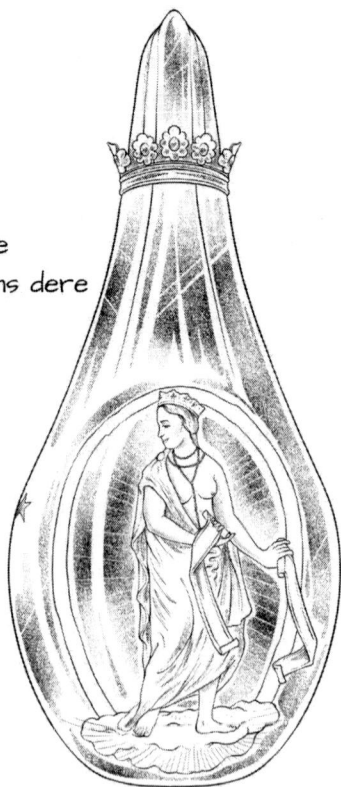

CHAPTER 8

THE DARKNESS CONDENSED INTO a catlike shape. Its silhouette moved like oil, yellow eyes seething in the darkness. Claws clicked against the wood floor as if it were real, but it *couldn't* be real.

I shook my head, numb. *Not real.*

It wasn't real, because it was impossible. A black so dark it drowned everything it touched. Too big for a normal cat, even a mountain lion. The shadow growled, and metal jangled in response—my bedside lamp trembling.

I understood now that old saw about blood freezing. Everything about me felt frozen—my limbs, my heart, my lungs. The shadow crept closer.

I was trapped. The impossible darkness stood between me and the bedroom door. I was hallucinating. It couldn't hurt me. It was the kitten's distorted shadow. Yes. That was it. Only a shadow.

"Here, Kitty." My voice cracked on the last syllable, and I was breathing again. My head spun. I was hyperventilating, pulse racing.

HISS. A tiny shadow bolted from beneath the desk. The kitten leapt, yowling.

The big cat vanished.

The striped kitten landed where the darkness had been. He sniffed the floor, sat, and licked a paw.

A strangled laugh emerged from my throat. My legs folded, and I sat hard on the edge of the bed.

Shakily, I forced myself to stand and tottered to the light switch. I turned it on.

My borrowed bedroom flooded with golden light. The wardrobe. The sissal carpet. The desk. The unmade bed, mounded with white duvet and sheets. All normal.

Bracing one hand on the bed, I made my way to the end table and its carafe of water. I managed to refill the glass without spilling and drank, water dripping down my chin.

I wiped it away with the back of my hand. I was awake. This was real.

Could I have been sleepwalking? Could the cougar or panther or what-ever-the-hell-it-was have been part of a walking nightmare?

The kitten stopped licking its paw and shot me a disdainful look. I checked the door. The window. All closed and locked and panther-free.

Though it was after three AM, I dressed in stretchy khaki slacks and a coffee-colored knit turtleneck, turned on my writing tablet, and sat at the desk. I was too shaken to return to sleep.

I typed my sister's name into the web browser app. A black panther raced across the screen and vanished at its edge.

I rubbed my eyes. Obviously, I'd imagined *that*. It had been a mental fragment of leftover fear, a trick of the eyes after all that darkness.

But could I have imagined the cat in my room? I glanced at the note-book and bit the inside of my cheek. My gaze bounced to the kitten, now licking his other paw.

I'd imagined it. That was all. That was the only thing that made sense.

I scanned the list of articles. I'd read them before—one a targeted advertisement from a lawyer suggesting Sarah's family sue for wrongful death. I opened the police notice posted in the local paper.

NEVADA DEPARTMENT OF PUBLIC SAFETY – 2.2.2024 *Fatality Crash in Douglas County*

By Editor | February 2, 2024 | 0

Number of Vehicles in Crash: 2   Number of Injured: 0   Number Killed: 2

Date & Time: February 2, 2024, at 3:56 a.m.

County: Douglas.

Location: US-50, east of Stateline.

Posted Speed Limit: 55 MPH.

Road Condition: Wet.

Vehicle 1: 2020 Chevrolet Tahoe.

Driver 1: Deceased.

Mary Ann Frankel, 56-YOA from Auburn, CA.

Seatbelt: Yes

Pronounced dead at the scene.

Vehicle 2: 2021 Dodge Ram.

Driver 2: Deceased.

Sarah Carthart, 50-YOA from Auburn, CA.

Seatbelt: Yes.

Pronounced dead at the scene.

Description: Preliminary investigation indicates that vehicle 1 was traveling eastbound when it veered off the highway to avoid a pedestrian. The driver of vehicle 1 overcorrected, causing the vehicle to cross into the westbound lane and strike vehicle 2 head-on. This investigation is ongoing, and no additional information is available.

Investigated by: R. Linnel, DS.

The kitten mewled and dropped from the desk and into my lap. Absently, I rubbed his orange head.

Sarah's killer had been from Auburn too. In a weird twist of luck or fate, Sarah and Mary Ann had known each other. Though that hadn't stopped Sarah's husband from suing Mary Ann's estate for wrongful death.

Since Sarah had earned all the money and her husband had spent it, he probably had a good case. Payouts in those sorts of cases were based on the financial loss to the survivor.

My heart squeezed so hard I had to force myself to breathe. I'd helped clean out my sister's closet after her death. The soles of her shoes had been worn through. She'd walked in tattered shoes while her "retired" husband had used her money to buy a new sports car and the best power suits she could afford.

I re-read the report by Deputy Linnel. Deputy Linnel, who'd been to Dragon House after Devin's death. Was it coincidence that he'd investigated Sarah's accident too?

But the deputy hadn't been the anonymous caller who'd told me about Wingate's role in the accident. The caller had been a woman.

That morning, I grabbed a bagel to go and left Dragon House before I could hear more of Wingate's excuses. He'd show me the rest of the scroll when he was good and ready. The more I pestered him, the longer that would likely take.

I drove to the wood-timbered mini mall where I'd seen the photographer with his mountain lion. If the big cat in my bedroom hadn't been a figment of my imagination, then it must have been real.

I'd thought the cat had been black, but in the darkened room, I couldn't be certain. And maybe the photographer made money off his mountain lion with more than photography.

I didn't know how someone could have slipped a mountain lion in and out of my room without me noticing. But it beat the alternative—that my visions were worsening.

But neither cat nor photographer were at the shopping center. I asked the woman behind the counter at a nearby Irish pub, but she just shrugged.

Frustrated, I wandered outside and stopped short in front of the pub's sandwich board, decorated with a shamrock:

IT'S NOT ABOUT LUCK. TRY COUNSELING.

I snorted a laugh. The message was a coincidence. It was an Irish bar. It was a no-brainer that there'd be something with shamrocks and luck on their signboard.

I looked away, across the highway. A familiar black SUV sat in the lot opposite.

Crossing the busy highway, I climbed the stairs of the wooden building to Riga's office. I knocked twice, tried the knob, and walked in as Riga emerged from the doorway to the small reception area.

"I thought I might see you again," she said.

"Unless Wingate fired you, it was a good bet. You have to return to Dragon House when he brings out the rest of the scroll." If *he brings it out.*

"I meant I thought I might see you *here.*" She opened the door to her private office. "Come on in. Do you want some coffee?"

"No thanks." I sat in a leather chair, my back to the stone fireplace. "What do you know about the mountain lion that was over there on Tuesday?" I nodded in the direction of the shopping area across the street.

"Not much." She walked around the desk and sat, her back to the window and the lake behind it. "I've never had my picture taken with the cat, though the eight-year-old in me has always wanted to. But it seems wrong, somehow. Though I've heard the cat's well taken care of."

"Do you know where I can find him?"

"The photographer is at the shopping center every Tuesday. Why?"

"There was a... It looked like a big cat was in my bedroom last night," I said, the words rushed.

She leaned back in her leather executive chair. Bracing her elbows on its arms, she steepled her fingers. "Interesting."

I stared. I'd just told her I'd seen or imagined a mountain lion had been in my bedroom. My story was ridiculous. Insane. "Interesting? Not impossible?"

"Well, either you're lying, which is interesting, or you're not, which is even more interesting. You said you didn't *see* things."

I pressed the flat of my hand to my stomach. "I don't. I mean... I could be crazy." And why did I want Riga—of all people—to tell me I wasn't?

"Do you think you're crazy?" Riga asked.

"No, but isn't that what crazy people say?"

"I'm a metaphysical detective, not a psychiatrist."

"Yeah," I said, "you mentioned that." I drummed my fingers on the arm of the leather chair. "How *does* one become a metaphysical detective?"

"By looking for answers, no matter where they take you."

"Even into the supernatural?"

"The supernatural is sort of implied," Riga said, wry.

"Like ghosts?"

Riga shrugged, the shoulders of her white blouse lifting and falling. "Sometimes."

I leaned forward. "Do *you* see ghosts?" Hope fluttered in my belly. Could she see Sarah? Was Sarah here? Would Riga tell me if she were?

"When they're around and want to be seen, yes."

Tell me she's here. "Are *they* very interesting?"

She smiled. "Most are confused, though their cases are interesting. Some are obsessed with everything they can't do, which is pitiable but boring. The most interesting thing I heard from a ghost recently was that it's all love. I'm still not entirely sure what she was talking about, but it's food for thought."

Rubbing the back of my head, I slouched in the chair. My pulse thudded in my throat. Sarah wasn't here, or Riga wouldn't tell me. Or Sarah was here, and Riga couldn't see her.

But it shouldn't matter. I should be able to call Sarah to my dreams. Why couldn't I?

Maybe it didn't matter. Maybe I was deluding myself. I lowered my chin and studied my sneakers. I wanted to believe the dead people I saw in my dreams were spirits. But were they just my imagination?

A squirrel scampered along the wide ledge outside the window. Its tail flicked in a question mark.

I swallowed. An imaginary sister was better than none. "Did this ghost come to you because of unfinished business?"

"Not all ghosts have unfinished business. Sometimes they have a hard time letting go. Or the people they love have a hard time letting go."

My throat tightened. Was I keeping my sister here? A part of me wanted Sarah here, wanted her to reach out to me. Another part realized how unfair that was.

"Has anything else weird happened?" Riga asked.

I hesitated. That panther that had flitted across my notebook's screen... Could my writing tablet have been hacked? Or had it been a creation of my sleep-deprived mind? The remnant of a nightmare?

"My notebook behaved strangely last night," I said slowly.

She leaned forward and set her elbows on her desk. "Oh? How?"

I shook my head. "Just... Strangely."

"As in magically strange?"

"I don't—" I gave a short laugh. "A magic computer?"

Riga's returning smile was slight. "Sure. Technomancers use technology for their magic. Chaos magicians could also incorporate it. Actually, anyone with access to the internet—"

"It was probably a computer virus," I blurted.

"Computer viruses are a lot like spells. They exist to cause an effect. Their operation is hidden. There are defenses and protections one can use against them. Certain spells can even propagate like a virus. And both can have unforeseen consequences."

"It wasn't magic."

"Says the woman who thinks Fortune is a living, physical force."

"I don't know if it's living. And it's just a hypothesis," I said, rattled. How had we gotten on this track? "And why do you keep asking if I *see* things?"

Riga looked away. "There's something about you that reminds me of a shaman I know. The more... courageous shamans do more than travel to lower and upper worlds. They can also see middle world."

"Middle world?"

"The spirits and other... things around us." She made a looping motion over her head with one hand.

I huddled deeper in the soft leather. *Other things.* That darkness I'd seen last night, the thing on the beach after Sarah's death... "I don't see ghosts."

"But you see other things?"

"No," I said. "I can see—when I want—the departed in my dreams." *Tell me about Sarah.*

"Do you have big dreams?"

"Lucid dreams." And they hadn't been doing me much good lately.

"You can become aware that you're dreaming? You can control your dreams?"

I nodded.

Riga leaned back and steepled her fingers. "Interesting. I've never been able to lucid dream on command."

She wouldn't or couldn't tell me about Sarah. I changed the subject. "Could my appearance at Dragon House and Devin's murder be related? Is that synchronicity? Or was Devin murdered because I arrived when I did?"

"Or because of who you are? Or maybe *you* murdered Devin."

My jaw hardened. "I barely knew the man."

"But you wanted a look at his uncle's scroll. Devin was killed outside Wingate's library, where the scroll was stored."

I'd known Riga had reasons for letting me take up her time. I didn't like that an interrogation had been one of them, but I'd walked into that. "Someone came from outside the house," I said. "The security videos proved that."

"Do they?"

"You haven't seen them yet then?"

"Actually, I have." Studying her palm, she massaged it with the thumb of her opposite hand. "A man climbing over a stone wall lined with broken glass, crossing to the rear patio, breaking more glass to enter the house, and then leaving the house and retreating over the same wall, all around the time of Devin's murder."

"How did he get over the glass studding the wall?"

Riga met my gaze. "Quite easily. It didn't seem to bother him. At all."

Strange. I tugged at the collar of my blouse. "How did you get involved with Wingate?"

"Involved? That's an interesting way to put it."

I waited.

She relaxed in her executive chair. "He's mob, you know. He claims he's ex-mob, but I don't believe it. I'm not sure they have much of a retirement plan. His *organization* was running some fortune tellers—"

"Fortune tellers? They're a mob thing?"

"They can be." She crossed her legs, and the fabric of her slacks rustled. "Often the little shacks you see along the road with palms and Tarot cards painted on their sides are mob run. They give honest psychics a bad name."

"I had no idea." If Wingate had been involved in running mob fortune tellers—and he must have been for Riga to have gotten involved—then he wasn't just an investment manager with mob clients. He was *in* the mob.

"Neither did my client," Riga said.

"Was she taken advantage of by a fortune teller?"

"She *was* a fortune teller. She said she had no idea what she was getting into. I helped get her out. Or I thought..." She trailed off, frowning.

"How did you get her out?"

Riga's smile was taut. "Telling you would be more trouble for us both than it's worth. Hopefully, Wingate didn't hold a grudge."

"He mustn't have, since he hired you."

"Yes. But I didn't accept because I thought he needed my help."

Had she put a slight emphasis on the word, *he*? "Why did you accept?"

"Because I don't like being used as a cat's paw." Anger flashed like summer lightning across her heart-shaped face. There and gone and followed by... regret?

"Did you suspect there'd be trouble over the scroll?" I shifted on the soft leather.

"Some objects attract trouble. I hoped this wouldn't be one of them. But I was curious about the scroll—professional interest. And you know what they say about curiosity and cats."

I frowned. *Cats again.* Had that been a warning? A threat? Or had I simply implanted the idea of cats in her mind, and it had bubbled back up?

"Then you don't know the name of the photographer with the mountain lion?" I asked.

"No. He must have gotten permission from the mall owner to be there. You could ask her."

"I will." And I should have thought of that myself. I rose. "Thanks."

"What are you looking for?" she asked.

I paused beside the office door. "Answers, I guess."

"Yes, but is that all?"

"What else is there?" I walked out the door.

As it slowly swung shut behind me, Riga called, "Don't look at them directly—the things you see in middle world. It's best if they don't—" The door shut, cutting off her final words.

The management office at the alpine strip mall was closed. But I noted down the name of it, found the number online, and left a message.

It was a long shot. The more logical explanation was that I'd imagined the entire thing, including the panther racing across my notebook's screen.

But I *wanted* the cat to be real. And if Wingate or someone else had somehow snuck a wildcat into my bedroom—impossible as that seemed—I needed to know. I needed to know I wasn't crazy.

Could someone be gaslighting me? No. My chest tightened. The visions had started before I'd come to Dragon House.

In my SUV, I leaned my head back against the driver's seat headrest. *Luck. Fate.* Had the scroll brought me to Wingate, or had Wingate brought me to the scroll? Because his luck obsession had become mine.

My throat ached. Oh, yes, I wanted... not revenge exactly. But I wanted to know *why* he'd been on the highway. *Why* he'd caused the other driver to swerve.

And now I wanted to know why Devin had died too. Wingate was connected to a lot of deaths—many I no doubt knew nothing about. But he was connected to my sister, to the other driver, and now to Devin's murder.

Wingate had possessed that fragment of the scroll for years though. It was only when I'd brought my piece to him that Devin had been killed.

My hands tingled. I rubbed my thumb against the inside of the steering wheel.

Questions. Too many questions. And the biggest question of all: was I somehow to blame for Devin's death?

THE FOUR ELEMENTS

The spirit of water
Ethereal daughter
Mercury's restless sea
Pacified let thou be
Emancipate thy dewy dros
Release from myre that which was loste
And thou shalt find Fortuna's fame
Never speaking loud her name
Cease thou now, thy fervent deeds
Evene measure, fortune heeds
Judge the nature of the aire
Under skyes of clouds and faire
Steadfast in winds' harsh embrace
The man who wields this hath he grace
In fortune's eyes and fortune's renne
Cal the mone and claime the sunne
Embrace thy fate wyth all thy breth
Cast off your fear and flee not deth
Obedient to fortune's charge
Unerthe now thy ynnermost spark
Rise as phoenix from the ashe
And in sacred fyere thy soul must bathe
God grant ye strength upon the erthe
Endure the fiery furnace herth
Prick thou now the green lion bryht
Restore thyself in fortune's syght
Unerthe the Philosophre's stone
Descend thy airy mountain home
Ere thee succumb to fortune's blyght
Now seek within the inner lyht
Cast aside the shades of nyght
Else lost forever yet thou myght

CHAPTER 9

"IT'S YOUR FAULT," FORTUNA slurred, walking across the patio. The skirt of her elegant black dress fluttered.

A brisk breeze whipped whitecaps and ruffled her red hair. Waves lapped against the lakeshore in a frantic susurration. Thunderheads massed over the eastern Sierras.

I tensed in the Adirondack chair. It wasn't the alcohol on her breath that unnerved me. What unnerved me was the echo of my own thoughts earlier that day. *Was* I to blame?

I shifted my notebook in my lap. It hummed, the anti-virus program scanning. A pinecone dropped to the flagstones.

"Your fault." She dropped heavily into the chair beside me and stared at the mercury lake.

I opened my mouth to speak, but there was no reasonable response to being accused of murder. Or maybe there was—to walk away.

But a storm was moving in. I wanted to stare back at the lake while I had the chance and to prove I'd conquered my imagination. So far, I hadn't proved a thing. The lake had a... presence. I pulled my sister's furry vest tighter.

"He wanted it. They all wanted it." Fortuna scowled at me. "You want it."

"You mean... the scroll?" My stomach gave an after-lunch rumble. "Devin wanted the scroll?"

"It's the scroll's fault he's dead." She shifted, the legs of her chair scraping against the patio's weathered flagstones. "Wasn't very lucky for Devin, was it? Nothing at Dragon House was."

"Why did Devin want the Luck Scroll?"

"They thought he wasn't good enough," Fortuna muttered. "Just a financial analyst. He kept Wingate out of trouble. *Devin* did all the work that mattered." She checked her cell phone.

What sort of trouble? "What type of work?"

"Why do *you* want to know?" Fortuna made a sweeping gesture, and her phone clattered to the flagstones. She jerked forward, her breath noisy. "Are you spying on me too?"

"Hardly," I said, taken aback. "I think someone's been spying on *me*." Maybe Fortuna and I could bond over our shared paranoia.

"My phone." She scooped it up, leaning so far over the arm of the wooden chair that it tilted, two of its legs lifting off the patio. "They know everyone I call. Don't text me."

Fortuna lurched off her chair, and its legs banged down. Unsteadily, she walked to the rear door of the Dragon-style mansion and inside.

I checked my notebook. The program had finished—no viruses found.

I hefted myself from the Adirondack chair, and my phone rang in my pocket. It was a number I didn't recognize.

"Hello?" I asked cautiously.

"This is Veda at the Greenwood Management Company returning your call. About the mountain lion guy?"

"Oh! Yes." I balanced the notebook on the low, stone wall overlooking the lake. "Do you know how I could get in touch with him?"

"Sure." She rattled off a number.

Hastily, I scrawled it into my notebook, then repeated it back to her. "Thanks."

I called the number. This, too, went to voicemail.

"Augh." Instead of returning inside, I walked around the house, across the lawn, and into the pine forest. I wanted to be alone to clear my head, and the patio was too visible from inside the house. And from the lake.

Dry pine needles and the occasional pinecone snapped beneath my shoes. The darkening lake glimpsed me from between the pines.

Queasy, I gnawed my bottom lip. Did the sheriff really consider me a suspect? Did the others in the house?

Was that why Wingate was dragging his heels when it came to showing me the rest of the scroll? He'd said he wanted to keep an eye on me. As long as I stayed at Dragon House, I was also under the eyes of the others.

I stopped beside a lightning-struck pine. Could Wingate know he'd been responsible for my sister's death? I hadn't been mentioned in her obituary—Sarah's husband had seen to that.

It made the anonymous caller all the more curious. The woman had to be someone in law enforcement. They'd reached out to Sarah's husband after the accident, not to me.

But my sister'd had a photo of me in her wallet. She'd preferred printed pictures over photos on her phone, had thought they were more real. Was that how the caller had found me?

A chipmunk chittered at me from a branch above, and I moved on. Wind tossed the trees, and another pinecone dropped to the ground.

I rubbed my forehead. Wingate had done a background check on me. He knew about Joe. He could have turned up the connection to Sarah. The old mobster might know I had other reasons for being here. If he did, I'd bet he found it funny.

Something the color of a fortress wall emerged between the pines. For lack of anything better to do, I made my way toward it. It was a stone outbuilding with a peaked shingle roof and a green wooden door. A row of windows faced the stone boundary wall, their glass too warped to see through.

Highway sounds rose and fell on the other side of the stone wall. Car engines, the rumble of the occasional truck. The top of the wall glittered with broken glass. How *had* the intruder gotten over it?

Quite easily. It didn't seem to bother him at all. Riga's words echoed in my mind.

A shiver raised gooseflesh on my arms, and I rubbed my biceps. Surely the sheriff would have examined the wall where he'd gone over. The intruder must have left threads of clothing or blood or skin. There would be DNA evidence, and I would be in the clear.

I tried the outbuilding's thick, green door. *Locked.* Disappointed, I rubbed the back of my neck. Not that I thought Wingate was keeping the rest of the scroll in here. I was just bored and nosy.

I walked around the back of the building and scanned the boundary wall. Riga hadn't said where the intruder had climbed over.

I stopped short at a spiked metal gate, chained shut with a thick padlock. It would have been easier to attack the gate rather than climb over that broken glass. Its chain was rusted, but the shiny padlock looked new.

I turned. A security camera blinked red beneath the outbuilding's eaves. It was aimed at the gate. That might have stopped the intruder from trying the gate, but he hadn't avoided the cameras when he'd scaled the wall.

And why did I keep thinking of him as an intruder rather than a killer? I rounded the other corner of the building. A streak of white caught my eye. Curious, I moved closer.

An arrow had been chalked on the wall by the gate. It looked new, the chalk bright white, but there were traces of fletching that had been erased, as well as a faded arrow going in the opposite direction.

Footsteps crunched through the pines, and I tensed. Sam rounded a thick tree trunk.

"You scared me," I snapped.

Sam scanned me, his expression critical. "If you're scared, you shouldn't be out here alone."

I ignored that. "Did you draw this arrow?"

"What arrow?"

I pointed at the chalk drawing. The academic came to stand beside me. "No," Sam said slowly. "I've never been this way before." He ruffled the curling, salt-and-pepper hair at the back of his head.

"What brought you here now?" My breath quickened. Had he been following me?

"Just wandering."

"Do you wander often?"

He scratched his beard. "Whenever I want to think. My guess is the arrow's a secret message."

"You're kidding," I said flatly.

Sam grinned, and my face warmed. He *had* been kidding.

"Since you're interested in medieval texts," he said, "surely you've heard of *The Swift and Secret Messenger*?"

I hadn't. My interest was in luck and luck alone. And I'd look very silly if this text was about luck, and I hadn't heard of it. "What's that got to do with anything?"

"Spy craft." Sam nodded toward the arrow. "It's one of the earliest treatises on how to pass messages secretly. And of course, it has occult leanings. Strange how the occult and spy craft seem to go hand-in-hand. Like John Dee."

Now he was showing off, but I nodded. Dee had been Queen Elizabeth the First's advisor and top spy. If memory served, he'd also fancied himself a necromancer.

"Or look at the CIA with their psychic and remote viewing experiments," Sam continued. "Nothing's changed. We still want a magical answer to passing intel."

I hugged my notebook tighter to my chest. A *magical answer... Technomancers...* I glanced toward the gate, and the security camera aimed at it from beneath the eave of the small building.

Stop it. I shook myself. "Right," I said. "Because why use a cell phone?" But I remembered what Fortuna had said about her cell phone being tapped. Could that be true? "Why are you really here?" I blurted.

"I'm here to transcribe letters from the Estonian crusades. Why are *you* really here?"

"For the Luck Text."

"You gave up your high-powered job for what amounts to a treasure hunt?" Sam lifted a brow.

"And your only research assistant left you high and dry?" I asked. "No, that's not suspicious at all."

"You're projecting. You're accusing me of what you're doing—having ulterior motives."

"That's ridiculous."

"Is it?" He crossed his arms over his broad chest. "You want to sell your piece of the text, but not without seeing the rest of it. Why?"

"Because the text means more than money to me. I want to understand it, and there's no way I could afford to buy Wingate's portion. My best option is to copy his, sell mine, and move on."

One corner of his lips quirked. "I understand academic obsession. I've been in the grip of it too often. *Can* you move on?"

Could I? I closed my eyes and drew a slow breath.

I wanted to believe that someday my life would resume its normal course. I wanted to believe I'd be happy again. I wanted to believe, but I couldn't. My sister was dead, and nothing would be the same.

GRATITUDE

EVERYTHING IN THE UNIVERSE is interconnected. When we understand this and begin to *see* the world's connectedness, we can see the world magically. The corollary to this magical law is that if everything's connected, then we should appreciate everything that touches us, both good and bad.

And if we can feel gratitude for the things that haven't happened yet but that we'd *like* to happen, we're seeding the universe with our good intentions.

But what about the truly awful, the unforgivable things? Is it possible to feel grateful for even the worst of situations? Why would we even want to? Wouldn't that just attract more problems into our lives?

The answer is: *while it may not be possible or even desirable to feel gratitude for the experience, we can feel gratitude for the lessons learned and challenges overcome.* And when the witch can manage this, it becomes easier to release the energies of negative experiences and the memories that may be keeping her from her magic.

This isn't about forgiveness. This is about freedom. We can recreate the meaning of what happened to us and make it empowering—or at least, *more* empowering.

Admittedly, this type of gratitude isn't always easy. But these challenges can add meaning to our lives. They provide a sense of contrast, expanding our appreciation for the good times. They also bring a sense of joy and fulfillment once we *do* solve a problem. Strange as it may seem, feeling gratitude for problems helps us focus on solving them.

Action item: Contemplate a negative experience from your past. Now list the positive lessons or ideas that may have come out of it on the downloadable worksheet. You'll probably find at least a few, though you may have to do some mental stretching to find them. Then contemplate the meaning of the Gratitude card, below.

SCAN ME

Gratitude

Gratitude. Recognition. Paying it forward.

If what we pay attention to expands, counting our blessings helps them grow. But there's more to gratitude than that. Gratitude inoculates us against despair. It's an antidote to resentment, and resentment is the route to mental and spiritual hell.

Gratitude isn't, however, a random emotion. It's a practice. So take time today to consider the good things in your life, from the roof over your head, to the birds outside, to the things and people that bring you joy.

The symbols:

Hands over her heart in gratitude, a woman holds a chrysanthemum. A hummingbird pauses to feed from it, pollinating the flower at the same time. Gratitude is a gift for everyone involved.

The questions:

Are you able to receive others' generosity with gratitude? What do you have to be grateful for? Can you be grateful for how far you've come?

Where Can You Find Gratitude?

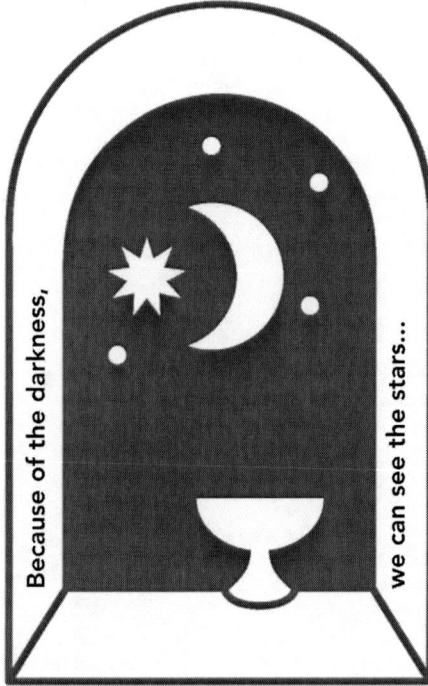

Because of the darkness, we can see the stars...

CHAPTER 10

DISGUSTED, I CURSED AND tossed the new card onto my pillow. The kitten picked his way across the snowscape of duvet. He sniffed the card then looked up at me.

"Some guard kitten *you* are."

I glared at my writing notebook and the mystery school email on its gray screen. *Gratitude*? I was supposed to feel gratitude? For what? A dead sister? Should I be happy that Devin had been murdered instead of me?

"I want to know about luck, not gratitude," I told the kitten. And I could always unsubscribe from the emails. But could I unsubscribe from Riga leaving cards on my pillow?

I stormed into the hallway and ran headfirst into the man I was looking for—Tobin. I staggered back at the impact. The estate manager did not.

"In a hurry?" Tobin quirked a dark brow.

I smoothed the front of my top, heat stealing into my face. "Looking for you. When was Riga Hayworth here today?"

He blinked. "She wasn't."

"How can you be sure?"

Tobin angled his dark head. "I know who comes in and out of Dragon House."

I said nothing. He hadn't known when someone had climbed the wall and murdered Devin. Spots of color darkened his high cheekbones.

My brow puckered. If the killer's entrance and exit had been caught on video, why hadn't an alarm been tripped?

"Isn't there an alarm?" I asked. "How did that guy get in here to kill Devin and no alarm went off?"

"He used a jammer." Tobin ripped out the words, impatience razoring his tone.

"How—?"

"I don't know all the technicalities, but our tech guy told me it was possible. It's the only explanation, outside of magic." His upper lip curled.

"But he didn't jam the video," I said slowly.

"He didn't have to. No one can tell who he is from that video. I get an alert if there's been a breach—the video is motion-activated. I didn't get the alert. It's not like I'm sitting around watching video monitors all night. Or day, for that matter. Don't worry, you're safe. We've corrected the vulnerability."

"But... You're *sure* Riga wasn't on the grounds this afternoon?"

"She wasn't here today at all. Do you want to watch the videos yourself?"

"Yes," I said. "I do."

"That wasn't a serious—" He rolled his eyes. "Fine. This way."

He led me down the stairs and pressed a wood panel beneath the staircase. A hidden door swung silently open, and I exclaimed.

"Yes," he said with a cool detachment. "I am the boy beneath the stairs." Crouching slightly, he ducked inside. "Come on in," he called. "There's plenty of space."

I hesitated then walked inside. It was a wide staircase, so I shouldn't have been surprised by the depth and width of the sloped room. A bank of video monitors hung from the back wall. A spartan metal desk with a computer, a notebook, and a pen stood before a chair.

"The videos are time-stamped," Tobin said. "When do you want to start looking?"

"From the moment I returned from my errand this morning. Around eleven o'clock."

He folded his long arms, his biceps bulging. "Heaven forbid you miss a free lunch."

"I haven't seen you turning your nose up at them," I said sharply, and he grinned.

He bent to the computer and tapped in commands. The monitors flickered.

"Security," Tobin said.

"Yes, Tobin?" a feminine voice responded.

I shifted my weight. The voice had seemed so real it was unnerving. I almost preferred the more mechanical mispronunciations of my car's navigation system. At least then I knew what I was talking to.

"Display videos of everyone entering the estate from eleven AM today until this moment," Tobin said.

"No one entered the estate from eleven AM this morning until this moment," the voice responded.

I stared at the monitors. "Is that—?"

"The AI," Tobin said.

"But the AI was tampered with before," I said. "You said it was jammed. How can you tell—?"

"Security," Tobin said. "Has your programming been altered in any way today?"

"No, Tobin," the AI responded. "My programming has not been altered in any way within the last twenty-four hours."

"That's how I know," Tobin said.

"But... What if it *has* been altered, and the AI doesn't know it?"

"You're not going to be satisfied until you've looked at the entire video feed, are you?"

I crossed my arms over my chest. "No."

"Fine. Security, display video from all the monitors starting at eleven AM this morning up until..." He checked his watch. "One-thirty today."

"Beginning now," the AI purred. The images on the screens jumped.

Tobin motioned toward the monitors. "Have at it."

I shrugged out of my vest, hung it over the back of the metal chair, and sat. The chair lurched sideways on creaky wheels, and my breath hitched. I steadied the chair. "Er, is there a way to watch at double speed?"

"Security," Tobin said. "Run the video at two times the normal speed."

"Yes, Tobin."

I watched 90 minutes of video, and Tobin watched me. He stood close enough for me to feel the heat from his body.

I watched myself on the patio with Fortuna. I watched myself amble into the woods. I watched Sam find me by the outbuilding. But I did not see anyone enter or leave the estate.

"Satisfied?" Tobin asked after I'd finished.

I stretched in the wobbly chair. "No. You admitted something funny was going on with your cameras."

"And that we'd fixed it." He scowled. Reaching over my shoulder, he tapped the keyboard, and the screens blinked.

"Yeah," I said, "but how can you—?" I inhaled a hiss. In the driveway, a black-and-white Fortuna opened the door to a Jaguar. Pushing back the metal chair, I stood. "Fortuna was drunk earlier."

"She looks fine now." He motioned to the monitor.

"We have to stop her." I stood and grabbed my sister's vest off the back of the chair.

"You think I can stop Fortuna? I'm just the hired help."

I slipped into the furry vest. "Call the sheriff." I hurried from the room beneath the stairs, across the foyer, and out the front door. Fortuna's turquoise Jaguar drifted down the gravel drive.

Cursing, I jogged to my SUV and got inside. Fortunately, I'd gotten into the habit of keeping my key fob in my pocket and a license and credit card in my phone, which I had now. I started my car and followed Fortuna.

What would I accomplish by following her? I wasn't dumb or desperate enough to risk trying to get in front of her Jaguar to slow or stop the car. But I couldn't let her drunkenly take someone else's sister, mother, friend.

She pulled onto the highway. I drove onto the winding road behind her and honked. She didn't notice—or at least she didn't slow. I glanced around, hoping to see a sheriff's car.

Fortuna was driving slowly, carefully. She drove like someone who knew she'd had too much to drink and thought she could get away with it. I honked again. She kept driving, oblivious.

We drove past a roadside memorial, a cross garlanded with a faded wreath of pink, plastic flowers. My hands clenched on the wheel.

There were so many of those sad roadside memorials. I hadn't noticed them before my sister's accident. Now I couldn't stop seeing them. They were everywhere.

No one had put up a memorial for Sarah though. Sarah had thought they were tacky. My vision blurred, and I blinked rapidly to clear it.

I scrubbed a hand over my face, my stomach burning. Fortuna continued on the lakeside highway, oblivious to my honking, until we reached South Shore. Then she pulled into a shopping area and parked.

It took me a little longer to find a spot. By the time I did, she'd vanished into a big-box computer store. I unbuckled my seatbelt and strode toward the store.

Fortuna emerged with a familiar-looking young man—Tobin's hot young tech guy. His hand on her elbow, he propelled her around the corner of the wooden building.

I trotted after them. Before I rounded the corner, I came to my senses and slowed. I peeked around the building.

He'd backed Fortuna against the wall in an embrace. They were too involved to have noticed me.

Embarrassed, I turned away and stumbled into Sam. I yelped. Where had *he* come from?

Over my shoulder, he studied the couple. His mouth twisted. "That explains the problems with Dragon House's security system."

"How—?" *Oh.* Had the tech guy been sneaking onto the estate to see her? Shutting down the cameras so he wouldn't be caught? "What are you doing here?"

"I followed you and Fortuna, obviously. She was drinking a lot at lunch. I didn't think she had time to process all that alcohol. Why were you following her?"

"Same reason."

"And what did you expect to do?" Sam scratched his beard.

Good question. My mad chase seemed silly now. I adjusted my collar. "I guess, talk to her when she stopped and make sure she was okay. And if she wasn't, give her a ride back."

"Sure." His blue eyes flashed with derision. "She would have gone for that. Why didn't you call the cops?"

"Because I asked Tobin to do it."

Sam snorted. "And you really think he did?"

"Of course. It's his job to protect them."

"It's his job to protect *Wingate*. Ratting out his niece to the cops would have made things more complicated."

My gut plummeted. I should have called 9-1-1 from the car. "Hold on, why didn't *you* call the cops?"

"I didn't think of it," he said. "Anyway, she's with her boyfriend now. She'll be fine. Let's go."

Reluctantly, I walked with Sam toward my car. "Thanks for coming after us."

He grunted. "I've got to get back to my work before—" Sam stiffened.

"What?" I turned to follow his gaze.

Fortuna tottered across the parking lot toward her turquoise car.

Sam swore. "I'll take her home."

"But—"

"She'll go with me." He strode across the lot, intercepting Fortuna beside her Jaguar.

And Fortuna *did* go with him. I was quite certain it was impossible for me to see the fluttering of her lashes or hear her grateful sighs when she leaned against his chest. It was all in the subtext. And the subtext was really annoying.

CHAPTER 11

Sam and Fortuna drove off, her head on his shoulder. She *could* have been just that exhausted, but I doubted it. A gust of chill wind ruffled my hair, and raindrops spattered the parking lot's pavement.

I shivered, unlocked my SUV, and got inside. But I didn't follow Sam and Fortuna to Dragon House. I sat in the car and stared at the computer store.

This wasn't any of my business. Not unless I was a suspect. And I couldn't be a suspect, because the killer had come from outside the house.

But I'd found Devin's body. I was a stranger in Dragon House. And I wanted to see Wingate's Luck Scroll. All of it.

Grimacing, I stepped from the SUV. Thunder rumbled. I darted into the computer store, and rain began to fall in earnest.

The gray-carpeted store wasn't crowded. I spotted Fortuna's side piece at the register with a dark-haired woman who looked to be in her mid-thirties.

"Two thousand dollars?" She gripped her Fendi purse. "But I can't afford that."

"Sorry," August said. "I thought I told you the price earlier. We can find something less expensive, if you like."

"But can't you give me a discount?" The woman leaned closer and batted her fake lashes.

He flashed a bashful smile. "I'm just a lowly computer tech. No discount power here."

"But I'm getting divorced and don't have any money." She licked her lips and leaned closer.

Fortuna's boyfriend crimsoned. "Honestly, there's nothing I could do."

She trailed one manicured finger along his arm. "Are you sure? I *really* can't afford this."

It was as blatant an attempt at discount-through-seduction as I'd ever seen. Though she may have had earthier reasons for the attempt. The computer tech's broad shoulders and muscular biceps strained against his white button-up shirt.

"You can talk to the manager," he said, "but I don't think there are any discounts on this today."

I'd been prepared to despise Fortuna's lover. Instead, I found myself feeling a little sorry for him.

Her finger reached his wrist. She jerked her arm away as if she'd been shocked.

"Excuse me," I strode forward. "I'm looking for the manager."

The look of relief that touched down on the man's face was comical. "I'll get him for you both." He backed from the register. Movements graceful as a cat's, he walked toward the back of the store.

I followed him. "I don't really need a manager," I said in a low voice.

He turned and shot me a startled look. The name tag on his shirt read: *August.* "What?" Around one wrist, he wore a bracelet made of metal and some translucent material which seemed not quite like plastic.

I nodded toward the woman fuming at the cash register. "I thought you needed an escape."

He gusted a breath. "Thanks. Let me get the manager for her, and I'll be right with you."

I waited beside a display of boxed monitors on sale. After a few minutes, August returned. "How can I help you?" His coffee eyes met mine.

Flustered, I straightened off the stacked monitors. *Damn.* I should have been thinking up a story while I was waiting instead of imagining Sam's fraught drive to Dragon House with Fortuna. "Ah… My writing tablet screen's been flickering."

August nodded thoughtfully. "If it's flickering, I might be able to fix it." His voice was low, and I found myself leaning closer. "Why don't you bring it in?"

Because there's nothing wrong with my writing tablet. "I'm, ah, getting kind of sick of my writing tablet. That's such an unusual bracelet. What's it made out of?" My face warmed.

His expression flattened. "Computer circuits and other materials."

Dammit. Now he thought I was hitting on him too. A woman pushed a shopping cart stacked with boxes past us, and we edged aside.

"I'm a friend of Fortuna's," I said. "She said you did some amazing work at her uncle's house."

August's broad shoulders relaxed a fraction. "Oh?" he asked warily.

"I'm assuming it wasn't through the store though?"

"No. I do some consulting on the side. AI tech, mostly." Little wonder he'd caught Fortuna's eye. I could understand her attraction, even if he was too young for us both. Also, she'd been married.

But his magnetism wasn't only due to his muscular form, it was the way he listened. His dark-eyed gaze hadn't wandered from mine since we'd begun speaking.

I laughed uneasily. "I'm a little worried AI will put me out of a job."

"But all sorts of new jobs will be created. AI's going to transform the world. It'll help us make better decisions, be more efficient and effective, and free up our time for bigger-picture things."

"Or distort the picture entirely. I can't believe anything I see on video anymore." *Or believe my ears.*

He gave a half smile. "True. Most people can't tell the difference between an AI deep-fake and the real thing. AI's that good. It's a tool, and any tool can be used for good or evil. But the potential of AI for good—as a catalyst for personal growth, as a method to liberate us from outmoded belief systems—is incredible. Everything can be personalized and individualized with AI—from healthcare to spirituality to philosophy. AI's the next step in human evolution."

My gaze flicked to the hanging fluorescent lights. I couldn't have been the *only* person who'd watched *Terminator*. But in the end, technology was going to move forward regardless of how I felt.

I coughed. "Right now, I'm more worried about my writing tablet screen. Would it be possible to connect a bigger screen to my tablet?"

An intercom pinged. "August, to customer service. August, to customer service." There was a loud, mechanical screech, and I winced.

"Maybe," August said, "depending on your setup. It just seems clunky. Why not get a laptop?"

"They don't seem to last long for the cost."

"If you're worried about the cost, you could get a minicomputer with a portable monitor. The whole setup would cost you less than a writing tablet with the same computing power."

"What would that entail?"

August walked me to the aisle with minicomputers, roughly twice the size of my mouse. He told me about RAM and ROM and terabytes.

I nodded wisely and told him how I used my writing tablet. Could I get out of here without buying anything? Six months ago, I could have bought it all without blinking. Today, I was blinking.

"How did you meet Fortuna?" he asked.

"At her uncle's house," I said, unthinking. "I haven't known her long. So much has been going on there—I'm sure you've heard—I feel like we've trauma bonded."

Trauma bonded? What was I saying? My face and neck tingled with heat. "Sorry. That sounded flippant. I didn't mean it to."

"No," he said quickly. "It isn't. Fortuna and I bonded over our shared rotten childhoods." He studied the small box in his hand for a long beat and swallowed. "My parents died when I was a kid. Boating accident."

"Not on Lake Tahoe?"

He nodded.

I studied the thin carpet. I wasn't the only person who'd faced loss. At least I'd had forty-five years with my sister. He'd only had a few years with his parents. "I'm sorry."

"It made me who I am. So maybe some things really are meant to be."

Heat flared in my forehead. I was sick of hearing that. It seeemd so... arrogant. "I don't—" I caught myself. I was here to learn, not to lecture. "Maybe."

"I know that sounds narcissistic," August said. "That my parents died so I could have some spiritual experience. But since I've started reframing it, looking for the positives, it's taken some of the sting from it." His smile was wry. "Is it pathetic that there's still a sting after all these years?"

"No. They say the pain eases, but the loss never goes away." My throat tightened, the backs of my eyes burning. "You always miss them." *Not now, not now. I couldn't cry now.*

But I could feel the tears coming and knew I couldn't stop them. "Sorry." I turned away. "I had a recent loss and catch myself crying at odd and inconvenient moments."

"There's a ladies' room in the back right of the store," he said. "Why don't I write up a spec sheet for a new set-up? No charge."

"Thanks." I fled to the bathroom.

I knew the grief would lessen. Someday, I'd be able to get through a conversation about loss without tearing up. I hoped that day would come soon. Blotting my eyes with the rough paper towels, I made myself think of other things.

Like August's apparent lack of suspicion. I'd appeared on the heels of a romantic rendezvous with Fortuna. I'd also admitted I'd been in the house where Devin had been killed. August had seen me there. Was I really that unmemorable?

In the mirror, my face was blotchy. Mascara gone. Eyes pink and puffy. My silvery hair had been flattened by the rain. The grief weight puffed my face, rounding my chin. I looked my full fifty-two years, and they weren't pretty.

I glanced toward the bathroom door. And I wondered if he'd mentioned Fortuna's rotten childhood by accident, or by intention.

CHAPTER 12

THE RAISED VOICES BEHIND Dragon House's paneled front door should have been a warning. I walked into the foyer anyway. A blur of white shot toward my face, and I ducked.

CRASH.

Cold seeped down the back of my brown turtleneck. Cautiously, I straightened.

Fortuna and Tobin stood beside the now-empty round table. Water darkened the near-black wall beside the door where the vase had hit and puddled around my shoes. Masses of autumnal flowers lay scattered across the wood floor.

Fortuna pulled a guilty face. "Sorry. But honestly, you'd throw things too if you knew what he did." She jerked her thumb toward an expressionless Tobin.

I plucked a mass of yellow strawflowers off my damp shoulder, glad my sister's vest was 100% faux-fur. "Oh?"

Her eyes bulged. "He sent Sam after me because he thought I was driving drunk."

You were. And that wasn't what Sam had told *me*. The tall estate manager shook his head slightly, turned, and strode through the wide doorway with an ornate, flattened arch.

Fortuna jogged after Tobin into the lounge, her heels clicking. "Don't you walk away from me. This isn't over."

I brushed another damp leaf from my chest and turned toward the stairs.

"You," Wingate roared from the lounge. "What do you know about this card?"

Card? Tensing, I stopped inside the wide entryway to the lounge. The gas flames in the firepit flickered.

Wingate threw an oversized card onto the bar. Had he been getting UnTarot cards too?

Tobin picked it up and dropped it. "Looks like a Tarot card."

"How did it get into my bedroom?" Wingate snarled.

"No one's been on the grounds but the people you've invited," Tobin said. "And since you refuse to allow video inside the house, I couldn't tell you."

"An UnTarot card?" I asked from the doorway.

"The Eight of Swords," Wingate said. "Do you know anything about it?"

I pressed my hands to my stomach. It wasn't an UnTarot card then. As far as I knew, that deck didn't have normal suits. Wingate had received a *real* Tarot card. But the coincidence of us both getting divination cards...

"No. I don't know anything about Tarot cards." I hurried upstairs to change my clothing. The orange kitten shot me a drowsy look from my pillow. "It's a good thing you sleep most of the time."

But the cat toys I'd left had been moved, and my heart pinched. He needed more interaction, more play time, even if it was only with a lowly human. "This is temporary," I assured him. "We'll leave soon, and I'll find you a real home."

The kitten growled, a comical noise coming from his tiny chest. I brushed the damp from my sister's vest and hung it in the wardrobe to dry. Then I changed into a black knit top with overlong sleeves.

I played with the kitten and topped up his water and food bowls. And when he fell asleep, I went downstairs.

The shouting had stopped. I returned to the lounge. A fire blazed silently in the open firepit, warming the chocolate-colored walls and their modern metal sculptures.

Sam hunched in a curving, beige chair near the fire. He hid his craggy face behind a cloth-bound book.

Looking thunderous, Wingate stood behind the long, gray-granite bar and mixed himself a drink. His pewter swizzle stick clinked against the glass.

"I can't *believe* you sent Sam after me," Fortuna snarled at Tobin. Impassive, the big man stood, hands loose at his sides.

Fortuna had been lucky it had been Sam and not the cops, I thought sourly. I recognized her tactic though—attack generally beat defense.

"Enough," Wingate shouted, and Fortuna fell silent. "It's a good thing he did send someone after you," he continued. "I don't need more trouble with the sheriff."

Fortuna blinked rapidly. "Wingate," she said, voice soft.

He exhaled slowly and adjusted his gray-silk cravat. "All right. Come and have a drink. Looks like we both need one."

She walked to the bar. Wingate handed her his glass then made himself another—ice and an amber liquid that could have been whiskey.

Fortuna said something to him too low for me to hear. Wingate came around the bar, and she buried her head against his chest.

Tobin met my gaze and shrugged.

"Brandy," Wingate said over Fortuna's shoulder, "can I get you a brandy?"

"No, thanks," I said, ignoring the joke. I moved to the bar. A black card with gold foil lay atop the granite. Eight swords surrounded a woman. I bent closer, and my breath caught. The woman in the card was bound and blindfolded.

Wingate plucked the card from the bar and slid it into the inside pocket of his sports jacket. "I understand you were looking through our security footage today."

My face heated, and I lifted my chin. "Someone was in my room this morning."

"Riga Hayworth wasn't at Dragon House today." Wingate swirled his drink.

I glanced at Tobin, my shoulders heavying. So he'd told Wingate about my suspicions as well. And why wouldn't he? Wingate signed his paycheck.

"Riga comes when called," Wingate continued. "And I didn't call."

Somehow, I doubted Riga was in the habit of playing lackey. Judging by Wingate's frown, I guessed he knew it too.

"But there have been problems with the security system," I said. "The night of Devin's murder, for example."

An inarticulate sound emerged from Fortuna's throat. Tobin stiffened.

Wingate took another slug of his drink. "Someone used a jammer to keep the alarm from sounding, that's all. We've fixed the problem." His smile was arctic. "Haven't we, Tobin?"

"Yeah," Tobin said.

"The good news," Wingate said, "is Ezra is on his way over with the restored section of scroll. You'll be able to look at it tonight, if you like."

"Of course I'd like," I said. "I want to finish up and get out of here."

My host grinned. "I thought you might. I expect he'll show up in time for dinner. Ezra's clever that way."

I glanced at the clock on the wall. It was six. Dinner would be in thirty minutes if past history was anything to go by. "Then I'll have that drink."

"Tobin," Wingate said. "Take care of that." He maneuvered Fortuna from the room.

Tobin walked to the gray bar, and I trailed after him. "What do you want?" he asked me.

"It's okay. I can get my own drink." I motioned toward the bottles lining the shelves behind the bar.

"Wingate asked me to do it. What do you want?"

I hesitated. Suddenly, I felt drained, hollow. "Got any red wine?"

"What kind?"

"Pinot?" It had been Sarah's favorite. She claimed she drank it for health reasons—lower calories, more antioxidants, and fewer sugars. But I thought she favored the stuff because of the wine-lover's movie *Sideways*.

With a wicked, short knife, Tobin expertly peeled the foil off the neck of a bottle. He uncorked it and poured the wine into a tall goblet.

"For someone with so much security," I said, "Wingate seems casual about its recent failure."

Tobin's voice sharpened. "It wasn't a failure. It was an attack."

"Which should be even more disturbing."

His face tightened, his dark brows drawing closer. "Not much disturbs Wingate."

"The security system's new, isn't it?" I asked.

"An upgrade."

"When was it upgraded?"

"Last February. Why?"

February. The worst month.

"Why?" Tobin repeated.

I shook myself. "For someone who isn't worried, switching to a high-tech AI security system seems like overkill."

"Considering what happened three days ago, it obviously wasn't."

And yet someone had gotten in and Devin had died despite the upgrade. "You think Wingate anticipated someone might be trying to harm him? Or trying to steal the scrolls?"

"He didn't anticipate," Tobin said. "He's careful. You should be too."

Wingate and Ezra walked into the lounge, and my chest hitched. I'd finally get to see the rest of the scroll. Eagerly, I moved toward the two men.

A sheriff's deputy walked in behind them, and I stopped short. The deputy removed his broad-brimmed hat and looked around the high-ceilinged room. His gaze landed on me. "Ms. Bounds?"

My skin went cold. "Yes?"

"The sheriff would like to speak with you."

What did the sheriff know? "Why? Am I being arrested?" I swallowed.

"No. It's just a conversation. For now."

"Don't say anything," Wingate warned me. "Not without a lawyer."

Thank you, Captain Freaking Obvious. Innocent or not, only a fool would talk to the cops under these circumstances. "Thanks for the advice. Mind if I grab a jacket?" I asked the deputy.

"It's probably a good idea," he said.

I hurried upstairs, made sure the kitten was comfy, and grabbed my sister's vest. It was still a little damp, but I wanted her with me.

I returned to the foyer. The deputy drove me to the station. I didn't bother to ask what this was about. I knew, and I shoved my hands into the pockets of my sister's vest to hide their trembling.

I could do this. This was for Sarah.

The station was a charming, low, cabin-like structure surrounded by dark pine woods. Its interior was more businesslike. The deputy ushered me past rows of office desks and into a cinderblock interrogation room with a metal table and an enormous circular hook in its center for shackles.

He motioned me toward the chair facing the door, and I sat, hands still in my pockets. And then he left me.

I sat there a good thirty minutes. I know, because the clock above the door told me so, each tick echoing off the cement floors and white-painted walls.

They hadn't taken my purse. I needed a distraction. And a lawyer. I didn't know any criminal attorneys, but my estate attorney might.

My heart was a drum, pounding out a frantic rhythm. I fumbled in my bag for my phone. My fingers touched hard paper, and I recoiled as if I'd touched a live wire.

Swallowing, I reached into my purse again and pulled out an UnTarot card.

COURAGE

As magical practitioners, we explore the unknown, uphold ethical principles, and face inner and outer demons, limitations, and weaknesses. Courage is required, because the path of least resistance will never bring us meaning.

Do you have the courage to face uncomfortable emotions, or do you run from them? We need to face our suffering to get through it. If we don't, all sorts of nasty things get stuffed down into the unconscious to pop out and cause us problems later.

Too often we push hard emotions away, crushing them down into the dark recesses of our psyche, in order to soldier on. The problem is the emotions fester, causing mental, physical, and spiritual sickness—a critical challenge for the witch. When we don't face our emotions, when we repress them, they boil in our unconscious, feeding our shadow selves and subverting our intentions and spells.

The irony is that when we *do* face our difficult emotions, they fade within only a minute or two. They may return for another round, but the pain of confronting them is much shorter than that of pushing them away. And once we face our fears and traumas, the work becomes easier. Courage grows like a muscle when you exercise it.

Courage is not the absence of fear but the willingness to act despite it. It empowers magical practitioners to take control of their lives, destinies, and spiritual journeys. Embrace your fears as stepping stones to courage and to personal growth.

Action Item: Using the downloadable worksheet, identify three fears or challenges you've been avoiding and write them on the stones. Contemplate what you'll gain by contemplating what you'll gain by facing these fears, and what step you can take to face each. Take one small, courageous step towards confronting one of those fears today.

SCAN ME

And now, we invite you to meditate on your latest card:

Courage

Bravery. Growth through struggle. Persistence. Resistance to despair.

Courage is one of the four Stoic virtues, because it takes courage to live the other virtues. When we act with courage, fear can no longer keep us from doing the right thing, whether that's living authentically, speaking truthfully, or acting justly. It enables us to act according to our values, and this in turn helps us find and stay on our true path. Courage enables us to grow and be our best selves.

Courage is also contagious. After the infamous Stanford Prison Experiment, which demonstrated how ordinary people could do awful things, the author, Philip Zimbardo, switched his research to what makes people heroes. The answer? It only took one person to step up and do the right thing for others to follow.

Who can you encourage today?

The symbols:

A woman in a raincoat, her shoulders set, faces an oncoming storm. Her resolve is bolstered by the symbols of courage around her – the sunflowers and the bear. She can pass through the storm, if she's willing to face it.

The questions:

What are you afraid to do? If you did it, where might it take you?

Your fears can be stepping stones to personal growth.

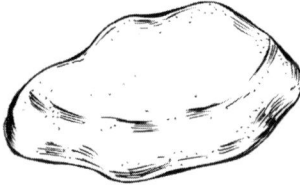

What will I gain by facing my 3 biggest fears?
What steps will I take to face them?

_____
_____
_____
_____
_____
_____

CHAPTER 13

MY PULSE THUDDED IN my throat. The email on my phone's too-small screen pulsed with light. How? *How?* The clock on the cinderblock wall ticked loudly, echoing off the metal table, the shackles hook, the linoleum floor.

The card had been at the *top* of the things in my purse. That meant it had been put there recently. Had someone gone into my room again?

Or had someone slipped it into my bag while I'd walked past with the deputy? The latter seemed more likely, timing-wise. And more terrifying.

But I needed courage now. Because it was never a good sign when you were "invited" to a police station.

That's not what this card is about.

I pushed the thought away. Of course that was what it was about. *Courage. Police station.* It was obvious.

The phone's display flickered. A black cat glowered from the screen, its eyes yellow with malevolence. I sucked in a breath. The cat vanished, and the email reappeared.

I rubbed my jaw, my stomach tightening. It had happened so fast... I'd imagined the cat. The flicker had been too quick for me to really see anything. There was a kitten hiding in my bedroom, so I had cats on the brain.

But my skin crawled, as if something unpleasant had slithered across my flesh. "Cats," I muttered, wanting to hear a human sound, even if it was only my own voice.

The door opened, and the bearlike sheriff ambled into the room, a file folder beneath his arm. His graying head was bare, but he wore his dark-colored sheriff's jacket. "What's wrong?" he asked, blue eyes marble hard.

"Ah, nothing." I jammed the UnTarot card and phone into my purse.

He scraped back the chair opposite me and sat. "Thanks for coming in."

I hadn't had much choice, but I nodded, maintaining the illusion. "What's this about?" I rubbed one long black sleeve of my knit top.

"You. Are you comfortable? Would you like some coffee?"

"I'm fine, thanks. What about me?"

The sheriff opened the folder on the table. "After Mr. Wingate was killed—Devin Weald—we went through his computer files."

I bit back a grimace. Wingate must have loved that. What secrets had his financial analyst/nephew kept about their criminal activities?

He glanced at me. "Aren't you curious about what we found?"

"I presume you'll tell me when you're ready." I wasn't telling him anything. I was learning. That was all. I could do that without a lawyer.

"Devin had ordered a background check on you."

Wingate had already hinted at that. But how deep of a background check had he run? My insides quivered. "And? I am who I said I am."

"The check included mention of your sister's accident. She was killed not far from here. I remember that accident. It was a bad one. Two dead."

My throat tightened. And that was it. The sheriff knew. Worse, Wingate knew. "Yes. Last February."

"It was strange," he continued. "The background check contained more detail on that accident than on any other part of your past. Why would Wingate's nephew be more interested in your sister than in you?"

My heart banged against my ribcage. I'd learned from some disreputable distant relatives that there are two tactics when dealing with the police. The first is to never lie simply by staying silent. The second is to lie your ass off.

The latter only worked when there were no witnesses and no evidence, and you'd better be damned sure there were no witnesses and no evidence. I chose silence.

After a moment, the sheriff continued. "According to a witness, there was a pedestrian in the road."

"Do you know who that pedestrian was?" My voice was a whisper.

"The witness gave us a detailed description at the scene, but later said she couldn't be sure. She wasn't able to definitely identify the person, and no one else came forward." He tapped his thick finger on the pages inside the folder. "The strange thing is, her original statement described someone we both know to a T."

"Oh?" I croaked.

"It described Wingate Weald."

CHAPTER 14

THE CLOCK'S SECOND HAND made one tick backward on the cinderblock wall. I fought for calm. Wingate knew he'd been responsible for my sister's death, and he knew I knew it.

And Wingate had invited me to his home anyway. Did my sister's death mean so little to him? Or did the Luck Scroll mean so much?

A blot of today's lunch had left an oblong stain on the sheriff's dark jacket. The eyes in his lined face were hard as marbles. The sheriff *had* to think I'd come to the Dragon House for revenge. That Devin had confronted me, and I'd killed him.

Except none of that was true. At least, *almost* none of it. I hadn't come for revenge. I'd come to understand. To understand what twists of luck or fate had put Wingate on that highway at that moment.

But if that was all I'd wanted, why hadn't I asked Wingate about that night yet? My heart thudded dully in my chest. I'd wanted to understand the Luck Scroll too.

The clock gave a mechanical sigh. Its second hand resumed its forward motion.

I hadn't been honest at Dragon House, and now I was paying for it. I wasn't the type of person to sneak around. It was why I'd been successful in my career. People knew they could count on me. They trusted I'd act according to my values. But lately, I hadn't been. I hadn't been playing the right game.

I'd thought Sarah had known she could count on me. But my sister hadn't told me the full truth about her unhappy marriage. And though I'd seen hints of it, I hadn't said anything to her. I'd thought I was being circumspect, not interfering.

Now I wished to hell I'd been more upfront. It might not have saved her. But maybe...

The metal door opened, and a pretty young woman with a pink streak in her hair leaned in. "Sheriff—?"

"Not now, Peggy," he barked.

She flushed and withdrew. The door banged shut. I frowned, a memory pinging. But a memory of what?

"Well?" the sheriff prompted.

"Who was she?"

"Dispatcher."

I swallowed, my mouth Mojave dry. "I'd like to speak to a lawyer."

The sheriff shook his head. "Did you ever wonder what Wingate was doing in the middle of the highway?"

It was *all* I'd wondered. "I want a lawyer."

He leaned back in his chair. It creaked beneath his bulk. "You're free to go."

I blinked. *Free?* "What?"

"You couldn't have killed Devin Weald. But you're either involved somehow, or you're in danger. Or both. Go back to the Bay Area, Ms. Bounds."

My eyes widened. "You're telling me to get *out* of town?" Wasn't he supposed to tell me I couldn't leave it?

"Would you rather be under arrest?"

"No." I stood so fast my thigh struck the edge of the metal table, and I winced. "I don't know what happened to Devin or who was involved. The fact that I was there was—"

"Bad luck?" He quirked a bushy brow. "What do you know about Wingate Weald?"

"I know he's an investment manager. Rumor has it he's managing investments for the mob." And why the hell was I talking? Only idiots talked to the police. *Stop talking.*

"It's more than a rumor. Go home, Ms. Bounds."

I strode to the door and into the hall. Peggy and the lanky young deputy from the murder scene jumped apart.

I shook my head slightly. "Do I know you?" I asked the woman.

"No," the deputy said. He was the same deputy I'd seen at the murder scene. The same deputy who'd investigated my sister's death. R. *Linnell, Deputy Sheriff.*

Peggy hurried down the corridor. She glanced over her shoulder at us then turned a corner and vanished.

Deputy Linnel rubbed his nose. "This way." He motioned with one long hand in the opposite direction Peggy had taken. I followed him down the hallway. I had to trot to keep up with his long legs.

"You investigated my sister's car accident," I said. "Sarah Carthart. Last February second. A head-on collision on Highway 50, east of Stateline." There was no sense in playing coy now. The sheriff knew everything.

Linnel stopped and angled his head down to meet my gaze. His caramel-colored eyes were somber. "I'm sorry for your loss."

"We spoke on the phone after the accident." And again, that strange twinge of memory chorded through me. But memory of what?

"I remember," the deputy said.

"You said the accident investigation was ongoing. Is it still?"

"The investigation hasn't been closed," he said carefully.

But I'd bet they weren't looking very hard for new information. It had been an accident, after all, and they had actual crimes to investigate. "The man in the highway who caused the other driver to swerve. You had a description."

"There are a lot of well-dressed, older gentlemen in Lake Tahoe."

"One lives quite near the accident scene. Wingate Weald."

"There were witnesses placing him at Dragon House at the time of the accident," the deputy said.

Witnesses like Tobin—whose loyalty was paid for. Or Devin and Fortuna, and they knew who buttered their bread too. "And if I told you I had a witness who could positively identify the man as Wingate Weald?"

Rolling his shoulders, he rocked in place. "Do you?"

The woman who'd called had been anonymous and likely for good reason. You didn't narc on the mob. "No," I admitted. I bit my bottom lip and glanced down the hallway, where Peggy had vanished.

He turned and continued down the hallway and through the rows of desks. Deputy Linnel opened the half-swinging door to the lobby for me. I walked past him and from the station.

The parking lot lights gleamed amber, dulling the colors of the cars. I climbed inside my SUV, but I didn't start the car. Distracted driving was no longer a theoretical problem to me, and I was distracted after the sheriff's interview.

Why *had* Wingate been in the middle of the highway at that hour? I'd assumed he'd been up to no good—drunk after a late night, playing chicken to feel alive, testing his luck.

But those answers no longer made sense. I rubbed the flesh behind my ear. Wingate was arrogant and devious, but he wasn't stupid.

I started my car and drove from the station. And I managed to keep my eyes and mind on the road all the way to Dragon House.

Two familiar cars sat parked in the circular driveway, and my shoulders relaxed. Ezra was still here. I wouldn't have put it past Wingate to come up with another excuse not to show me the last fragment of scroll. And Riga was here too.

I strode inside and found them gathered in the massive lounge area. They were all there—even Tobin, pouring drinks at the bar.

Riga and Ezra stood deep in conversation by the firepit, firelight flickering off their wine goblets. Tonight, Riga wore wide-legged tan slacks, a white blouse, and a green scarf knotted around her neck. She looked like she'd stepped from a 1940's movie set. Ezra looked like he'd come from a funeral.

Sam read the same book in the same chair by the window. He ignored us all.

Fortuna stared out the window toward the sullen lake. A wan, silvery light behind the clouds hinted at a full moon.

"Good, they didn't arrest you." Wingate waved from the bar. "What did the Sheriff want?"

I braced myself. It was time to ask. *Just ask.* "He asked me about my sister's car accident. The one you were involved in."

The room fell silent. Wingate stilled. "Pardon me?"

I clutched my purse straps in both hands, low and in front of me. "It was February 2nd, 3:58 AM," I continued, reckless. "You were standing in the middle of the highway, not far from here. A car driven by Mary Ann Frankel swerved to avoid you and drove head-on into my sister's SUV. They were both killed at the scene. What were you doing on the road?"

"I wasn't," he said coldly. "I don't know what you're talking about."

"If you're worried about my brother-in-law suing you for wrongful death, don't. He doesn't know, and I have no intention of telling him. I just want to know what put you on that stretch of highway at that exact moment."

Fortuna turned from the window, and I nearly stumbled back. Raw hatred etched her beautiful face. But her rage wasn't directed at me. She glared at Wingate.

"You're insane," Wingate said.

"Maybe," I agreed, lowering my voice. "I get that you don't want to tell me. I wouldn't want to tell me either." I couldn't force him. I could only convince, cajole. "But I hope someday you will. For luck's sake. May I see the scroll now?"

He barked a laugh. "Sure. It's in the library. Tobin, take Riga and Brandy to the library. You know what to do."

Ezra set his glass on the edge of the open fireplace.

"No, Ezra," Wingate said. "Stay. You're done with the scroll."

Ezra's lips whitened. His jaw set. Wingate had spoken to him as he'd command a misbehaving dog. I wouldn't have liked being talked to that way either.

Riga and I followed Tobin to the library door. He patted us both down, took my purse, and let us inside, closing the door behind us. Since he didn't join us in the library, I guessed he was standing guard outside.

"What the hell was that about?" Riga hissed.

I set my electronic notebook on the long, wooden table. "The Sheriff thought I'd come here for revenge," I said, voice thick. "I haven't. I wanted answers. I thought it was time to get them." Or to try.

She swore and clawed a hand through her auburn hair. "And.... What? You thought blurting that out in front of everybody would keep you safe? Because it may have done just the opposite."

"Right now, I just want to copy the scroll." Weary, I walked to the table. This portion, too, was behind glass.

Riga leaned against a bookcase and watched me.

"Have you seen it already?" I sketched the image.

The goddess of Fortune sat in the center, both hands brandishing scrolls with illegible writing. Kings rose and fell on the wheel. One sat on top, one was crushed beneath.

"Of course," Riga said. "We all got a good look at this piece while you were at the sheriff's station."

I copied the text beneath the wheel into my electronic notebook. It took time. I'd have hated to try and transcribe it before it had been restored—if Wingate had been honest about it being out for restoration.

Finally, I looked up to meet her gaze. "And?" I asked.

"And what?"

"Did you read this?" I motioned jerkily with my stylus toward the scroll. "Yes."

"What do you think?"

One corner of her mouth quirked upward. "I'm not a Ripley expert."

I straightened away from the table. "Bullshit. You may not be an expert, but don't tell me you didn't read his other texts. You would have had to before Wingate would let you anywhere near this."

She stepped away from the bookcase. "I read them."

"This is different." It wasn't his usual instructions in poetic form. It was a folktale. "Did Wingate fake this?" Was he hiding the real scroll fragment from me?

She drew a deep breath and exhaled. "Not to my knowledge."

I stared.

Riga rubbed the back of her neck. "It has the same... energy—for lack of a better word—as the other portions of scroll," she continued.

"Is that your *metaphysical* opinion?"

"You're studying luck," she pointed out. "While I admire your skepticism, there's a point where you're going to have to decide where you stand."

"Where I stand on what?"

"On if there's magic in the universe or not."

If there was magic, Sarah had had it. She'd loved life, and it had loved her back. Until it hadn't.

I lined up the three portions of scroll along the long edge of the table. With two under glass, it was impossible to square them up perfectly. But the torn edges *seemed* to match.

"I wish I could photograph these together," I muttered.

"Too bad you promised not to."

"Yes." A headache flared, and I rubbed my temple. Even though Wingate was no doubt lying to and cheating me, I wouldn't let him turn *me* into a liar or a cheat. I hadn't told Wingate all my motivations for coming here. But what I *had* told him had been true.

"What are you going to do next?" Riga leaned one hip against the table.

"Next?"

"You've got what you wanted, at least as far as the scroll goes. But you didn't get what you needed, did you?"

"Do *you* know why Wingate was on that highway?"

"No, but it's curious. Wandering around a highway at four a.m . seems out of character. It's definitely out of the ordinary. And the out-of-the-ordinary bears looking into."

The library door snicked open. Wingate strolled inside, a slip of paper dangling between two fingers. "So, are we done?" He handed me the paper—a cashier's check.

I stared at the number longer than I needed to. What could I say? I had what I wanted, but not, as Riga had said, what I needed.

"Yes." I folded the check. "We're done."

THE WHEEL OF FORTUNE

CHAPTER 15

WINGATE HAD WON. My arms dropped heavily to my sides. I ran my thumb across the edge of the check in my hand.

Wingate had won, and I'd failed. I'd failed, and I hadn't even had a definite goal to miss. I lowered my head. Outside the library window, the clouds moved closer, blotting out the moon, turning the lake to a pool of black ink.

"It's late," Wingate said. "There's no sense in you packing up now. Why don't you stay the night?"

I hesitated. A mobster, generous in victory? But I was done with Dragon House.

Beside the long, wooden table, Riga shifted her weight. She made a short, negating motion with her head.

The answers I needed weren't at Dragon House, and I had my money. I could afford now to stay at the best hotel on the lake. But I was tired, and I was here, and I didn't know how I'd smuggle the cat out.

Outside, a long, impossibly large feline shadow slunk along the edge of the patio. I tensed. "Thanks," I said. "I'll spend the night."

Riga's lips pressed tighter. "Are you returning to the Bay Area tomorrow, or do you plan to stay at Lake Tahoe?"

"I'll go home." There was a reason Sarah had died, a reason she and Wingate had been on that road. And I'd learn it eventually. Maybe I should take my money and hire Riga to figure it out. Though I was tired of relying on other people for answers.

"There's no rush," Wingate purred. "I hope you'll at least stay for breakfast."

The Dragon House caterers *did* provide good breakfasts. I slipped the cashier's check into the rear pocket of my jeans.

The mobster snapped his fingers. "We've been overlooking a prime source on the scroll."

I canted my head. "Oh?"

"Sam," he said. "Before you leave, I'd like the three of us to sit down tomorrow morning and get his take on it."

"I thought his area of expertise was the Estonian crusades," I said.

Wingate smoothed his silk cravat. "That's only one area. He may not be a Ripley expert, but he's a scholar and has studied medieval documents. I'd like his input."

I shook my head. "I don't—"

"Don't tell me you've lost interest in luck?" Wingate asked. His tone was a challenge.

My luck quest was all I had left. I raised my chin. "No." I tapped the notebook with my stylus. "This is a beginning, not an ending."

"We'll see you tomorrow then." He pivoted and strode from the library.

Riga studied his departing back. "Strange he didn't recommend getting Ezra's opinion."

"I imagine he already has it."

She grunted an agreement and faced me. "I'm sorry to hear about your sister."

"Did the Sheriff tell you?"

"I told *him*."

I believed her. Not because I thought the sheriff was incompetent—far from it. But I believed she'd been the one to uncover Sarah's death, and my connection to Wingate.

"What was your sister like?" Riga asked.

"She was a poet and a damned good investor. The latter's where she made her money, the former was her passion. I wish..." I swallowed.

I wished I could have shown her the scroll. She'd no doubt have a comment on the structure and rhyme scheme. She'd bored me often enough on the topics—on odes and acrostics, cantos and canzones.

I scrubbed both hands across my face. Because I wished now I hadn't been bored, hadn't been too busy, hadn't *pretended* to listen. They'd been things that *she'd* cared about, even if I had not.

"I have a sister," Riga continued in a low voice. She studied her tan boots. "We're very different and don't always get along. Don't *usually* get along. But I can't imagine losing her. Not now. And I understand wanting to learn more, wanting to make sense of things. But the attempt at sense-making can be a trap, keeping you attached to your loss. You know that, don't you?"

"But I haven't made sense of anything." I wandered along the library's bookshelves and trailed my finger across their leather spines. "I still don't know why Wingate was on that highway." Or my sister. Her husband hadn't been able or hadn't wanted to explain it.

"But you know he was there."

Dropping my hand, I met her gaze. "Yes."

"And you came here with the scroll—your price of entry into Dragon House. That speaks to a certain amount of determination."

"Would you believe it was a lucky coincidence?"

"I don't usually believe in coincidences," Riga said. "Though I do believe in luck. I'm afraid yours may be on the verge of running out."

"Don't worry. I'll leave tomorrow." Clutching the slim notebook to the front of my black knit top, I left her in the library. My footsteps were heavy as I ascended the stairs to my room and opened the door.

The kitten bounded toward me. I scratched his striped head, checked his food and water, and played with him for a time. Then I sat at the desk and studied my copy of the Luck Scroll.

The first two sections were clear enough—at least clear enough for an alchemist. The author had used the ouroboros—in this case two dragons eating each other's tails—as a metaphor for the cyclical nature of Fortune. It was an echo of Fortune's wheel.

I studied the creatures I'd copied. One had wings and one did not. Was it a dragon eating a snake instead of two dragons? How did that change the meaning?

The next image showed a crowned, robed man. A hangman's noose dangled from the cloud above. The man pointed with one hand to the sky, with the other to the ground.

"As above, so below," I muttered.

The kitten meowed, as if recognizing the famous alchemical phrase. The poem here seemed to be saying that aligning oneself with the universal flow could influence one's luck. But how? Through virtue?

But instead of clarifying, the next image—Wingate's missing piece—depicted the cruel wheel and included a folktale, *The Queen Bee*, about three brothers seeking their fortune. Because the youngest and simplest—a *jestour*—was kind to the animals they encountered, at a crucial moment, the animals came to assist the youngest, who saved a cursed kingdom and won the hand of a princess.

The folktale was a strange divergence. Though the writing style seemed the same, the addition of a fairytale was out of character for Ripley. I rubbed my burning eyes.

The rest of the scroll continued as if the folktale hadn't existed at all. There was a discussion of alchemy's four elements and how they balanced the different aspects of life to achieve a favorable outcome with Lady Luck.

Next was an image of a woman holding a Caduceus. That symbolized the alchemical alignment of one's actions and intent with luck.

It was all standard alchemical imagery. But instead of using alchemy to align oneself with the Divine, it was used to align oneself with luck. The instructions were vague, and that, I knew, was intentional. Alchemists cloaked their instructions in symbols to hide their secrets.

Now all I needed to do was learn alchemy. *Ha.* Lightly, I tapped the end of my stylus on the desk.

There was a faint knock at my door.

I checked my watch. It was after midnight. I'd been at it for hours. "Come in," I said.

The door opened, and Riga stepped inside. The kitten trotted to her and sniffed her low-heeled boot.

I twisted in my chair. "I thought you'd left." I'd *hoped* she'd left. There was something disturbing about the woman.

"I had some things to do here first." She scooped up the kitten and ruffled its tiny head with the back of her finger. "And I thought you might still be up. You have a cat."

"For now. I'm looking to adopt him out. I don't suppose you—"

"I have a dog and two toddlers. No."

I slouched in the leather chair. *Figures.* "This folktale in the Luck Scroll—it's out of place."

"It's late, and you're trying to force things," Riga said. "It won't work."

"I know, but the story, it's... weird." I twisted further, cracking my back.

She set the kitten on the wood floor. "And things that are out of place deserve the most attention."

Like my sister and Wingate on that highway. My hands went limp on the chair arms. "Did you know Wingate upgraded his security system to AI after the highway incident?"

"Did he now?"

"Do you think he was... frightened onto the highway?" Had my sister been?

"Maybe. But he's not talking. And you're leaving tomorrow," Riga reminded me.

I stood and glanced at my writing tablet on the desk. The screen reflected the massive head of a snarling black cat. I gasped and jerked away, and then it was my screen background again—a photo of a sand labyrinth on an Oregon beach. I exhaled shakily.

"Have you been to the accident site?" Riga asked in a low voice.

"No. I don't see the point." I didn't want to see the place where my sister had died. There would be no cross for Sarah, no roadside memorial, and a fist squeezed my heart so hard I nearly gasped.

"Do you ever see things that aren't there?" I asked abruptly.

"What do you think you've seen that isn't there?"

I laughed shortly. Had my question been that obvious? "I keep thinking I see... This is stupid. I keep thinking I see a panther or puma or something."

"Has it been in your room again?"

"No." How could she ask that question so casually? "I thought... I don't know what I thought. That the photographer's mountain lion had gotten loose and had looked black because it was dark?"

Riga walked to the window overlooking the drive. "You've only seen it at night?" She opened the wooden blinds and peered out.

"Yes. No. I mean, I've seen it on my notebook."

She shut the blinds. "Your notebook? You found an image of the cat?"

"No, it prowled across the screen. I mean, it *didn't*, obviously. It was that virus I told you about, or I've been seeing things. It's stress. Since Sarah died... It's a brain blip."

"You've been seeing things, and you doubt your senses. It's the intelligent, rational thing to wonder. You *have* been under stress." Riga walked closer. "What else have you seen?"

None of her damned business. Yet I found myself telling her about the creature on the beach, the shadow people, the changing landscape.

When I finished, I clamped my mouth shut. Was she a witch? Had she charmed me into confessing?

A long breath escaped her mouth. "I think you should leave Dragon House with me tonight."

"What?" What did she know? "Why?"

"Because I don't trust that AI security system. Because I don't believe the killer came from outside these walls. Because of the things you've been seeing. And because you joined the mystery school."

"That's—What does *that* have to do with anything?"

"You joined the school for a reason," Riga said.

"Yes, it was part of my luck research. And it was free. Not that it's helped much."

She ran one hand down the smooth, wardrobe door, and studied its grain. Did she see faces in it, like I did?

"Are you sure about that?" she asked.

"There's nothing useful about luck in those emails."

She tore her gaze from the wardrobe. "The point is, people who have an interest in magic usually have some magic in them. And I don't think the things you've been seeing have been stress delusions."

I groaned. *Stop speaking in riddles!* "Then what are they?"

"Come with me tonight. You can stay at my place. My husband won't mind. The house is embarrassingly big, though you'll have to contend with two toddlers in the morning. And an extremely large dog. None of them understand the concept of quiet time."

"Thanks for the offer," I said, "but I'd rather stay here."

"I don't think you heard me. Something's wrong at this house. This isn't over. And the threat most likely isn't coming from the outside."

"You think he's—Devin's killer—is here."

"Or she." She glanced at the closed wardrobe. "You can't believe your eyes when it comes to video. Not anymore."

I nodded curtly. "I'll lock my door."

Riga looked as if she were going to say something, but she shook her head and left.

I turned back to my notebook and puzzled over the symbols for another two hours. And when I finally stumbled into bed and slipped my hand beneath the pillow, I touched hard paper.

I froze, heart thumping, and briefly closed my eyes. Then I forced my cold and trembling fingers to pull the card free.

NATURE

While nature is a great creative force, it doesn't *force* creation. It allows. Even its supposed failures—the forest fires, the droughts—make way for new growth and sometimes new types of growth.

Likewise, the witch does not force. She doesn't force her will on others, and she doesn't force her magic or manifestations. Instead, she opens herself to the universe, gets clear on what she wants, and enters into co-creation with the universe.

This does not mean the witch takes *no* action. She acts with clarity, decisiveness, and love, because these types of actions—even the actions which don't seem to directly lead to her goals—seed her manifestations.

But she does not force the outcome, because she admits that she may not know the best outcome for herself or for others. Instead, she focuses her will and intentions on her desires and has faith that the universe will hear and co-create with her, achieving an outcome in her greatest and highest good.

If you find yourself frustrated, if your will seems thwarted at every turn and your magic isn't magicking, ask yourself: Am I trying too hard? Am I co-creating, or am I trying to force my will on the universe?

But there is another magical concept around nature, and that is working *with* its energies to make magic. This is why witches pay attention to the phases of the moon, the cycles of the sun, and even the weather and spirit of the place when it comes to spellcasting. It takes subtle energy to do magic, and it's easier to work with natural energies than against them.

Play with the attached worksheet. What have you been trying to force? What can you allow?

SCAN ME

Nature

Creativity. Allowing. Abundance. Chaos. Wonder. Groundedness. Instinct. Sex. Cycles.

Nature is a great teacher. It's in constant motion, growing and withdrawing, creating and dying, blossoming and rotting. And we're a part of it without even trying, taking place in those same cycles simply by existing.

Nature is also implacable. We can grind our teeth at the unfairness of life and wish for things to be different, but nature grounds us. Nature doesn't care about our opinions of how the world should be. Nature *is*.

That truth helps ground us too, settling us both mentally and physically. Time spent enjoying nature keeps us aligned with ourselves and our world. It helps us get out of our heads and return to our own bodies, which are a part of the natural world. Time in nature also helps us regulate our nervous systems and instill a sense of wonder. It's one of the quickest ways to find beauty.

The symbols:

A woman sits in a lush jungle scene. A parrot, a symbol of intelligence, adaptability, and spirituality, flies above her. A ladybug of good instincts and pleasure perches on her shoulder. A butterfly, a symbol of rebirth, cyclical transformation, and positive change, covers her eyes—the woman is seeing through the eyes of nature.

The questions:

Are you trying to force things? Should you allow things to unfold? What can you create? Are you in your body or in your head? Are you working with the flow of nature, or swimming against the tide?

What Will You Allow?

Inhale gratitude. Exhale gratitude. Get present. Inhale deeply. What do you smell. Relax. What do you hear? What do you feel against your skin?

Say: "I don't have to force anything. I can allow." Inhale gratitude. You are part of an amazing, evolving creation. Say: "Life is happening for me, not to me." Breathe deeply. It's okay to relax and let go. Let life be fun.

I will allow: _____ Thank you!

I will allow: _____ Thank you!

I will allow: _____ Thank you!

CHAPTER 16

I DIDN'T THINK I'D slept late so I could extend my stay at Dragon House. I'd sabotaged my sleep by staying up until the wee hours puzzling over the Luck Scroll, though I hadn't intended to. Because I'd *wanted* to sleep.

I'd wanted to see Sarah.

But that night, when I finally did sleep, I failed again. I'd been flying above a tropical island. Realizing I was dreaming, I changed the scene to the woods around Flathead Lake.

Smoke rose from the cabin's chimney. I told myself she'd be inside this time.

But the silver-haired woman in Slavic dress waited for me instead. "You won't find her until you let her go," she said.

The flames rose in the brick fireplace, roaring. I awoke to a warm weight and tiny daggers digging into my stomach. "What the—?"

The orange kitten gave me an injured look.

"S'okay," I mumbled, lifting him from my stomach. The sheet clung to his claws, and I disentangled the cat. "Leaving today. I'll find you a home."

The kitten growled. From downstairs came an angry shout.

"Don't worry," I told him. "I'm done with the drama, too."

Taking my time, I dressed in a blue sapphire knit top and jeans, checked the kitten's food and water, and walked downstairs.

At the base of the wide staircase, a red-faced Wingate swore fluently and creatively at Tobin. My host's button-down shirt was as rumpled as his ivory hair. I recognized the outfit from the night before. For once, Wingate hadn't bothered with a suit jacket or cravat.

"—on my pillow! He was in my bedroom." He flicked a black card at Tobin.

The card hit Tobin's chest and landed face-up at his feet. The younger man didn't bother looking down at it. "Would you like to add cameras inside the house?"

Wingate's chest heaved. His fists clenched at his sides. "No," he gritted out. "I would not. I would like to know how he *got* inside."

"We could add cameras to the passages," Tobin said.

Wingate's nostrils flared. "I want—"

I stepped from the last stair, and the floor creaked beneath me. The men seemed to notice me and fell silent.

"Hi." I sidled past them and glanced down. A gold skull grinned from an ebony Tarot card. Wingate bent and snatched it off the parquet floor.

I moved on to the breakfast room, overlooking the gloomy lake. A blue and white motorboat bobbed beside the dock.

"Is there a visitor?" I asked Sam, who was shoveling food into his mouth at a table near the window.

His paper notebook sat by his elbow. Flat across its open pages lay a child's drawing on pink construction paper—a stick figure waving at what looked like a flying cat.

The academic glanced at the lake. "No," Sam said, "that's Wingate's. It's usually in the boathouse."

I walked to the sideboard and grabbed a bagel. "There's a boathouse?" My exploration of the grounds had been sub-par, because I hadn't noticed one.

"For a place like this? Of course, there's a boathouse." Sam motioned to the south. "It's hidden in those trees."

I stuck the bagel in the toaster and walked closer to the window. I squinted at a stand of pines. "Why park the boat here when he's got a boathouse? Isn't that the point of a boathouse?"

"The word is *dock*." Sam grinned, his salt-and-pepper hair curling damply around his ears. "And Wingate's lazy. He didn't want to walk over there, so he had Tobin bring the boat here."

I pointed to the construction paper drawing on his notebook. "Is that a—?"

"Unicorn." He shut the notebook. "My niece drew it. She thinks I hunt unicorns and other mythical creatures. I keep trying to explain, but archaeomythologist is a little above the head of a four-year-old."

My heart pinched. Sam must be the male version of Sarah—the beloved uncle. "Do you have kids of your own?" I asked.

"No." The word was as final as a slammed door.

Since I could take a hint, I returned to the sideboard and loaded my plate. It would be my last breakfast at Dragon House, and I was determined to enjoy it.

My bagel sprang from the toaster. I slathered it with cream cheese and walked to Sam's table. "Mind if I join you?"

"Have at it."

I sat across from him. "Did you read the entire scroll?"

"Of course I did. I'm a medieval scholar. I'm not going to turn up the chance for a look at a rare artifact from that period."

"What did you think about the new section?" I bit into the bagel. It was sourdough and delicious.

"Usual magical nonsense." He shrugged.

My mouth puckered, and I swallowed. "*Is* it nonsense?"

"Sorry. The alchemical act isn't nonsense. Sure, the idea of turning lead into gold is bunk, but that wasn't the point, was it? It was about turning your spiritual lead into gold. What I meant was, the text itself. Alchemical texts were written to intentionally obfuscate. Alchemy was considered too dangerous for the common mind. Everything in alchemy is symbolic, and the symbols mean one thing under certain circumstances and different things in others. Only someone deeply schooled in the art could interpret them."

"And you are?" I raised my brows.

He rumbled a laugh, a pleasing sound that reverberated low in my chest. "Hardly. I know enough about alchemy to be dangerous, but that's all."

"But wouldn't an archaeomythologist be interested in that sort of thing?" I braced my forearms on the edge of the white-clothed table.

"Yes, but I'm interested in the cultural and mythological significance of the text, not in transforming myself into a shimmering being of light."

"What's the cultural and mythological significance of the Estonian crusades?" I asked.

His gaze met mine. His eyes were the most amazing shade of blue—Nordic blue? "My crusader encountered the pagan Estonians," he said, "including one of their shamans."

"And it's the shamanic beliefs you're interested in," I said slowly.

"Exactly," Sam said.

Shamans can see Middle World. Wasn't that what Riga had said when she'd asked if I was one?

And now an expert at shamans was at Dragon House. *Luck? Coincidence?* Outside, Canada geese skimmed across the lake, honking, coming in for a landing.

I shook myself. "Like what?"

He shoved the notebook aside and braced his elbows beside his plate. "Today, Estonian shamans use singing to get into a trance state and experience their visions. I'm trying to learn if this is a modern innovation."

"How do shamans usually do it?"

"It depends on the culture. Drumming, drugs, dancing... Some even travel using lucid dream techniques."

I sucked in a breath. *Lucid dreams?* I'd been able to lucid dream since childhood. But my day visions had begun after Sarah's death. "How does one become a shaman?"

"Typically, through some form of dismemberment. It could be literal or figurative, like a trauma."

"Like losing a loved one?" I held my voice steady.

The geese honked outside. The massive birds floated near the bobbing motorboat.

"Yeah," he said. "But there's all sorts of shamans and all sorts of shamanism. Hell, there are even people calling themselves techno-shamans now."

And... we were back to technomancers. "How do *they* work?"

"Don't know, don't care. My field is the past, not our brainless present."

Warmth crept across my cheeks. *Right.* I was getting off track. "Okay." I braced my elbows on the table. "From an archaeomythological perspective, how would you approach the Luck Scroll?"

"I'd start with the text itself, specifically the language, structure, symbols, and any narrative structure. Then I'd do the same for the images and dig into any deeper symbolic connections between symbols and text that might not be obvious. Knowing the historical and cultural context is crucial too. Ripley lived in England in the 1400s, but there's a question as to whether he actually created the original Ripley Scroll, which was lost long ago. All the world has now are 16th and 17th-century copies. Even if this scroll was created by the same hand, we can't assume it was Ripley."

"But the copies we *can* date," I protested, enjoying the argument. When was the last time I'd truly enjoyed myself? Hell, this was beyond enjoyment. I was having *fun*, and that hadn't happened since... before Sarah.

"And there *is* evidence for the first *copies* dating to the 16th century," I continued, stretching in my chair.

"Which isn't helpful, because you can't compare your scroll to the original original, which was lost. Only to the copies."

I folded my arms. "Well, phooey."

Sam laughed again, and I found myself leaning closer. I liked that I could still make someone laugh, even if I couldn't find the heart for laughter myself.

Wingate strode into the breakfast room. Our host had changed from yesterday's rumpled clothing into a charcoal suit that looked like it had been cut to fit. He poured a cup of coffee from the sideboard.

"That said," Sam said, "comparing this scroll to other 15th-century scrolls could help you determine if what you have is an original from that period. And you'd have to compare the alchemical myths in this text to the writings of the original Ripley."

"But the Ripley scroll doesn't include any folktales. It's all poetic instruction."

"Ah. I noticed that too. That's a mark against your scroll being by the same person."

"My scroll now." Wingate came to stand beside us and stared out the big windows at the lake. "I know I suggested you confer with Sam about the scroll, but I wanted to be there for it."

"Then sit down." Sam motioned toward the chair facing the window.

"I can't right now." Wingate checked his gold watch. "But I do want to hear this. Brandy, stay for lunch. The three of us can talk afterward."

My neck tensed. It was one delay after another with Wingate, and it was all a power play. He liked being the king, liked pushing others around. "No, but thanks. I have to go."

"We're having steak salads."

Whoa. I loved steak... I shook my head and pushed back my chair. "It was nice meeting you, Sam."

The academic grunted and bent his head to his notebook.

I hesitated. I hadn't made many inroads on my breakfast. But I'd made my point about leaving. Dallying to finish my eggs would make me look silly.

Returning to my room, I packed my bags. I was stumped when I got to the litter box. I didn't want to take a full litter box in my car, but I couldn't exactly dump the contents in the wastebasket. That would be gross for whoever had to deal with it.

I stomped downstairs in quest of a heavy-duty garbage bag. Eventually, I found Dragon House's enormous kitchen.

Tobin, in a ruffled apron, was cleaning up. He pushed up his sleeves. "What?"

At least he wasn't insecure in his masculinity. An old-fashioned electric coffeepot perked on the white tile counter. "Oooh, coffee." I reached for the handle.

Tobin slapped my hand away.

"Ow!" I rubbed the back of my hand. "Fine, keep your private stash. What do I care?"

"The cord's frayed." Gingerly, he picked up the gray cloth cord from the middle. A spark flew from its exposed wires. "It'll give you a helluva shock. I'll get you a cup."

"Never mind. That's not what I came here for anyway."

"What *did* you come here for?" His dark eyes narrowed.

"May I have a garbage bag?"

"Why?"

"Litter box."

He bent and opened a cupboard beneath the old-fashioned sink, closed it. "We're out. Hold on. I'll find you one."

Whipping off the apron, he strode from the kitchen.

Stacks of dishes teetered in the sink. Coffee splashed in the clear glass top of the electric pot. I shuddered and trailed after him. But Tobin had vanished down one of the long halls.

I ambled to the lounge. Maybe deep brown hadn't been such a bad fashion choice. Though the lake was grim and gray outside, the lounge had a certain cozy warmth. But that was largely due to the gas fire flickering in the open pit.

Fortuna sat in a corner wearing oversized sunglasses and drinking a Bloody Mary. She didn't look up at my entrance.

I walked to the windows. The motorboat pulled from the dock, Wingate at the helm. I didn't have to worry about Wingate seeing me smuggle the kitten out after all.

"He's doing it on purpose," Fortuna said.

I turned. "Doing what?"

"Dragging everything out. Keeping you here. Did you ever wonder why?"

"I assumed Wingate enjoyed jerking my chain."

Fortuna snorted. She raised her sunglasses to the top of her head. The skin beneath her eyes was the color of an old bruise. "You're not the only one. He nearly killed Devin with the stress. At least *you* can leave."

"And Devin couldn't?"

Her laugh was harsh. "You don't retire from this sort of work."

"You mean the m—"

The lounge brightened. A boom rattled the windows. Fortuna cried out, leaping to her feet, and I flinched backward.

Smoke plumed from the lake, wood and metal raining into its unforgiving waters. The motorboat was gone.

CHAPTER 17

A MOTORBOAT WITH SHERIFF on its side bobbed on the sullen lake. The sheriff himself leaned over the edge and spoke to a black-clad diver. The diver nodded and vanished beneath the surface.

Nauseated, I hugged my arms. The temperature had dropped, and I stepped from side to side, clapping my feet together as if that would keep me warm. I couldn't imagine how cold the lake would be.

"Creepy Tarot cards, got it," Deputy Linnel scribbled in his notebook. "And you're sure you saw a flash and *then* heard a boom?"

I forced my attention back to the deputy. He probably didn't mean to loom, his head bent to his notebook. Nonetheless, he was a loomer.

I wondered about that notebook. The deputy wore a recording device attached to the lapel of his thick jacket. Either he was just that careful or the recorder was broken.

"I... Honestly, I'm not sure of anything," I said. "It happened so fast. I didn't know I was supposed to be paying attention." The last came out higher pitched than I'd intended, and my face and neck heated.

I wanted to leave Dragon House. I wanted to be done with this. I wanted to put my sister's death behind me and move on. Wingate was dead. Even if I'd had any ideas of revenge, it was a moot point now.

"All right." The deputy tapped his pen on the notebook and shut it. He slid it into his jacket's inside pocket. "We know where we can find you."

Taking that as permission to leave, I hurried into the house and upstairs to my room.

The kitten sat in the window and studied Dragon House's front lawn. His striped tail lashed expectantly. He glanced over his shoulder at me, then resumed his contemplation of the lawn.

I came to stand beside him. The driveway was filled with emergency vehicles. A coroner's van drove off, empty. The body hadn't been recovered. After that explosion, I doubted there would be much left to recover.

"Ready to leave?" I asked the cat.

He gave a tiny growl, and I smiled at the sound. Then I realized I still didn't have the promised bag for the litter box contents.

Leaving the kitten enclosed in the bedroom, I walked downstairs and to the kitchen. I opened the cupboard beneath the vintage sink, hoping Tobin had put the bags there. But all I found were cleaning supplies.

Because safety first, I unplugged the coffee pot and got a nasty shock for my troubles. This made me feel slightly more warmly toward Tobin. He hadn't been kidding about that frayed wire.

I wandered from the kitchen and down the hall. Tobin had to be around here somewhere. I'd seen him talking to the deputies. But he wasn't in the lounge, wasn't in the dining room. I stopped outside the closed library door.

Its heavy, paneled wood was made for privacy. I shouldn't go in.

I tried the knob. It was unlocked. I glanced down the hallway. No one was there. I crept inside and hurried to the long table, where two thick frames lay.

I don't know why I wanted to see them one last time. What did I expect to get from a final glimpse of the Luck Scroll?

I leaned over the table. Sucking in a breath, I stepped backward. Empty frames lay on the dark wood.

"They're gone," Tobin said.

I jumped, clutching my chest. "What? Where—?"

He emerged from a shadowy corner near the door. For such a large man, he was surprisingly proficient at stealth. "The scroll's gone. So's the scroll case you brought. I assume the thief used it to carry away the rest. Was it you?"

"I didn't—if I'd stolen the scroll, I wouldn't have come back here to admire the crime scene."

Tobin tilted his head. "No, but you're here, and you're here for the scroll."

"What are *you* doing here?" I sputtered.

"I have a right to be here. You don't. Why are you here?"

"I wanted to see the pieces together, one last time."

He snorted. "Sure. That's believable."

"Believable or not, it's true," I snapped. Had it always been about the scroll? Devin had been killed outside the library after someone had broken in. My room had been rifled on more than one occasion—by someone looking for my section of the scroll?

I hunched my shoulders. They'd gotten the Luck Scroll. They'd killed again, and this time, they'd gotten the scroll.

"The sheriff knows," Tobin said.

My neck turned so swiftly the bones in it cracked. "What?"

"He knows the scroll was taken. You said you'd come here to sell the scroll. Now you've got a fat cashier's check, and the scroll's missing. It's convenient."

"You think I came here to rob Wingate and steal the scroll?"

Tobin folded his arms and leaned against a bookcase. "There weren't any problems until you arrived."

The top of my head heated. Oh, there *hadn't* been? "What was Wingate doing on the highway the morning of February 2nd?" I countered.

His expression flattened. "It's November now. February was a long time ago."

"So, something *did* happen to him that sent him onto the highway."

Tobin didn't respond. I moved to the French doors overlooking the lake. On the patio, the IT guy, August, showed Deputy Linnel something on a tablet computer.

"Are there cameras in the boathouse?" I asked.

"No," he said shortly.

Then that was probably where the bomb had been planted in the motorboat—where no one would see. Because it had to have been a bomb. Boats didn't just explode.

"You were lucky," I said. Tobin had been the one to pilot the boat to the dock. It could have exploded with him in it. Unless someone had lain in wait, watching for Wingate to get inside, and then had set the bomb off remotely.

"This doesn't feel lucky to me."

Heels clacked on the floor behind us. "There you are," Fortuna said. "Thank God. What a mess." She clawed her hand through her red hair and knocked askew the sunglasses atop it. Her eyes were red and puffy, and mascara streaked the skin beneath them.

"You were looking for me?" Tobin asked.

She adjusted the sunglasses on her head. "No, for Brandy. You can go."

With an ironic bow, Tobin left. He didn't close the library door.

Fortuna slammed it shut hard enough to ruffle the hem of her little black dress. "I can't deal with this." She paced to the French doors and gnawed her bottom lip. "How am I supposed to deal with this?"

"I don't know." I swept my hair from the side of my face. "I'm assuming... Do you *have* to deal with it?"

"This is my *home*." She massaged the palm of one hand with her thumb. "And now there are police everywhere, and another murder. I don't know who I can trust." She turned and walked to the library's long, wooden table.

"Well, you won't have to worry about me anymore. I'm leaving."

"No!" Fortuna clutched my hand. The life had fled from her porcelain skin, leaving it ashen. "You can't leave me alone. Not now."

I itched to pull free, but how could I? "I don't think I can stay." I shifted my weight. "I was a guest of Wingate's, and—"

"Now you're my guest. This is my house now. I say who comes and goes."

"That's, ah, kind of you. But—"

"Sam's staying too."

He would. Sam hadn't finished his research. My mouth twisted. "Then you don't need me."

"You'd really leave me alone in this house full of men?"

I doubted it was the male company that worried Fortuna. Why did she really want me around? "I'm sure you'll be fine."

"How can you say that? My husband was killed. And now his uncle—"
She hiccupped a sob and turned from me.

Guilt burned my chest. "I'm sorry. I can't imagine..." But I could. I knew
the devastation of a loved one's unexpected death.

"People are always asking if there's anything they can do," Fortuna said.
"But you *can* do something. You can stay."

I knew this too, and a cold weight filled my chest. After Sarah had died,
I'd received plenty of offers of support. Most had been genuine. But I
hadn't known what to ask for. And I'd felt worse for not being able to give
my well-wishers something to do.

"I can't stay. I have a cat," I blurted.

She made a high-pitched sound and bent double. It took me a moment
to realize she was laughing.

"Ah," I said, "are you okay?"

Bracing one hand on the library's long, wooden table, Fortuna straightened. "You're worried about the cat?" She laughed harder and wiped her
eyes with her free hand. "I still can't believe you brought one. He *hates*
cats."

Hated, I silently amended. "I tried to take him to a shelter, but they
didn't think the odds of placement were good."

"I could use a comfort animal. May I see him again?"

I shrugged. "It's your house." I led her upstairs to my room.

She scooped the kitten off my bed and held him to her chest. "You're
a darling."

"I don't suppose you want to adopt a cat?" Absently, I brushed white
dust off my palm. Where had I picked that up?

"No." She held him out to examine him. "I'm more of a dog person."

"Well, darn."

The cat gave me an injured look.

"I'll have Tobin get a scratching post," she said. "We wouldn't want him
to damage the furniture. What's his name?"

"Trouble," I said, unthinking. "But you don't—"

"My kind of cat." She set him on the bed's fluffy duvet. "You'll stay, won't you? Please say you'll stay? Just for a few days, until things settle down. I don't have anyone else. Please?"

I hadn't had anyone else either. My son had been so angry after Sarah's death that he hadn't wanted comfort and hadn't been in the mood to give any.

And Sarah's husband... He'd said all the right things, but I hadn't believed them. Leaving me out of the obituary had spoken volumes.

I might not be able to fix things with Sarah's husband. In truth, I didn't want to. I didn't like him.

But I *was* to blame when it came to my son. I was the one who'd been so busy working, so busy pleasing everyone but the people who counted, that I'd neglected our relationship. That was on me.

My throat hardened. "Yes. I'll stay."

JOKER

Seeker:

There are trickster gods across time and cultures. Mercury and Hermes for the ancient Romans and Greeks. Coyote for certain American Indian tribes. Loki for the Norse. The Monkey King in Chinese mythology. The Magician in Tarot.

The lucky break, the unlucky disaster... These gods are maddening—tripping up mortals and their fellow gods alike. But most of us can't help admiring their devious ways.

That's because tricksters and the chaos they bring are catalysts for change. They frequently appear at our lowest or highest moments—to force us to do better or to knock us back down to earth.

They cross boundaries—walking between the worlds and sometimes pushing up into our boundaries.

Tricksters cause mayhem, forcing us to drop our masks and to wake up. We can roll with the curves these tricksters throw us, looking for the hidden opportunities they may provide. Or we can become tricksters ourselves.

We are **not** advocating deception or manipulation. Instead, we ask how you can take on the manifesting energy of the Joker? How can you take on that energy of resourcefulness, adaptability, and inspired action? How can you ride the waves of fate and fortune rather than be swamped by them?

The answer is to live within the connection between the spiritual and material realms like the fox in the Joker card, suspended between heaven and earth. We reach this state through consistent practice of a combination of emotional elevation and meditation, i.e. contemplation + joy.

While in this state, it is important to focus on your true goals rather than trying to direct the *means*—the how—of accomplishing an action. Instead, have faith that the universe has a greater understanding of how to manifest your intentions.

The Joker understands that the separation between magical/spiritual and material is an illusion, and it's the *belief* in that illusion that keeps those realms separate in our lives. Our minds—our beliefs—can either unite our body and spirit or keep them isolated.

Are you willing to believe?

Download the attached spell sheet and raise your vibration!

SCAN ME

Joker

Wildcard. Trickster. Cleverness. Deceit. An outside perspective.

Every deck needs a joker, a nod to the trickster god Mercury. In a card game, the Joker can either play as a wild card or stand outside the game, giving him a different perspective. We chose the trickster fox to represent our deck's Joker. And in true trickster form, that's all we'll say on the matter today.

Raise Your Vibration

1) Get into a meditative state. Relax and breathe deeply. Get present and feel the aliveness of your toes.

2) Visualize a pink and green mandala spinning in your heart space. Breathe love and joy into the mandala, and visualize it growing larger and brighter. Exhale love and joy into the universe.

3) Fold your hands over your heart. Continue to breathe love and joy into the mandala, and visualize it growing larger and brighter. Exhale love and joy into the universe. Do this until the mandala expands to fill the room.

4) Contemplate the things you are grateful for. Say to yourself: "I am connected to Source, and Source is love. I am love."

5) Conclude the meditation. Do this daily for five minutes this week, and whenever you need to raise your vibration.

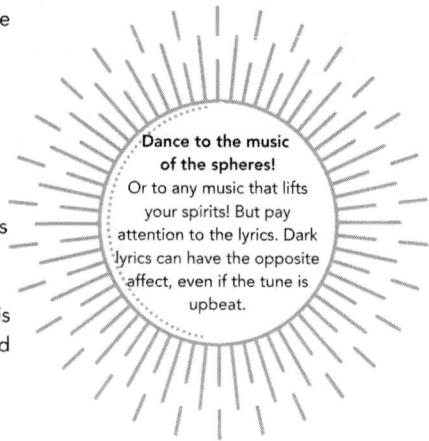

Dance to the music of the spheres! Or to any music that lifts your spirits! But pay attention to the lyrics. Dark lyrics can have the opposite affect, even if the tune is upbeat.

CHAPTER 18

JOKER. THE CARD LAY on my pillow beside the Courage card. The description in the email mentioned luck, but it was as oblique as the scroll.

A shower of rain pebbled the windows behind the wooden blinds. The kitten curled in my lap.

Phone to my ear, I hunched on my bed, and tossed the card onto the ski moguls of the duvet cover. "I'm in Tahoe. I just wanted to see how you were doing."

There was no response to my pause, because I was talking to my son's voicemail. I rolled my eyes at myself. But I hadn't expected a response. I'd been struck with an attack of uncertainty.

I should have admitted to myself sooner that Joe's affectionate distance was a shell. A shell he'd built to keep from being disappointed by me again.

I'd been avoiding this admission. Avoiding it because it had been easier to run along the same old relationship tracks, pretending things between my son and me were fine.

But they weren't fine, and they wouldn't be fine unless I changed things. Unless I changed. The kitten's claws dug into my thigh.

I swallowed. "And I want to... Losing Sarah has made me think a lot about our childhood and about *your* childhood. And I wanted to tell you I'm sorry we didn't spend more time together. That was on me. I'm glad you had Sarah, but I should have been there more."

I exhaled slowly. There was so much more I could say, should say. But I couldn't bring myself to do it in a voicemail. "Anyway. I'll be home soon. I have a lot to tell you. Call me when you can. I love you. Bye." I disconnected.

My hand holding the phone fell limp to the coverlet. It couldn't be too late. It had been too late with my sister, but it couldn't be too late with my son.

A dark image raced across the screen—a blur of pixels, there and gone. I drew back against the brown leather headboard.

Had it been another illusion, or had I been hacked? I rubbed the skin beneath my bottom lip. Was the cat a virus that had gotten past my cleaning program? But how had it migrated from my writing tablet to my phone?

The kitten rolled over and off my thigh. He flopped to the duvet, and his cognac eyes briefly widened with dismay. Then he rolled to sitting and groomed himself as if nothing had happened.

"Pretend all you want," I said. "I saw a big cat."

Ignoring me, Trouble turned away and continued his ablutions.

I crossed my legs and settled against the headboard. What had Tobin meant when he'd asked Wingate about installing cameras in the "passages."

It was ridiculous to think he was referring to secret passages. But I'd grown up on a diet of old Abbot and Costello movies and Nancy Drew mysteries, so that's where my mind went.

Secret passages. Ridiculous.

I tilted my head. On the other hand, deputies were still wandering the house. It was too wet for a ramble. I was also a little afraid of the monster cat appearing again if I wasted the rest of the afternoon online.

"Secret passage search it is." I stood. "Want to come?"

The kitten responded with a disdainful look.

"Right," I said. "I'll let you know how it goes."

I walked to the window overlooking the circular drive and pressed my fingers against the cool glass. If I were going to build a secret passage, I'd have one leading from the master bedroom. But I couldn't search Wingate's room now. Not with the police around.

Where would a passage from the master bedroom lead? To another bedroom for a clandestine rendezvous with a winsome Hollywood guest?

Feeling foolish, I walked my bedroom's perimeter, pressing the edges of the flat, blond-wood panels on the wall. None opened. I tapped the back of the wardrobe and felt around inside that too.

Straightening, I banged my head on the metal hanger bar. "Ow." I lurched sideways and fell hard against the wardrobe's back. The wood gave beneath my shoulder, and I pitched into darkness.

Before I could scream, I landed hard, sprawling on my side. I lay, catching my breath, and sneezed a swear word.

Adrenaline rushed through me. Holy crap, there *was* a secret passage. To my *room*. Maybe I *had* seen a physical cat inside my bedroom the other night? Could it have escaped through here?

The passage was dark, dwindling, and very, very dusty. Chest light, I scrambled to my feet and sneezed again. The shadow of my sister's furry vest on its hanger swung across the sliver of light from my bedroom.

The light only penetrated the first few feet of the passageway. The rest was lost in blackness.

Returning to my room, I grabbed my phone off the desk. I switched on its light, stepped into the wardrobe, and closed its doors behind me. I didn't want Trouble exploring in here and getting lost.

Mouth dry, I shuffled deeper into the passage and a shiver rippled my skin. Whoever had built the passage hadn't bothered with heating.

My phone's flashlight shone dimly through the swirling dust motes. I moved slowly, scanning the walls with my light. Still, I almost missed it. A latch embedded in a wall and only the faintest outline of a door.

I laid my ear against the wall and listened.

Silence.

But the walls had to be fairly soundproofed. If someone were sneaking around in the passage, they wouldn't want to be heard.

Grimacing, I hooked two fingers beneath the latch and pulled. The door swung backward, and I stared into an empty wardrobe. I stepped inside, rattling hangers, and pushed open the wardrobe doors.

A bare-chested Sam gaped, button-up shirt dangling from his fingers. A few curls of gray hair lay flat against his muscular form.

Heat flushed through me. "Oh! Sorry." I backed toward the passage. A hanger pinged off its rod and clattered to the wardrobe floor. "I didn't realize this was your room."

"Hold on." He grasped my arm and hauled me into the bedroom.

I stumbled a bit stepping from the wardrobe and fell against him. His arms, hard and strong, came around me, and this time my shiver wasn't from the cold.

"What the hell?" His breath tickled my ear. "Is that a secret passage? What have you been doing?"

Holding his gaze, I straightened away from him. He released me as if I burned.

I smoothed my hair. "Exploring."

He moved me aside and stepped into the wardrobe. "Where does it go?"

"I don't know, but one of the entrances leads to my bedroom."

He turned, his jaw set. "That explains a lot."

"What the hell does it explain? Has a giant cat been in your bedroom too?"

Sam blinked. "No. What? You've seen a giant cat?"

My chest heated. "I, ah, thought I did. It was probably a trick of the light. Or the dark."

"I *thought* someone had gone through my papers." He motioned toward the blond-wood desk and the laptop and papers piled beside it. "Not that there's anything of interest to anyone but a... Wait here."

While I looked discreetly away, Sam shrugged into his shirt and buttoned it up. He switched on a small but professional-looking flashlight.

"Where did you get that?" I asked.

"I never go anywhere without one. Or a knife." He aimed the light towards the passage floor. "Damn. If someone else came this way recently, I can't tell. You've stirred up all the dust."

I grimaced. I hadn't thought to look for recent footprints when I'd started exploring.

Sam pushed past me in the wardrobe. He strode into the passage.

"Hey." I hurried after him, rattling more hangers. "Wait up."

"The Dragon House was built in 1932 by a dissolute actor, Max Sterling," Sam lectured. "He was of Norwegian descent. Changed his name to fit into Hollywood. Not that it helped. His career was a flash in the pan. He wouldn't have had it at all if it hadn't been for the family money financing his pictures."

He was right. Max Sterling was only famous today for his connection to the Dragon House. "Yeah," I said, "I—"

"There were rumors Max was involved in the occult. In fact, there are rumors that rituals were held here, at Dragon House."

I tugged down the hem of my knit top. "I hadn't heard that."

Sam turned and shined his flashlight upward, illuminating a demonic grin. "Don't worry. I doubt the place is haunted." He turned and continued down the passage.

"I don't," I muttered.

He stopped short, and I bumped into his broad back. "This is not good," he said.

"What?"

Sam edged to the side and directed his flashlight at a pile of fallen beams and broken wood. He rubbed his hand across one. "This passage is a deathtrap."

I cleared my throat, my palms damp. "At least they've braced it." I pointed to a metal beam that ran from floor to ceiling.

He shook his head. "Leaving this wood here though—it's a fire hazard."

We retreated the way we'd come. Sam aimed his beam to the right. "Stairs." He vanished down them. "Have you been down these?" he called up.

"No." I took a hesitant step.

He turned to shine the light on the stairs beneath me so I could see. "Well," he said, "someone has. And recently."

The stairs were steep and creaky. Lightly, I rested my hand on Sam's shoulder for balance. It was reassuringly solid.

We wound down three levels to another hallway that extended north and south. At least I *thought* it did. I was disoriented after the descent from the dark and twisting stairs.

"I accused you of projecting earlier," Sam said. "I shouldn't have, and I'm sorry."

"Forget it."

"I can't. I was the one projecting. I was the one who buried myself in work to get away from—" He shook his head.

I didn't ask what he'd been avoiding. An ex-girlfriend? With his looks, he probably had a string of them plus a load of co-eds after him. I stumbled. Sam swiftly turned and took my arms, steadying me.

My skin tingled from the contact. I stepped away.

Sam dropped his hands to his sides and cleared his throat. "I'll take the north passage," he said.

How did he know which way was north? I shook my head and followed. It would have been more efficient for me to take the opposite. But the passages were cold and stifling, and there was something comforting about Sam's presence.

A gleam of metal caught my eye. "Wait. Here."

Sam turned. "What did you find?"

I pointed at the latch he'd strode past. He scanned the wall with the flashlight, illuminating the faint outlines of a door. He pressed his ear to the wood.

"There could be someone inside," I said. "I didn't hear *you* when I walked into your wardrobe."

"We're not doing anything wrong. There's no reason we shouldn't check it out." He tugged on the latch. The door swung open—not into darkness—into the library, cobwebbed with shadows.

Sam loosed a quiet whistle. "I'll be damned."

A door beyond our field of vision snicked open. "We'll take prints of the cases," the sheriff was saying.

My gut spasmed. *The sheriff.* I reached past Sam and pulled the hidden door shut.

CHAPTER 19

SAM FLICKED THE BEAM of his flashlight upward. Dust motes swirled in front of his bearded face. His bearded, *irate* face.

I hung my head. We should have stayed in the library. We *hadn't* been doing anything wrong. Now we'd look guilty if we got caught.

Sam reached for the latch, and I caught his arm before he could open it. He looked a question at me.

"How much was the complete scroll worth?" the sheriff asked.

I shook my head then cocked my ear toward the secret door. I wanted to hear this, and I doubted the sheriff would let us listen in.

"The last Ripley Scroll on alchemy sold for nearly 600,000 British pounds in 2017," Ezra said. "But there are 23 16th and 17th-century copies of that scroll. Wingate's scroll is unique. But it's not complete."

I straightened. *Not complete?*

"There's a piece still missing," Ezra continued. "If it could be found, and if this is indeed a second scroll by Ripley, it could be worth millions. The original Ripley scroll was lost. All that exist are 16th and 17th-century copies."

Sam's brows gargoyled downward. I winced again.

My financial advisor had warned me not to make any big financial decisions within a year of a loss. I'd ignored him and sold my overpriced Silicon Valley condo to buy my portion of the scroll. But my bet had paid off.

I'd gotten my money back and more in the form of Wingate's cashier's check. Though as my son had pointed out, I had taken quite a chance. I brushed back my hair and choked back a cough from the dust I'd disturbed.

"I can't believe anyone would be so reckless as to put the whole scroll in that metal case," Ezra fretted. "It's centuries old."

"But it would be hard to carry it from the house in those frames," the sheriff said. "Not without being seen."

"They're hermetically sealed!"

Dust tickled my nose. I pinched my nostrils shut, and the urge to sneeze subsided.

"What else?" the sheriff asked.

"Argon is pumped into the frames—"

The sheriff snorted. "Not about the frames, about the scrolls. I know Wingate has a thing about luck, but a million-dollar scroll seems a bit much, even for him."

"He likes the best." Ezra's voice dropped, and I leaned closer to the hidden door.

Sam aimed his flashlight downward. Our footsteps really had made a mess in the floor's thick dust.

"And?" the sheriff prompted.

"He thought the scroll would tell him how to control luck."

"Did it?" the sheriff asked.

"Of course not," Ezra sniffed. "You can't control luck. Attune thy spirit—what nonsense."

"Pardon?"

"It's one of the poems in the scroll. The Caduceus, I believe."

"Nonsense or not, Wingate bought Ms. Bounds's section anyway."

"He had an opportunity to have a complete scroll—the only such of its kind, as far as anyone knows. He wasn't going to walk away from that. The value of the scroll increased exponentially with the addition of Ms. Bounds's section."

"You were at the house yesterday, weren't you?" the sheriff asked.

"Yes. Briefly."

"Did you see anyone on the beach? Anyone at the boat house?"

"No."

"That's too bad," the sheriff said. "I heard you went for a walk along the shore yesterday."

"I wasn't on the beach yesterday," Ezra said.

"You didn't walk to the boathouse?"

I pinched back another sneeze. Sam gave me a warning look.

"No." Ezra's voice rose. "And you can't claim anyone saw me, because I didn't do it."

"You saw no one, not even when you were in the lounge? The windows overlook the shore."

I shifted my weight. A floorboard creaked beneath my feet, and I stilled, heart pounding. Sam's blue eyes bulged.

"If you're implying the bomb was planted yesterday," Ezra said, "while I was here, you can hardly think I did it. What do I know about bombs? I'm a specialist in occult texts."

"I understand you worked as a marine mechanic in your younger days."

"If you know so much, why are you asking me?"

"There was an incident with one of the boats you were repairing. It exploded. You were nearly killed."

"I don't see what that has to do with anything," Ezra said stiffly.

"Really?" the sheriff asked. "A boat explodes, and you've been personally involved in a boat explosion caused by a fuel leak. You don't see a connection?"

"Any idiot could guess that placing a bomb near the fuel tank would cause more damage."

"How do you know it was a bomb and not an accident?"

Ezra sighed. "This is Wingate Weald. We both know his reputation. It stretches the bounds of belief to think this was an accident, especially with the Luck Scroll gone. You need to get that scroll back. It's an important historical artifact."

I sneezed. Sam widened his eyes at me, disappointment lining his craggy face.

"What was that?" the sheriff asked.

"Probably one of your clodhopping deputies. Are we done?"

"I understand your explosion was caused by a gas leak," the sheriff continued. "The port bypass fuel shutoff hadn't been closed properly. Could that have caused the explosion on Wingate's boat?"

"How should I know? We needed an arson specialist to tell us what happened all those years ago. I wasn't responsible for that investigation, and I wasn't responsible for this explosion."

A door slammed. Silence fell.

Sam cleared his throat. In a low voice, he said, "Maybe we should, uh…"

"Go back?" I whispered.

"Yeah."

We retreated. But we must have missed our turn, because our retreat dead-ended at a blank wall.

It was silly to panic. We'd find our way back. But butterflies kicked off in my gut.

Sam scanned his flashlight beam across the wall. "There's got to be another latch here. The passage wouldn't just stop."

"Right. Of course not. Why would it? It's not like this is the Winchester Mystery House or anything." Sarah Winchester *had* to have been unique in that particular form of madness. Hadn't she?

"Brandy?"

"Yes, Sam?"

"You're not claustrophobic, are you?"

"Please," I scoffed. "I'm as comfortable as a cat in a cardboard box."

"What *is* it with cats and boxes?" he asked, continuing his scan. "Why are cats so intent on sitting inside them?"

"The cardboard box is the feline version of a fortress of solitude. Never underestimate the power of a good, solid box."

He huffed a laugh. "I won't."

We scanned the walls and felt along them for a latch. CLICK. Sam turned to me, his expression smug.

The door in front of him glided silently open, and we stepped out behind a juniper bush. Rain pattered onto the earth. Sam pushed the branches aside, revealing the lake shore.

He turned and ran his hands along the door, then closed it. It fit seamlessly with the wood plank sides of the yellow-painted house.

"I hope you know how to get back into the house," I said.

He grunted. "The front door, if necessary."

But it wasn't necessary. Sam ran his hands along the door again and pressed a knothole. The door swung open. His smile this time was even more insufferable than the last.

I frowned. "Anyone could get inside this way." Was that how...? I shook my head. No. Devin's killer had broken a window in the library's French doors to get inside.

"Anyone could get inside who knew about the secret door," Sam said.

"Tobin knew."

"Tobin wouldn't have to use a secret door to get inside. He lives here."

"Really?" I asked. "Where?" A part of me had thought he might have lived in a hidden cabin on the estate. A groundskeeper's cottage—wasn't that what they were called?

But Tobin was no groundskeeper. I wasn't convinced he was even an estate manager.

"Room next to Wingate's."

I folded my arms. "How do you know that?"

"Wingate told me." Sam stepped inside the passage. "I think it was his way of warning me off trying to murder him in his sleep."

I hoped Sam was joking. I *thought* he was joking. Because it worried me that Wingate thought Sam might have wanted to kill him at all.

THE CADUCEUS

Clense thy vessell of drosse and impurities
Attune thy spirite wyth supernalle symphonies
Lest in the divine ballance
Fickle Hermes, god of chance
Betwene seene and unseene realms
Bestowes favoures for the ille
So aline thyself wyth Holy will
Ye shal fynd perfecte harmony stylle

Hold the sacred caduceus hye
Above the serpentes' wings devine
Prudence holdes her gentille sway
To her honoure thee must pray
For Fortune favoures not the brave
But to ascende from the darke grave
Thee mouste make the grevous choice
Of wysdom and counterpoise

CHAPTER 20

SAM SAW ME THROUGH the passages to my bedroom. I didn't protest. I wasn't confident I'd find the winding way on my own.

I stepped through my wardrobe and turned to sag against the opposite, sand-colored wall. The Scandinavian-modern style I'd sneered at before seemed welcoming after our journey through the mansion's veins.

Trouble dropped off the couch and trotted to me. The kitten sniffed my sneakers.

Sam stuck his head inside the bedroom and looked around. "You brought a cat? Huh. I didn't know that was allowed." He retreated before I could explain. The hidden door inside the wardrobe clicked shut, hangers rattling.

An unexpected pang of loneliness gripped my heart. I'd never been lonely before. I enjoyed my own company. I *liked* being alone. Alone, I got more done. Alone, I could do what I wanted, when I wanted.

There was no way a husband would have gone along with selling our home to buy a Luck Scroll. Or infiltrating a mafioso's mansion to get... *What? Closure?* I pressed the wardrobe doors, making sure they were shut.

I was better off on my own. Besides, Sam wasn't my type. And he definitely wasn't a murderer. He was a scholar, a researcher. It was dumb luck that he'd come here. His research assistant had had to stay home for the birth of his child.

Dumb luck.

I dropped onto the fluffy bed. And I wasn't completely alone. I had my son, Joe—

Do you?

Okay, Joe had his life too, and that was as it should be. I checked my phone. *Think of the Devil, and he appears.* Joe'd finally responded to my text:

Don't get morbid on me now. Neither of us are built for that. My childhood was footloose and fancy free.

An ache pierced my chest. *His childhood with Sarah.*

Stop ruminating. I strode to the desk and opened my electronic notebook's leather case.

Why would Ezra have thought the scroll wasn't complete? I'd studied the edges of the vellum. They'd *looked* like they fit together, but I hadn't tested that assumption. I couldn't while they were in their frames.

And the text... It seemed complete as well.

What had Ezra seen? What had I missed?

The kitten crouched in front of the wardrobe. He stared at its closed doors.

"No one else is coming out of there," I said testily.

Trouble glanced at me then resumed his study of the wardrobe doors.

During my exploration of the passages, I hadn't found Wingate's room. Not that it mattered—the scroll wouldn't be inside it. The sheriff's deputies would have searched it by now, leaving it empty.

"I should go back," I muttered. If the room was empty...

The kitten growled.

"I know," I told him. "Devin's dead. Wingate's dead. Sarah's dead. Everyone's dead. This should be over. But it doesn't feel over. It *isn't* over, because someone killed Wingate and Devin, and I'm here. The murders happened when I was here, and now the Luck Scroll is gone. Somehow this is connected to the scroll, and that makes it connected to me. I need to know."

Like I'd needed to know about the chain of events that had led to Sarah's death. A month ago, Joe had laughingly told me I'd become obsessed. With Sarah. With luck.

I'd gone along with the joke. I hadn't believed he might be right, that it might be a problem... until now.

"It doesn't matter if I'm obsessed or not." I stood and strode to the wardrobe. "I can quit anytime. I just don't want to quit *now*." I reached for the doors.

The kitten hissed.

"It's only a secret passage. It's not an interdimensional portal." Though it *was* spooky as hell.

I stepped inside the wardrobe and opened the door at the back. A wave of cold rippled out, raising the fur on Trouble's back. There was something clammy and rotting about that cold, and I took an involuntary step away.

I swallowed. The air flowing from the passage was cold because the builder hadn't bothered to heat it. That was all. It wasn't supernatural or haunted or cursed. It was just... cold.

I hesitated then stepped inside, turning to shut the doors. Baring his tiny teeth, Trouble hunched his back.

"I'll be back soon." I closed the doors so he couldn't follow.

On this trip, I moved swiftly through the passage and in the opposite direction I'd gone before. The cold pressed against my back, urging me onward.

I found the latch to Wingate's room easily. It was shinier than the others. It must have gotten more use.

I pressed my ear to the door. All I heard was the thumping of my own heart. I tiptoed inside another, larger wardrobe. Forcing my way through a thicket of men's dinner jackets, I stepped into the room.

The lights were off, twilight shadows gathering in the spacious suite—a massive bedroom and a small work area. Inside the latter was an elegant, Gustavian desk—a table with spindly legs and on one short side, a cabinet of drawers. If a chaise longue had been turned into a desk, it would look like this.

I moved to the desk. It sat atop a flat-woven kilim with a wheat-colored background. I tried the desk drawers. They were locked.

The desk was an antique. I didn't have the heart to try to force it open.

Beside the desk, a wicker wastebasket lay on its side. I knelt to study the contents. The two ebony Tarot cards Wingate had received had been tossed into the basket. *Death and the Ten of Swords.*

I knew not to touch them, and not because I was superstitious. I'd told the deputy about the cards today. At some point the sheriff would get around to retrieving these and taking fingerprints. I snapped a picture of the cards in the basket with my phone.

Something else lay inside the basket. A leather-bound journal with gilt paper edges. I glanced behind me. I'd been in Wingate's bedroom a long time.

Wishing I had gloves, I pulled the long sleeves of my knit top over my fingers and retrieved the journal from the bin. Carefully, I opened the book.

My eyes widened. Wingate had kept notes on the Luck Scroll too. And not only the scroll—he'd kept clippings of lucky incidents—lucky incidents regarding crimes. People who'd avoided getting shot by pure luck. Criminals caught in lucky breaks for the cops.

He'd annotated the stories with phrases like *childlike belief, confidence,* and *openness/opportunity.* They were phrases I recognized. Lucky people tended to be confident and outgoing. They trusted things would work out, and so they were open to opportunities.

That didn't explain what had happened to my sister though. She'd had all of those qualities. Fortune had ended her life anyway.

Hastily, I snapped pictures of his notes on the Luck Scroll. Wingate had made drawings of its images too. They were cruder than mine, but clear enough.

The Luck Scroll had been more than a vanity purchase for Wingate. He'd been obsessed. *Like me.*

Not that his obsession had saved him.

I turned to the final page, dated yesterday. Triple underlined in red was an angry scrawl: *Missing piece???*

I sat back on my heels. Wingate had believed the scroll was incomplete too. *Huh.*

Men's voices rose in the hallway, and I froze, crouched over the basket. *The Sheriff.*

Dropping the journal into the wastebasket, I scuttled to the wardrobe and stepped inside. I closed the doors behind me as the bedroom door clicked open.

Heart pounding, I shuffled through the soft jackets toward the back of the wardrobe. My head struck hangers, and they rattled. I winced, biting back a curse.

"What's that?" Deputy Linnel said.

"What's what?" the sheriff asked.

Heart banging, I ducked inside the passage. I gingerly shut the secret door, turned on my phone's light, and speedwalked toward the hidden door to my bedroom.

It wasn't there.

Frowning, I retreated, scanning the passage with my light. The door had to be here somewhere. I must have gone too far. Or not far enough...

The cold came first. A smothering cold dark with malice. A feline shadow stretched along one wooden wall.

I stilled. I couldn't have moved if I'd wanted to, tentacles of freezing air wrapping me in their choking embrace. The shadow's definition sharpened, a cat, its head low to the ground as if sniffing.

A tremor wracked my bones. It wasn't real. It had to be another hallucination or middle-world spirit.

The shadow raised its head. Its ears twitched.

Don't look at it. My shallow breathing quickened. The shadow prowled closer.

I blinked, sweat stinging my eyes. This was... It was silly. Trouble must have found his way into the passage. I mustn't have closed the wardrobe tightly enough. I'd have to rescue the kitten, that was all.

But I couldn't move. The cold, black and bitter with spite, had me in its grip. The shadow skulked closer. *Don't look at it.*

"You can't hurt me." My voice quavered.

HISS. The sound was unnatural, sickening and sinister. Nausea swam up my throat, and I pressed my hands to my ears.

Swaying, flesh pebbling, I braced one hand against the wall. I snatched it away, gasping. The dusty wood was so cold it had burned my palm.

My phone's light dimmed and went out. A low growl, too deep and too loud to be Trouble, sounded in the passage.

I wanted to bolt, wanted to run. But if I did, I'd never find my door in the dark. I backed away. Real or unreal, I couldn't stay in the passage with this...thing.

Movements jerky, I forced myself to lay my palm on that awful, cold cold cold wall and feel. There would be a latch. The others had been hip height. I'd somehow missed my door, but it would be there.

The growl came again. My head swam. Maybe it was adrenaline, but my eyes seemed to adjust to the darkness, and I glanced over my shoulder.

A low, black shape stalked steadily toward me. Not a shadow. Something real. Something here. The world lightened, going gray, my own feminine shadow shooting toward the thing.

I backed away and stumbled against something warm and hard, and I cried out. A broad hand grasped my shoulder and whirled me around.

Tobin, holding a flashlight, frowned down at me. "What the hell are you doing?"

"We have to get out of here." I wrenched free and turned to point. "There's a jag..."

The long passage stretched before us.

It was empty.

CHAPTER 21

MEEK, I LET TOBIN escort me into my room, clothes hangers in the wardrobe rattling behind us. It's not as if anyone had *told* me the passages were off-limits. But I knew I'd been trespassing.

Tobin moved toward my paneled bedroom door and opened it. "Next time you want a midnight adventure, do it somewhere else. You're making my job way too interesting."

"Why was Wingate so obsessed with luck?" I asked.

He paused, hand on the knob, and turned. "He didn't tell you? It's no secret. He's always been lucky. With his life. With women. With mon—" His lips flattened.

"With money?" I finished for him, and he nodded.

"There was no one like Wingate for finding dropped cash on the street," Tobin said.

But I had a feeling that wasn't what he'd meant to say.

I leaned one hip against the desk and crossed my arms. "If he was so lucky, why did he need the Luck Scroll?"

"He didn't need it. He *wanted* it," he said sharply. When I didn't respond, he continued, "Wingate thought people only had a finite amount of luck in their lives."

"Like a cat with nine lives?" I glanced at Trouble on the bed. The kitten watched Tobin warily from the white folds of the duvet.

"Yeah," Tobin said. "Once it was out, it was out."

"And was Wingate's running out?"

"Wingate didn't need luck," he said. "Wingate was smart."

"The boat accident wasn't very lucky."

"It was no accident."

"Winding up in the middle of a dark highway was either a very lucky or unlucky thing for him," I said, and Tobin blanched. "Lucky he wasn't killed." *Like my sister and the other driver.* "Unlucky he was there at all. Was he trying to test his luck?"

Tobin's jaw hardened.

"No," I mused, answering myself. "You don't test your luck if you think there's only a limited quantity available. You hoard it. What was he doing out there?"

"I'd tell you to ask Wingate, but that's impossible now."

"What's impossible?" Fortuna drawled. She leaned against the frame of the open door, her little black dress swaying provocatively. Fortuna gave Tobin a slow up-and-down look.

He pivoted and strode past her and into the hallway.

"Tobin's a dedicated lone wolf." Fortuna watched his departing form, then she met my gaze. "I wouldn't bother."

My face heated. "I'm not interested in Tobin," I said shortly.

"In Sam then?" She shook her head. "Too damaged."

"What do you mean?" Sam seemed fine to me. As fine as anyone else and better than most. Better than me.

"He made one too many good guesses about my childhood last night in the lounge. I think he was trying to sympathize with me, but I don't need sympathy."

"You lost your husband. Take the sympathy."

"Not about that."

"Then what?"

"The poor baby was neglected by his parents," she cooed.

My stomach clenched. After my husband had abandoned us, I'd been so determined to build a stable career that Joe hadn't gotten the attention he'd needed. Not from me.

It hadn't been neglect. Joe had always known I had his back. But I hadn't gone to his baseball games, hadn't been there for the teacher conferences. I'd wanted to, but there just hadn't been the time.

And if I was being honest with myself, financial need wasn't the only reason I'd thrown myself into work. My ego had been bruised by my husband's desertion. I'd been... unwanted.

And I'd been determined to prove that feeling wrong, determined to be wanted somewhere, to be useful, to be needed on the job.

But Joe was the one who'd needed me the most.

I stared at her, my gaze fixed. "Being sympathetic doesn't mean he was neglected."

Fortuna's expression hardened. "It was obvious. When I confronted him, he confirmed it. He thought—" She tossed her red hair. "But I got over my childhood. And you really should lock your door." She straightened off the door frame and swished into the hall.

I got over my childhood. Somehow, I doubted that. Fortuna's lover had mentioned she'd had a troubled childhood. And... what? Like called to like, and Fortuna had somehow recognized Sam's troubled past?

I shut the door. Trouble meowed and clambered onto one of the pillows. A colorful card slid from it to the snowy duvet.

Tensing, I strode to the bed and picked up the new card. *Generosity.*

I closed my eyes. If someone was going to the trouble to put UnTarot cards on my bed, why were they leaving cards that were so... banal?

Cards. The Tarot cards.

I hurried to the desk. Tossing the UnTarot card to the bed, I picked up my writing tablet and did an online search for the meaning of the Ten of Swords. *Betrayal. Backstabbing. An ending.*

"Huh." I sat back in the gently curved chair. The meaning of the Death card Wingate had received was obvious enough. But his angry reaction had implied the cards were a threat, so I hadn't learned anything ground-breaking here.

But Tarot cards... Could they have been related to the fortune tellers Wingate's mob bosses had controlled? Or to Riga's fortune teller in particular?

The kitten dropped from the bed and jumped onto the low, sand-colored sofa. He hopped onto the desk and pawed at my notebook.

"Good idea." I opened my inbox. Sure enough, there was an email from the mystery school, subject line: *Generosity*. Feeling perverse, I scanned my other emails instead.

There was one from the CEO of my old company, asking if I'd think of returning. Apparently, the people he'd hired to replace me weren't working out.

I smiled bitterly. And who was the fool? Him for convincing me to work two more-than full-time jobs, or me for accepting the challenge?

I opened the Generosity email and read it. *That stupid mystery school.* Why had I bothered? Oh yeah, because I'd been following a hunch, and the school had been free. Well, that hunch had been a bust.

I dug out Riga's business card and called her. It went to voicemail, and I disconnected. My cell phone rang in my hand a few seconds later.

I clapped it to my ear. "Hello?"

"This is Riga. You called?"

"Yeah. That fortune teller you helped out—did she read Tarot cards?"

"No, she was into astrology and palmistry. Why?"

So much for the Tarot card clue. Though they still made excellent fortune-teller-themed threats. "Wingate received another Tarot card this morning. Or maybe he got it last night, I can't be sure. But he was upset about it and implied someone had gotten inside the house to leave it."

"Let me guess, the Death card?"

"Yeah." I spun my stylus between my fingers. "How'd you know?"

"It's a little on the nose, don't you think?" she said dryly. "Did you tell the sheriff?"

"The deputy knows." I fumbled the stylus. It clattered to the wood floor, and I bent to retrieve it. "But I wasn't the only one who saw the card. Wingate was pitching a fit about it. Could this be connected to those fortune tellers?"

"I doubt they would take on someone like Wingate. Besides, when they were trying to get loose of their... contracts, he was only the go-between for me and his *clients* who were controlling them."

"His clients? The mob, you mean."

"Yes. They're his likely killers. The mob or a rival. A boat explosion has the feel of a mob hit to me."

"Is that what the sheriff thinks?"

Riga laughed softly. "Alas, he doesn't confide in me." She disconnected.

I picked up the Generosity card again and began to slide it into the pocket of the notebook's leather portfolio with the others. Instead, I pulled the others out and laid them on the desk as if I were doing a Tarot reading.

The Game. Gratitude. Courage. Nature. Joker. Generosity.

I frowned. *There was something...* Why did they send a ping of familiarity through me?

First the cards, then Peggy the dispatcher... Had turning fifty doomed me to the constant feeling that I'd forgotten something important?

I studied the jester's hat on the Joker card and sucked in a breath. *The jester's hat.* A jester—or *jestour* —had been mentioned in the Luck Scroll's folktale. And so had gratitude, courage, and generosity.

A jester hadn't meant the same thing in the 15th century as it did today. Jesters hadn't been court buffoons then. They were closer to wandering magicians.

I flipped through my notebook and scanned the poem. Nature and a game were mentioned in the scroll as well.

No. It *had* to be a coincidence. After all, these weren't concepts from the modern era. It wasn't surprising Ripley—or whoever'd written the poem on the scroll—had used them as well. But it was an *odd* coincidence.

"A coincidence," I said firmly and closed my notebook's leather case.

The kitten shook his head.

GENEROSITY

SEEKER:

Generosity is a magical act.

It's one of the quickest, most powerful ways to elevate our own magic, elevating our mood, our energy, our alignment. And when those three things are in place, manifestation comes easily.

However, generosity needs to be sincere. Generosity for the sake of getting something, especially for getting magical mojo, doesn't have the same *oomph* as true generosity.

To the ancients, generosity of spirit meant giving without any expectation of return. This concept is critical for the witch, because magic is not transactional.

Non-transactional magic may seem odd at first. In magic, we do certain things with the intention to get certain things, such as a better life. But magic is an act of co-creation with the universe, and it is an act of attracting what you desire.

However, a transactional mentality is *not* attractive. In fact, it's a massive turnoff. But a generous spirit is hard to resist. Approaching *any* work in a generous frame of mind will move the witch toward her goals.

We cannot have the idea in the back of our minds that our generosity will *trick* the universe into getting what we want. However, a habitual practice of generosity *can* train our minds and hearts to approach the work with a freely loving mindset. And like any other magical practice, the more you do it, the easier and more enjoyable it becomes, until it becomes second nature.

So, practice random acts of kindness in your daily life. It's easy, because you'll find they uplift you as well.

These acts could be as simple as offering a helping hand, giving someone your full attention, or speaking highly of someone. Be sure to infuse these acts with positive intentions and magical energy for extra *oompf*.

And try on the attached incantations for size, or create your own.

SCAN ME

And now, we invite you to meditate on the next card.

Generosity

Giving and receiving. Open heartedness. Kindness. Unselfishness.

We can be generous with our time. We can be generous with our attention. We can be generous with our resources. But true generosity is an act of love. It comes from the heart, without any expectation of getting something out of it for ourselves. Anything worthwhile is done for its own sake, and when we approach life with this generous attitude, our life force expands. Ultimately, generosity, like forgiveness, is something we do for our own peace of mind. But we also need to be generous with ourselves, but that can mean setting boundaries.

The symbols:

A woman extends a hydrangea as a gift against a background of maple leaves—all symbols of generosity.

The questions:

How can you be generous with the people around you? Are you giving freely, or deep down, do you expect something back?

Generosity

Incantations take affirmations to a different, magical level, by wiring certainty into your nervous system. When you incant, you speak the words aloud, from your gut and chest. You say them with bold certainty, over and over again. As you incant, emphasize different words. E.g.,

I *am* a channel for love.
I am a *channel* for love.
I am a channel for *love*.
I am a channel for love.

To create certainty in your mind, incantation also works well when you're doing some mindless exercise, like jogging, to drill it in with movement and extensive repetition as well. That said, you might not want to do it when someone is jogging past. 😄

How can you be more generous with those around you?

_____
_____
_____
_____
_____

Incantations:

- I am a channel for generosity, love, kindness and positivity.
- I am a willing vessel for the Universe to spread generosity, love, kindness and positivity.
- I give for the joy of it, without expectations.

CHAPTER 22

RAIN DRIPPED FROM THE eaves. It spattered the narrow window of Ezra's shop. Instead of cleaning the window, the drips obscured the shapes behind it even more and sent dark rivulets over the nameplate on the door:

EZRA BLACKTHORN

SPECIALIST, OCCULT TEXTS

I sighed. At least it wasn't snowing. I hated driving in snow.

My sister had hated it too, which had made her move to Auburn all the more inexplicable. Her husband had wanted to move to Auburn though, so move to Auburn they had.

But the roads had been dry the morning of her crash. And God, I missed her. Heat dampened my eyes, and I pressed my lips tight.

Last night, I'd journeyed in my dream again to the cabin. Once again, I'd been frustrated. Sarah hadn't been there.

My hands tightened on my borrowed umbrella. I should be able to see her. I was *good* at lucid dreaming. Why was it failing me now? Was my subconscious still too raw with grief?

Shaking out the umbrella, I opened the shop's door. I hesitated and stepped inside. The shop was as dim and dusty as its front window had implied, and I blinked, giving my eyes a chance to adjust to the gloom.

Bookcases with sliding glass doors lined the walls. The glass doors were dingy, giving the books behind them a warped look.

"Shut the door," Ezra shouted from somewhere in the back.

I shut it. Wrapping the tie around the damp umbrella, I edged deeper inside the shop. My footsteps were soft on the thin, gray carpet. "It's me," I said. "Brandy."

Ezra appeared at the end of the narrow aisle holding a leatherbound book open in his hands. Dust smeared one sleeve of his graveyard-black suit jacket. "What do you want?" His voice rose. "What are you doing with that umbrella?"

"It's raining," I said, surprised.

He glanced toward the front window, opaque with murk and condensation. "Oh." He snapped his book shut. "You don't have an appointment."

"I'm sorry, I didn't know I needed one."

"This isn't a bookstore. You can't just show up."

"The sign said OPEN." I nodded toward the front door.

"I'm expecting an important client." He walked behind the laminate counter and stared down his long nose. "What do you want?"

Down to business, then. "Why do you think the Luck Scroll is incomplete?"

"How did you—?" His long nose twitched. "It was obvious, wasn't it? The edges of the fragments don't match up."

"They looked like they matched up to me."

"You aren't an expert."

No, but I'd loved puzzles as a kid. "I sketched the scroll fragments, including their edges."

"And are you a trained artist?" he snapped.

"Yes, with a minor in art history."

His thin lips pursed. "You—You managed a tech company."

"But before that, I trained as an artist." Until my parents had convinced me it was impractical, and I needed to do something more lucrative with my life.

I didn't resent their advice. They probably hadn't been wrong, and I'd had a successful career in tech. I'd even enjoyed my work.

"Your sketches are hardly evidence." He sneered.

I raised a brow. "Evidence?" A draft of cold air chilled my skin, and I shivered.

He flushed. "I merely meant when dealing with historical artifacts, one shouldn't conjecture without... I'm telling you, there's a piece missing."

"I don't think so. The text flows naturally. None of the verses read as unfinished. The scroll is complete. The question is, why would you tell Wingate otherwise?"

"I never told him the scroll was incomplete."

"But you made Wingate think it was," the sheriff said from behind me.

Ezra's book slipped from his hands and hit the carpet with a thud. He ducked behind the counter to retrieve it.

I pressed one hand to my chest. "How—?" My gaze darted toward the door. *The draft*—the sheriff had come inside, and I hadn't heard.

The burly sheriff's smile was wintery. "I may not look built for catlike stealth, but I've still got a few tricks up my sleeve."

Clutching the book to his chest, Ezra straightened behind the counter. "Sheriff. You're early."

One corner of my mouth curled. *So much for a client meeting.* He'd been waiting for the sheriff.

"I can only think of one reason why you'd want your client to believe the scroll wasn't worth as much as he hoped," the sheriff said.

"Because Ezra wanted to buy it off him," I guessed.

"That type of game is a risk with someone like Wingate," the sheriff said. "Which implies you already have a highly motivated buyer. Who is it?"

"I never *said* the scroll was incomplete," Ezra whined.

"Who?" the sheriff asked.

Ezra grimaced. "A group of occult investors."

Wait. What? My jaw slackened. "There are occult investment groups?" My financial advisor hadn't mentioned *that*.

"Who?" the sheriff barked.

Ezra ran his hand up and down the spine of the book he held. "They're called the Brotherhood."

The sheriff pulled a notepad from the breast pocket of his near-black jacket. "Write down their contact info."

"I can't— I don't—" he stammered. "I don't know it."

"What do you mean you don't know it?" the sheriff asked.

"They're incredibly secretive. They're a black lodge."

The sheriff's pen hovered over the open leather notepad. "Black lodge?"

Ezra looked away. "An organization of... occultists."

"Like Riga Hayworth?" I asked.

Ezra's bony face contorted. "Her? They wouldn't let someone like *her* in."

"Why not?" the sheriff asked.

"She's not the right sort," the bookseller muttered.

What was the *right sort* of occultist? More importantly, what was the *wrong* sort?

"How'd you get in touch with them?" the sheriff asked.

"I don't. They contact *me*."

"And they contacted you about the Luck Scroll?" I asked.

The sheriff frowned but said nothing.

Ezra nodded. "When they heard your missing fragment had been found—"

"How'd they know that?" I asked, disconcerted. I hadn't advertised my find.

"I don't know." Ezra ran a hand over his thinning hair. "They told me a woman would be bringing a fragment to Wingate for sale. I should assess whether it was legit and if the scroll was now complete."

I rubbed my wrists, bile rising in my throat. Someone had known about my section of scroll? But I hadn't told anyone. Not even Joe. He'd known I was pursuing luck, but not the scroll.

The leak had to have been someone inside Dragon House, someone close to Wingate. Or the consultant who'd found the scroll fragment for me.

No. My consultant had left for a project in South Africa the day after he'd handed me the scroll. I hadn't told him about Wingate or what I'd planned to do with the find. Then how had they known?

"And *is* the scroll complete?" the sheriff asked.

Ezra swallowed. "It appears so."

There were outsiders interested in the scroll. Could that explain the break-in at Dragon House and Devin's murder? I hugged myself, and the umbrella over my wrist jutted outward, whacking the edge of a glass case. "But—?"

"You can leave, Ms. Bounds," the sheriff said.

I opened my mouth to object. The sheriff glared, and I thought better of my impulse. Wordless, I turned and left Ezra's shop.

The rain had lessened to a miserable drizzle by the time I returned to Dragon House and checked on the kitten. He sat on my white pillow with an expectant air. A dark card lay before him.

Dread pooled in my gut, but I plucked the UnTarot card from the fluffy pillow. *Fear.*

I cursed. Taking the striped kitten to the desk, I pulled my notebook from my satchel and checked my email. There was a new message from the Mystery School, which I'd begun to capitalize in my mind.

I read the entire email again then looked up the Brotherhood online. My search turned up a movie with a one-star review on Rotten Tomatoes, a whaling bar in Nantucket, and a book about the Freemasons.

"I don't suppose *you* know anything about the Brotherhood?" I asked Trouble.

The orange kitten sneezed.

I sighed. "I didn't think so."

I descended the winding stairs to find Fortuna. In the lounge, Tobin informed me she'd gone shopping.

That avenue of intel out of reach, I decided to pursue my own. I retrieved my borrowed umbrella from the stand in the foyer and opened the front door.

"Where are you going?" Sam asked from behind me, and I jumped a little.

I lifted and dropped my hands. "Why is everyone sneaking up on me today?"

"Who else sneaked up on you?" he asked.

"The sheriff, at Ezra's shop." Rain pattered on the flagstones behind me, and I shut the front door.

Sam scratched his beard. "What were you doing at Ezra's?"

"I wanted to know why he'd told Wingate the scroll was incomplete, when it clearly *was* complete."

The academic braced one shoulder against a dark wall. "Was Ezra trying to knock the price down?"

"Well, yes, that would be the obvious conclusion. But I wanted to hear it from him."

"Who did he plan to sell it to?"

"A group of occult investors."

"There are occult investment groups?"

"That's what I said." *Roughly.* "They're called the Brotherhood. Ever heard of them?"

"No. Are they online?"

"Not that I could find."

"I'll do some digging."

"You will?" *Why?* What did he care?

"I want to know what's going on. I'm a suspect in the murders too."

The words were a punch to the chest. *Too.* Sam thought I was a suspect. He thought I might have killed two people.

But it was the intelligent thing to think, and Sam was intelligent. I didn't trust anyone at Dragon House. Why should they trust me?

"I'm going for a walk," I said, hunching my shoulders.

"Where?"

"Around the grounds. Want to come?"

"In this weather? No thanks." He turned and vanished down a long hallway.

Unaccountably disappointed, I walked onto the front steps and unfurled the umbrella. Rain pattered its black fabric.

The collapsed sections of hidden passageways had gone *somewhere*, and Sam and I hadn't explored every turn. I had an idea that one passage might run all the way to the outbuilding we'd seen earlier. It would be a *long* passage. But if I were a rich, creepy occultist, I'd build one.

Thinking hard, I paced through the dripping pines. Wingate had caused my sister's accident, killing her. And that had set in motion my quest for understanding, and that had brought me to the scroll, and that had brought others to the scroll and to Dragon House. And then Devin had died, and Wingate had been blown up...

I glanced up. The pines shot to the gun-metal sky. The trees leaned inward as if listening, looming. I knew it was an illusion, knew the illusion was what was making me dizzy.

But I kept looking, caught between the lower and upper worlds. Tearing my gaze from the trees, I stumbled, disoriented, then resumed my trek through the woods.

I edged around a waist-high boulder. Wingate was a high-ranking criminal. Odds were good someone would have tried to kill him eventually. But I couldn't get around the fact that things had started spiraling when I'd shown up at Dragon House.

Was I a part of some giant Rube Goldberg contraption? Was that what luck was? Just a chain of random events? Cause and effect that we interpreted as connected because we humans liked seeing patterns?

A branch cracked behind me. Startled, I pivoted, scanning the pines and manzanita bushes. I exhaled shakily. It was probably a bird. It was incredible how loud they could be. Not like cats...

I swallowed and moved more quickly along the little trail. It hadn't been a cat. Of course not. I had cats on the brain, that was all.

Footsteps padded behind me, and I stopped short. I looked around. The woods fell silent, except for the steady dripping and occasional louder plop on my umbrella.

No bird called. No wind rustled the trees. No squirrel scampered over the nearby boulder, a barren island rising from the browning manzanita.

I continued. Footsteps echoed behind me, and I stopped. The echoes halted as well.

That... was no cat. The footsteps had been human.

FEAR

SEEKER:

Fear is a message to move forward. It's a message from our instincts that we can use to protect ourselves, preparing us to deal with threats. But too often, it's used against us as a tool of control—control by our shadow self or by malignant actors.

Fear can attack us from within and without. There are the fears rattling around in our unconscious. These fears keep us from our greatness and keep us playing small. To our unconscious mind, these fears seem rational and reasonable. But when we shine the light of conscious awareness on them, they evaporate.

Our shadow self may use fear to keep us in the comfortable cycle of making the same mistakes over and over, to keep us from breaking free of our bad habits and roles. The shadow doesn't mean to make us miserable. At some weird level, the shadow thinks it's protecting us. But it's rare to think clearly and act in our best interests when we're in a state of fear.

As witches, we spend a lot of time in our heads. While our powers of imagination and visualization make us powerful spellcasters, they can also make us more vulnerable to dark spells of fear and anxiety. It's easy for imaginative people to envision all the things that might go wrong.

The cure to this is presence. If we can spend time in our bodies in conscious awareness, irrational fears will naturally fade away. (There are, of course, rational fears, and being present can help us deal with those as well).

Yes, anything *could* happen. But you're a witch. You've dealt with chal-lenges in the past and you'll deal with them in the future. You've got this.

Until we voluntarily face our fears, we will be vulnerable. Face them. Don't give in to fear. Download the attached worksheet. Use it as needed.

SCAN ME

Fear

Fear. Nightmare. Analysis paralysis.

Fear needs to be put in its proper place. When managed properly, it's a useful warning that danger's at hand, giving us time to adapt and react. But when it governs our thoughts, it causes us to make bad decisions. It steals our potential.

Fear also makes us more malleable to being controlled, so it's frequently used as a tool of manipulators and sorcerers. Fear moves us away from meaning.

If you find yourself stuck in fear or anxiety, take a beat to sense where (or who) it's coming from. Your fear may represent a legitimate concern, or it may be a spell of control. But fear is only an emotion, and it doesn't have to rule us. We can overcome through faith, consciousness, or just lightening up.

The symbols:

A woman floats through a nightmare world in a state of sleep paralysis. She's frozen, paralyzed by fear. But this is only a nightmare. It isn't real.

The questions:

What decisions are you making (or not making) out of fear? Where does that fear originate? Are you making mountains out of molehills? How can you move past your fear?

Is This Real?

Make a list of your five biggest fears.

Once you have your list, review each item and ask yourself, "Is this a legit fear, or is it some unconscious BS? If it's legit, is it something I need to worry about now? How is this fear holding me back?"

I Fear	Is This Real?
_____	_____
_____	_____
_____	_____
_____	_____

Next, feel the fear that is still bothering you the most. Sit with the feeling of that fear. Notice how it feels in your body and where you feel the fear.

Visualize the fear as a childlike monster. Name the fear, e.g. "Hello fear of losing my money," and greet it as a friend.

Visualize yourself breathing in healing light and say to yourself: "May I release my fears." Exhale and say to yourself: "May all living beings release their fears."

Visualize yourself hugging the little monster. You don't need it anymore. Lovingly wish it peace. Hold it close and absorb it into your glowing heart space.

Thoughts become things. Focus on the good ones!

CHAPTER 23

A GUST OF WIND shivered the pines, tugging at my umbrella and sending a spattering of droplets to the needle-covered earth. The skin between my shoulder blades prickled.

"Who's there?" I called out and snapped my mouth shut. *Idiot!* If someone was stalking me, they'd hardly admit it, and I'd just confirmed my location.

I stood frozen, uncertain, unwilling to go forward and face my stalker or to run away, turning my back on him. Heart thudding, I stepped backward. No sound broke the dripping of the rain. I took another step, and another.

A deep growl sounded behind me. I stilled, hair rising on the back of my neck. Goosebumps sprouted on my skin, my breath catching in my throat.

But none of those clichés could adequately describe the terror that slicked my skin, snaked down my spine, throttled my lungs. Those were just words. My fear was a thing, a palpable force, sly and smothering.

I bolted and ran. I didn't look back. I ran, crashing through bracken.

Manzanita branches clawed my clothing. My foot twisted on a pinecone. I stumbled but didn't stop until I reached the front door of Dragon House.

And when I turned, panting, and scanned the curving gravel drive, it was empty.

I ate lunch without human company. The kitten gamboled at my feet in the expansive dining room overlooking the lake. With Wingate gone and Fortuna in charge, I'd brought Trouble out of hiding.

Behind the picture windows, the sun broke through the clouds, driving the last remnants of that unreasoning fear from my mind. *Fear.*

It *wasn't* a palpable force. And the only slyness to it was that of my own out-of-control mind, letting my emotions take over.

I propped my elbow on the long table, my head on my fist. How had I let things get this bad? How had I let myself be ruled by fear?

"That stupid email was right," I muttered.

The kitten made a sound eerily like a tiny laugh. I shot him a sharp glance. He sat up and licked an orange paw.

Pulling out my cell phone, I reread the email I'd found when I'd returned to my room on fear. I closed my eyes and breathed deeply.

I felt my toes. I focused my attention on my hands. I felt the air moving in and out of my lungs, the fabric of my top brushing against my skin with every rise and fall of my chest.

I felt my heartbeat, and I felt the anguish that gripped it. I'd known of this trick for dealing with emotions before. I'd tried it so many times before, so many times.

It had worked, briefly, but the anguish always returned. Was my grief bottomless?

I want to live.

My eyes blinked open. The thought had popped into my mind and hit me like a cannonball to the chest.

Because I realized I *did* want to live. Sarah was dead, but I wanted to go on, no matter how miserable life felt without her.

So, my son thought I was a foolish old lady? Someday, he'd be old too, and he'd understand. And I was alive, and I could repair our relationship. The time I had left was a gift.

And I wanted to live. Without fear.

Until we voluntarily face our fears, we will be vulnerable.

I nodded and scraped back my chair. *All right then.*

The site of my sister's accident shouldn't have been hard to find. Her car had taken out Lake Tahoe mile marker 38. The wooden posts followed the highway encircling the lake, starting at Fanny Bridge in Tahoe City and looping east.

The rain had stopped, though a few sullen clouds massed over the eastern mountains. At mile marker 37, I started watching my odometer. I pulled onto the highway's shoulder at one mile. The markers weren't exact, so I got out and walked until I found the cross.

Head bent, I studied the small wooden stake. A wreath encircled its crosspiece, droplets sparkling on the plastic flowers. And the name: *Mary Ann Frankel.*

My throat closed. *The other driver.*

Another family had lost a loved one to sudden death. My brother-in-law was suing them, of course, piling angst onto their agony. Until I'd learned about the man in the road, I'd thought he had a case. Now, I wasn't so sure.

The earth around the tiny monument was stained black. A pine stood sentry over the spot, bark gouged from it at bumper level. This was where Sarah had died. I placed my hand on the rough, raw wood and blinked back tears.

"Sarah," I whispered. "Why?" Why *her*? I covered my eyes with one hand and let the tears come.

But Sarah wasn't the only one who'd died. My pain wasn't unique.

I drew a shuddering breath and scanned the area, looking for... I didn't know what.

As expected, there wasn't anything new to learn here. The accident had happened in February, and it was early November. But I paced the highway's shoulder, walked through the nearby pines.

I found nothing but a faded beer can and a candy wrapper.

I sniffed and walked toward my car. Sunlight glinted off a picture window on the hillside across the highway, and I squinted, turning my head. Then I stopped and studied the window. Cars roared past.

The dark brown, A-frame cabin stood on the opposite side of the highway and roughly a hundred feet up the steep hill. There were no pines blocking its view of the lake. Or of the highway.

I gnawed my bottom lip. I'd assumed the witness to the accident had been another motorist. After all, the accident had happened just a few minutes before four AM in February—hardly the hour for a dog walker or bicyclist.

My arms tingled, hope bottling the breath in my chest. But what if the witness had been a sleepless homeowner? What if the anonymous woman who'd called me lived nearby?

Unwilling to cross the busy highway on foot, I returned to my SUV and drove until I found a place to cut across, into a gas station parking lot. I retreated the way I'd come and turned onto a street that I guessed would lead to the cabin.

It did.

I parked on the side of the slanting road and made my way to the A-frame, knocked on the door. No one answered. I found a doorbell and rang it.

The bell's trill faded, leaving highway noise and the faint soughing of the wind in the pines. I stood, shifting my weight. After several minutes, I reluctantly walked back to my car.

A petite, silver-haired woman walking a greyhound climbed the hill toward me. She wore a blue sweatsuit with racing stripes down the leg. "Looking for someone?" she asked.

"Yes, the owner of this cabin."

The woman stopped and looped the leash more tightly around her gnarled hand. "That's me." Her gray brows lowered, and she took a step sideways.

"There was an accident on the highway on February second," I said. "I was wondering if you were home then?"

The woman nodded.

"Did you happen to see anything?"

"No." She moved past me. "I was sleeping."

"The crash must have woken you up." I took a step toward her.

She walked to her front door, painted green metal. Pulling a set of keys from her pocket, she unlocked it. "I can't help you. Sorry." She walked inside.

"My sister was hit head-on. Sarah. Sarah Carthart," I said rapidly. "She'd invited me to spend Christmas with her since my son was going to be with his girlfriend, but I didn't go. I didn't like her husband. There was always some holiday drama between them. Instead, I was there for her birthday, on the 15th, when her husband was away. We had ice cream cake. I hate ice cream with cake. It ruins the texture. But Sarah loved the stuff."

Ice cream cake? Oh, God, why was I saying all this?

Because guilt was making me ramble. I should have spent Christmas with them. Just because Sarah made all the money and her husband spent it, just because he always had some TV program going full blast in the house, just because he swaggered around like the lord of the manor that my sister had paid for...

I could have stomached it for one day. And she'd loved Christmas. Over the holidays, her house looked like a high-end shopping mall had exploded, dripping tinsel and decorations from her trips around the world and a Christmas tree in every room.

But I hadn't been there for her final Christmas. I hadn't seen her since her birthday. And now I'd never see her again. The funeral had been closed casket.

My face crumpled, and I turned away. "Sorry. I'm sorry." I hurried to my SUV.

"Wait," the woman said.

I swallowed, took a deep breath, and turned.

The greyhound leaned against her thigh. She took a step sideways to steady herself. "I knew your sister," she said. "Come inside."

I rocked backward. She'd known... "What?"

"Come inside." She turned and vanished into the cabin.

Numb, I walked in after her. The decor was Sierra kitsch. Watercolors of the lake and mountains adorned the paneled walls. A pair of crossed skis hung over the stone fireplace in the living room. A cracked leather sofa and matching chairs were angled so you could stare at the cold fireplace or the lake, depending on your mood.

She released the greyhound from its leash. It trotted to me and sniffed my limp hand, then curled onto a rag rug beside a wood stove.

She dropped into one of the chairs. "I'd offer you coffee, but I'm out."

"You knew my sister?"

"Briefly." Her voice softened. "Why don't you sit down?"

I pressed my palms to my stomach. She had known Sarah. I perched on the edge of the sofa. "Had she come to Tahoe to see you?"

"No." She gave a decisive head shake. "Not like that. I was awake when the accident happened. I don't sleep much anymore. When you get older, you don't need to. Maybe it's nature's way of giving us more time on this earth. I was awake, and I was here." She patted the arm of the leather wingchair. "The lights were off, and I was watching the moon over the lake. I heard brakes screaming and looked down."

"You saw the accident," I whispered. Did I really want the details? To know what my sister had suffered?

"Yes," she said, "but not then. A big black SUV had stopped on the highway. A door opened, and a well-dressed man was pushed out onto the median. His hands were tied behind him, and there was a blindfold over his eyes."

"You could see all that?"

"There's a streetlight on the highway, just there." She pointed. "It's irritating. I have to concentrate not to look at it when I'm stargazing."

I gripped my knees and swallowed. I was going to learn the truth. Did I really want it? "I don't... And then what happened?"

"They left him there and drove off. A car came right after them—missed him by a whisker. And then another man came running up—I don't know where he came from—and raced toward the first. An SUV—a Chevy Tahoe, I think it was—rounded the bend and swerved onto the shoulder to avoid the newcomer. The driver over corrected, crossed the median, and drove straight into an oncoming pickup."

"My sister's pickup." My voice cracked on the final word.

"The crash was..." She looked away, her lips squeezing together. "I didn't think anyone could survive it. I called 9-1-1." She motioned toward an old-fashioned wall phone above the open kitchen's tile counter. "When I looked again, both men were gone."

"You said you knew Sarah."

"I put on my shoes and a coat and ran down the hill to the highway. Other cars had pulled over by then. I went to your sister's pickup. It had flipped. She was still in her seatbelt, upside down. I was afraid to try to move her. She was obviously badly hurt, but she didn't seem in pain. She seemed... peaceful."

"Sarah was conscious?" My eyes burned, my throat tightening. *Oh, God. No, no, no.*

"She looked at me. She said, 'Tell her it's all love. Tell her. It's all love.' I'll never forget it. The way she looked at me, just so..." Her lips crimped together. "I was holding her hand when she passed."

Blinking, I studied my sneakers. It was what I'd wanted to hear. That she hadn't died scared and alone and in pain. So why didn't I feel that burden had lifted?

"Maybe it's silly, or self-delusional," she continued. "I hope you don't mind I said I knew her. But I just felt... I felt like I *did* know her in that moment. I've thought of her quite often since."

It's all love. Riga had said that. Had she encountered my sister's ghost? Hope and jealousy stabbed my chest, though I knew both were wrong. Why hadn't Sarah come to *me*?

"Did you call me last April?" I asked. "To tell me about the man on the highway?"

"Call you?" Her blue eyes widened. "I didn't know you existed until today."

She was telling the truth. Her voice hadn't triggered any memories in me. She hadn't been the one to call.

"Thank you. Thank you for—for being with her. For telling me this." I cleared my throat. "There were two men on the highway, you say? What did they look like?"

She described Wingate to a T, right down to his expensive suit. The greyhound rolled onto his side and yawned.

"Did you recognize the man?" I asked.

"No. I told the police the same."

"And the other?" I asked, voice taut.

"An African-American gentleman. Tall, broad-shouldered, close-cropped hair. He wore a suit too."

Tobin. Tobin had been there. Tobin had saved Wingate and killed my sister.

CHAPTER 24

MY HANDS CLENCHED ON the SUV's wheel. *Tobin.* I'd never completely trusted him. So why was sick disappointment twisting my gut?

My car glided to the iron gates of Dragon House. I rolled down my window and pressed the intercom button. I waited.

BUZZ. The gates shuddered open.

I sped down the drive, gravel pinging off the SUV's undercarriage, and lurched to a halt in front of the house. Tobin knew what had really happened that night. He had to at least give me that.

I jogged up the steps and inside, my limbs trembling with fury. Masculine laughter burst from the lounge. The sound was a slap.

I stopped inside the chocolate-colored room's flattened arch entryway. The gas firepit was out. Sam and Tobin ate sandwiches at a square table overlooking the lake. Sam was out of his usual button-up and in a blue t-shirt and jeans.

I pulled back the free chair between them and sat. Tobin knew the truth.

"Hi, Brandy," Sam said.

I turned to Tobin. "You were on the highway with Wingate on February second. Who put him there?"

Tobin's face shuttered. "I don't know what you're talking about."

Sam leaned back in his chair. He studied the contents of his coffee mug.

"February second." My voice trembled, and I hated myself for it. "Three fifty-six AM. A car dumped Wingate, bound and blindfolded, onto the highway median and drove off. And then you appeared out of nowhere to save him and caused an accident that killed two women."

"I don't know what you're talking about."

"You're not an estate manager," I said hotly. "You're Wingate's body-guard. Or you were."

Tobin didn't respond.

"Who tried to kill Wingate last February?" I burst out. "Because that's probably who put the bomb on his boat."

"I am aware," Tobin ground out.

"So?" I asked.

Tobin pushed back his chair and stood. "I can't discuss it." Taking his mug from the table, he turned.

"My sister was in one of those cars."

Tobin faced me. "You had a real life." A muscle pulsed in his jaw. "You were at the top of your career. You gave all that up to wrangle your way into Wingate's house. For what? Revenge?" He strode from the room.

Sam exhaled slowly. "Brandy—"

"What?" I snarled.

"I'm sorry about your sister," he said. "I can't imagine how hard it must have been—how it must still be."

I stood, hands fisting. "It is." I strode from the room and scanned the empty hallway. Tobin owed me answers. He *owed* me.

My shoulders bunched. Though I wanted to chase after Tobin, that wouldn't get me the answers I deserved. I needed to wait and give us both time to cool off before tackling him again.

Pulse speeding, I climbed the wide, winding staircase to my room. Wingate was dead. Tobin hadn't put him onto that highway. He'd reacted.

What Tobin had done might not have made a difference. Whoever had put Wingate on the road was responsible for the crash. Tobin had to know who that was.

Trouble howled behind my bedroom door. I opened it slowly so as not to jam the kitten's paws. But he wasn't on the wood floor, wasn't near the blond-wood desk, wasn't on the sand-colored couch. Stepping into the bedroom, I shut the door behind me.

A howl echoed from the wardrobe.

I opened its doors. It, too, was empty. Frowning, I felt my way to the rear of the wardrobe and opened its secret door. Trouble bounded past me and into the bedroom.

"How'd you get in there?" I retreated into the bedroom, and a hanger pinged to the floor. Tossing it onto the desk, I shut the wardrobe doors with my hip.

The kitten meowed. I picked him up. His tiny warmth was comforting against my chest, and my breathing evened.

There was a gentle knock on my door. Setting the kitten on the bed, I opened it.

Sam stood in the hallway. "You didn't give me a chance to tell you what I learned about the Brotherhood." He ambled into my room.

He'd done it? I stood, astonished, mouth flopping open like a rainbow trout on a Tahoe shore. He'd found something?

Trouble hopped off the bed and trotted to him. Sam let the kitten sniff him. Trouble rubbed against the cuff of his jeans, leaving white and orange hairs on the fabric.

"How?" I asked. "I searched online and couldn't find a thing."

"I *didn't* search online. I called a friend who studies the occult. He's at Berkeley."

I folded my arms. "Okay."

"They're a secret society. There are all sorts of weird rumors about them—shadowy world domination stuff."

Sure. I rolled my eyes. And maybe the Illuminati were involved too. "Conspiracy theories, you mean?"

He shrugged. "It is a *secret* society. Rumors and conspiracies are all you're going to get."

Hope hunched out the door and left me, my shoulders sagging. "Is that all?" I asked bleakly. If they were that secretive, there was no way to prove Ezra's claim that they were after the scroll.

"I'm just saying the Brotherhood does exist." The wardrobe door drifted open and grazed his shoulder. He turned, scanned the interior, and closed it, rattling the handle to make sure it was shut fast. "How are you doing?"

My gaze focused. There was no twinkle in Sam's Nordic-blue eyes. No hint of mockery or pity or exasperation in his handsome face. There was nothing but a calm watchfulness very unlike the sense of watchfulness of the lake. That had been mildly threatening. Sam's was accepting. Open. As if I were being seen without judgment.

"I'm fine. Thanks." I glanced at the windows, weak light shining through their wooden blinds. My breath quickened, my face burning.

"Because no offense," he said, "but you don't seem fine."

"I'm fine," I said firmly.

Sam grimaced. "Right. If I learn anything more, I'll let you know." He walked to the bedroom door, paused, and turned. "For the record, I don't blame you for trying to learn more. But life is short. Shouldn't we live what we have left to the fullest, with the people and passions we care about?"

An ache bloomed at the back of my throat. I *wanted* to move on. But maybe a part of me—my shadow side—believed moving on was a betrayal?

I knew Sarah wouldn't have wanted me stuck in mourning. What I didn't know was *how* to move on. If learning why she'd died couldn't bring me closure, what would?

Sam nodded. He strode into the hallway, shutting the door behind him. Trouble meowed.

"I know I was short with him, but it's for the best."

The kitten's left ear twitched.

"If I think he's attractive, he's *got* to be bad news."

There was another knock at my door.

"For Pete's sake," I snarled and yanked it open.

Fortuna stood in the hallway. "So. Tobin covered for Wingate again." She strolled past me and into the room.

My gaze flicked to the beamed ceiling. I mean, I knew it wasn't *my* room. The house belonged to Wingate—or whoever his heir was. Fortuna seemed to believe it was hers. But still, why did everyone think they could just wander inside?

I leaned against the door frame. "You talked to Tobin?"

"No, I was listening in the secret passage."

My head jerked backward. "You know about those? Wait, there's a passage that leads to the lounge?"

"They go all over the place. Some of the passages are closed, but if you know which doors to use, you can find your way around."

"Why were you listening in on Sam and Tobin?"

She tossed her red hair. "I thought I might learn something useful, and I did. Tobin was always covering for Wingate, no matter who got hurt in the process."

"Like Devin?" I asked in a low voice.

Her face tightened. "Wingate and Tobin were both responsible for the deaths of people we loved."

"How do you figure Wingate was responsible for Devin's murder?"

Her lips flattened. "Isn't it obvious? The mob came after Wingate in February as a warning. The next time they came, my husband got in the way." Her smile was bitter. "I guess third time's a charm."

I braced one hand on the desk. The mob must have been the ones to have put him on the highway, setting my sister's death in motion. They'd killed him on the boat. I'd suspected it, Riga had suggested it, but hearing it from Fortuna...

She moved to the window and angled the wooden blinds. "Do you like your room? I can switch you to a better one."

"A room with a more convenient secret passage?" I cocked my head.

Fortuna turned and smiled. "That too."

"You said Wingate blamed Devin for something."

She examined her manicured nails. "Did I?"

"Something that went wrong with the investment company?"

Her head jerked upward. "How did you know about that?"

"Devin worked at Wingate's investment management company." Wingate hadn't hidden that. "If the mob wanted to kill Wingate over mismanaged funds—"

"Devin didn't mismanage anything," she said, shrill. "It was a pyramid scheme."

My mouth opened and closed. Wingate must have been insane. "He was running a pyramid scheme?" I choked out. "On the mob?"

"Devin found out too late. His only way out—"

"Was to inform on Wingate to the mob," I finished. *That* was what Wingate had meant about Devin betraying them. *Good God.* "And August?" I asked.

"What about him?"

"The chalk arrow on the wall by the back gate. Was that your way to signal a rendezvous with him?" A camera had been angled toward it. As their tech consultant, August might have access to it. And both had had chalk on their hands.

Fortuna whitened, then reddened like a cartoon Queen of Hearts. She stormed from the room, slamming the door shut.

I dropped limply on the bed. *The mob.* They were untouchable.

I had some answers, but there would be no justice, no closure. Not for Devin. Not for my sister.

CHAPTER 25

THE REST OF THE answers were here, at Dragon House, but they were as out of reach as Sarah in my dreams. My hands fisted. Everything I'd done—

The kitten butted his head against my ankle.

I stooped to scratch behind his ears. "You're right. I need to get out of my head and get some fresh air." The sky was iron gray outside the bedroom window, but the rain was holding off. There was time for a walk.

I jammed my notebook and phone into my businesslike leather satchel. Shrugging into my sister's furry vest, I double-checked that the wardrobe doors were shut fast.

"No more exploring hidden passages," I told Trouble. "They're dangerous."

My phone rang. Naturally, it had fallen to the bottom of my satchel and hidden itself behind a cloth grocery bag. Finally, I wrenched it free and answered without checking the number. "Hello?"

"Uh, Brandy? This is Sean. You called about my mountain lion?"

"Oh. Right! Thanks for calling me back." I paced in front of the window. "I wanted to know if you ever, er, take it out, aside from to the mall?"

"Sandy has plenty of space to roam," he said defensively. "I've got a five-acre plot of land, and it's fenced in."

"No, no. I didn't mean that. It's just... Do you rent Sandy out?"

"No."

"No?" I adjusted the angle of the wooden blinds. Fortuna had slanted them up, so anyone down below could look inside my room.

"Sandy's a mountain lion. No one handles her but me."

"And you've never taken her to other estates to, er, roam?" I sat on the edge of the bed.

"What are you asking me?"

"I'm asking if you've ever taken her to Dragon House."

"Why the hell would I do that?"

"For money?" I asked weakly.

He hung up.

I slid my phone into my vest pocket and grabbed my oversized purse. "That went well," I said dryly.

The kitten sneezed.

"Yeah." I strode from the room.

I hadn't planned on returning to that stone outbuilding, but my footsteps took me into the pines and in that direction. I wound between masses of manzanita and the occasional gray boulder rising like an island from the ground.

A few sullen drips plopped to the needle-strewn earth. I shivered and hooked the clasps on my sister's vest. The sound of the waves, soft and persistent, drifted through the pines.

I walked briskly, partly because it was cold and partly because I was feeling paranoid. But neither phantom cat nor human stalker trailed me to the outbuilding.

I looked through the high windows, but the old glass was too warped to see anything inside. I tried the green wooden door. To my surprise, it was unlocked. I walked into the small, stone building and stopped short.

I'd expected boxes, tree trimmers, maintenance equipment. What I found was a temple.

A marble table, much like an altar, stood at the eastern end of the small building. Behind it was a tile mosaic of a winged, white-bearded man holding a scythe in one hand and a screaming baby in the other.

The child was raised to his greedy, open mouth.

I knew enough Greek myth to recognize the old man—Kronos, god of time. He'd devoured his own children after being told one would supplant him. It was the past eating the future.

Dragon House's builder, the Hollywood actor, really *had* been an occultist. This must have been the site of his rituals. I turned from the mosaic in disgust.

And saw a card table. A wicker picnic basket sat beside a small camp stove, a half-empty bottle of wine, and a used dish and wine goblet. A cot leaned upright against the wall beside the table, and I sucked in a breath.

Someone had been living here. Would he be back?

Clutching my satchel, I hurried to the door and eased out. A pale flash of pine near the corner of the building caught my attention. Slowly, I walked toward the injured tree.

Someone had removed the bark from a section of the pine. A reddish symbol (blood?) had been carved into the raw wood. It was crude and simple—all straight lines and angles.

Occultists, killers, secret symbols... I needed to get the hell away from Dragon House.

But I'd come here for a reason. I wasn't running now. Pulling my notebook from my bag, I willed my trembling hands to still and sketched the symbol.

Returning my notepad to my purse, I started down the narrow trail. Tobin *must* know someone was living there. There were cameras all over the estate.

I glanced over my shoulder at the outbuilding, my forehead wrinkling. Unless the cameras had been tampered with? I veered around a waist-high boulder.

The cold came without warning. There was no shivering of the pines. No change in the rhythm of the far-off waves. No dimming of sunlight from a passing cloud. Only the cold, deeper than death.

And then I saw it. A dark shape cut through a stand of manzanita like a shark scenting blood.

I swayed to a stop beside a boulder, putting it between me and the thing gliding closer, though I knew the futility of that gesture. I wanted to shriek. Wanted to run. Instead, I stood paralyzed.

The ebony form parted the thorny bushes like liquid. A shiver raced from the back of my neck to the top of my head.

My skin crawled. A big cat—No. Though the creature creeping closer had the form of a puma or jaguar, this was no cat, no being of flesh and blood. Black as oil and slipping like an eel over the earth, it was bestial, but it was no beast.

This was *not* the tawny animal I'd seen at the mini mall. That cat had been older. And though I wouldn't have wanted to face the mountain lion in a lonely wood, it had been... clean. Something real and alive and natural. This was not.

Run.

My teeth chattered. I couldn't run. If I turned and ran, I'd have no chance. It was too close. It would catch me. I couldn't make it back inside the temple in time. I moved slowly backwards on the trail, unwilling to take my eyes off those bushes.

The dried leaves rustled. The thing slipped closer.

Hostility flowed from it, stilling the wind, hushing the waves, silencing the birds. Malice filled the quiet.

Two red-gold eyes gleamed from the dying manzanita branches, and a pantherlike head emerged. But it wasn't a panther. Wasn't natural. It had the shape and size and fur of a living cat, but it was not living, not a cat.

Its nostrils flared.

I backed away. "Nice... kitty." My heel hooked a thick branch. I stumbled backward then twisted, scooping up the branch that had tripped me. I swung it like a club. "Go away!"

Its mouth peeled back in a hiss. The creature glided closer, and something like muscles rippled beneath its fur. My shoulder struck a tree. I backed around it and saw the skinned bark, the strange symbol.

The creature hesitated. Its head tucked. It sank lower to the ground. The thing's tail lashed.

I walked backward. My shoulder bumped chill stone, and I gasped a sob. *The outbuilding.* The cat-thing growled, and the sound shuddered through my bones.

Legs trembling, I sidestepped to the corner of the stone building. Then I turned and bolted around that corner toward the green door.

The cat screamed. I whisked inside the temple and slammed the green door shut.

THUD. The door shuddered against the weight of the beast.

Swallowing, I dropped the branch. Bits of bark clung to my damp palms. THUD.

It couldn't get inside. I shook my head and backed from the heavy door. This was a physical thing striking the green door. The cat *wasn't* supernatural, wasn't an illusion. But now I was trapped.

I laughed hollowly. Story of my life. Trapped by a wildcat, trapped by my work. I'd given up everything for my career—my son, my sister, my life. And then I'd given up my work, and now I was trapped again.

I raised my chin. But I wouldn't be trapped long. This was the era of cell phones, and it was time to leave Dragon House. For good.

I pulled my phone from the pocket of my sister's furry vest and called the main house. Outside, a feline howl raised gooseflesh on my arms. I edged toward the marble altar.

No one answered the phone. I tried again and got the same result. Briefly, I closed my eyes.

At some point, *someone* would answer the damn phone.

Assuming, Tobin hadn't left on an errand.

A dark blur thudded against the window. I yelped and leapt backward. A black shape dropped from sight.

The warped glass rattled from the blow. But the sound came from far off, as if another window in another, darker place, had been struck. Was any of this real? The temple, the cat, my thumping heart?

My phone pinged, and I dropped it to the stone floor. Scooping it up, I released a small sigh. It hadn't broken. Eagerly I checked the notification, hoping Tobin had messaged me.

He hadn't. It was a notification that I'd received an email.

Which was impossible. I hadn't set up email notifications on my phone. Texts were annoying enough.

I glanced at the window's thick, rippled glass. The cat wasn't getting inside the temple, and I needed to calm down. *Distract yourself.* I opened my email.

SUBJECT: RELEASE.

My nostrils flared. *The Mystery School? Now?*

Something scratched at the door. I glanced at its thick, green-painted wood. That old occultist had built the door to last. I was trapped, and that was unnerving, but I was safe.

Tearing my gaze from the door, I noticed another email from my ex-boss. I opened it, read, and gave a dry, shaky whistle.

My replacements *really* must not be working out. Either that, or my ex-boss seemed to think my rejection had been a negotiating ploy. He'd offered me more money. I'd need it after shipwrecking my career for the Luck Scroll.

My two-handed grip tightened on the phone. Was I actually considering returning to my old career?

Going back could be the answer to everything. If I got busy with real life again, maybe I could finally move on.

Claws scraped the door. The scratching sounded as if it had come from under water.

Forcing my shoulders to relax, I sat against the marble table. *I'm safe. Think of something else.*

Go back. It made sense. My son was still in the Bay Area, still on the Peninsula.

I'd have to fix whatever damage my work replacements had done. And they must have done *some* damage or my ex-boss wouldn't be quite so conciliatory. But that would take time...

I glanced over my shoulder at Kronos, preparing to devour another young god. I could make time. I could figure this out.

Yes, I'd go back. It was so obvious, I nearly laughed out loud. I'd go back to my old life and everything—eventually—would return to...

Not normal. Normal was gone now that my sister was dead. But normal for the new circumstances.

I replied to the email: *Let's talk when I get back.*

Yes, that would do it. No promises. Keep him guessing. But a talk. A negotiation. I straightened off the table, and my blood chilled.

An UnTarot card leaned against the wine bottle on the card table.

RELEASE

AS WE'VE DISCUSSED IN other cards, the way to release fear is to let yourself feel the feeling, even if it's uncomfortable—*especially* if it's uncomfortable. Otherwise, it will bury itself in your subconscious. When this happens, it can influence your behavior in unexpected and frequently unpleasant ways.

But how do we release attachments? The same way.

We feel the feeling that comes with the loss of that attachment. We label it and say "yes" to it. We feel where it sits in our bodies and we breathe love into that space. We explore the meanings we've given to the attachment and reject any false beliefs.

The stronger the attachment, the more time this will take. But be patient, and trust that freedom will come.

For the witch, the harder task is not the challenges faced, but the emotions and thoughts those challenges are attached to. This is why a meditation practice is a cornerstone of any magical practice. It helps us recognize what we're thinking and feeling so we can manage those thoughts and feelings.

While we can't stay "high vibe" 24/7 (nor should we), we shouldn't dwell in negativity either. This is especially true since being in a positive emotional frame makes a more effective base when casting spells.

But recognizing our thoughts and feelings is only the first step in releasing them. The second is to differentiate those thoughts and feelings from our identity. For example, instead of thinking: "I am angry" (which is an identity), switch to: "I am thinking angry thoughts." Or instead of thinking, "I'm lonely" (identity), change the thought to "I am feeling lonely."

Once thoughts and emotions are recognized for what they are—simply thoughts and emotions—space is created between us and the feelings. We can then approach life more calmly and effectively.

And if you worry that this practice of release will turn you into an unfeeling automaton, it won't. In fact, the opposite happens. When the witch thinks to herself, "Oh, I'm feeling love," or "I was thinking happy thoughts," these higher-level emotions are strengthened.

Perhaps by releasing low-energy emotions, we make room for higher-energy emotions? Do our low-energy emotions repress the high-energy emotions? Or are high-energy emotions our true, natural state?

As you release to become more conscious, you'll raise the consciousness of those around you, empowering them. Consciousness is contagious.

Try the attached exercise to cleanse your chakras and release your attachments.

SCAN ME

Release

Letting go. Non-attachment. Feeling your emotions to move through them.

It's easy to hang on to things and to relationships even when they're not good for us. But to be emotionally healthy, we need to know when to let go, and we need to be able to trust that by releasing, we're making way for new and better conditions and people to enter our lives.

Release is closely connected to the concept of non-attachment. People often confuse non-attachment with not caring. But that isn't the case. We should care. Feeling things intensely means you're alive. It's one of the beautiful parts of being human. But everything end, and we should be ready to meet those endings, no matter how painful.

Through release, however, we can get through the pain of loss and other hard emotions more easily, ironically, by spending time feeling and accepting our emotions. This, combined with the exercise below, can help.

So, try the mantra: *Let go.* Use it when you're experiencing a strong emotion you'd rather not let get the best of you, and as you do, take a deep breath and let go of the tension in your body as well.

The symbols:

A hand reaches across a body of water and releases a burst of crocus blossoms and doves. Water represents emotion, and ultimately, release is all about emotional attachments—to habits, to people, to ideas about the way we or the world should be. The hand offers crocus blossoms—symbols of hope in the face of loss. Doves of hope, renewal, transformation, and love burst from the flowers, flying free.

The questions:

What do you need to let go of? Can you believe you can let go?

What must I release?

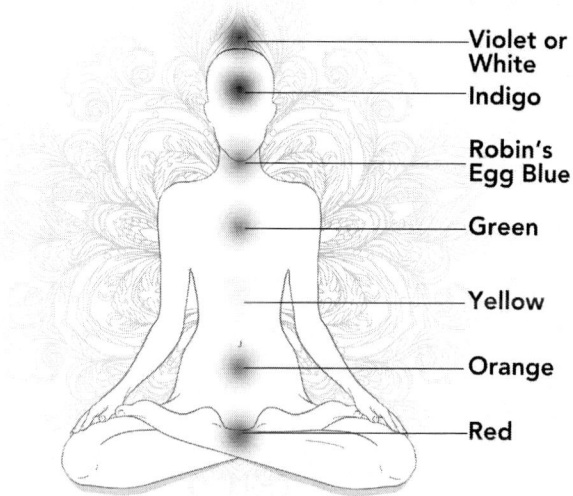

Violet or White

Indigo

Robin's Egg Blue

Green

Yellow

Orange

Red

What are you holding onto? How would life change if you let it go?

_____

_____

Relax in a meditative posture, either lying down or seated. Breathe deeply and visualize you are surrounded by a protective light. Starting at the red, root chaka, visualize healing light flowing into each chakra, one by one until they shine clear and bright.

Visualize an angel with a fiery sword cutting the ties that bind you to ideas, emotions, and people you are attached to. (Don't worry, this will actually strengthen your relationships with the right people). You don't need to identify these attachments. The angel knows. When the angel is finished, thank him or her for their assistance. Visualize a column of glowing white light flowing through the crown chakra at the top of your head, through your chakras, and out through your root chakra.

CHAPTER 26

I EDGED TOWARD THE card table. My hand trembled as I reached for the UnTarot card.

It *wasn't* magic. Magic wasn't real. The card hadn't appeared on its own. *Someone* must have put it inside the temple during that brief period when I'd been gone. But I couldn't have been gone for more than five minutes.

Something scrabbled behind the temple door. My hand jerked, knocking the card from its perch against the wine bottle and to the stone floor.

Whoever had left the card would be nearby. But how would they know I'd return for the card? Had *they* set the monster outside loose to drive me back into the temple?

I shook my head. There was no "they" about it. Riga was the Mystery School, and Riga held the cards. Literally.

But why? Why taunt me? It was sick and weird, and God, why was the temple so cold? It hadn't been this cold when I'd first arrived.

A tremor wracked my body. I dropped the card into my leather satchel and paced between the card table and the marble altar.

Riga was a metaphysical detective. Despite what Ezra had said, she *could* be part of the occult group that wanted the scroll. And she'd disliked—hated?—Wingate. He'd known all of that and invited her to Dragon House anyway.

I laughed shortly and clawed my hands through my hair. My jumbled thoughts were a manifestation of my fear, and none of them were helping. I worked to steady my breathing.

Pulling out my phone, I called the house again. No answer.

I could call 9-1-1, tell them a big cat had me trapped. They'd probably send animal control. But the thought of inflicting whatever was outside on an unwitting dog catcher stopped me.

Inflicting it on Tobin did *not* bother me, however. I was still furious about his role in my sister's death and more importantly, his refusal to take any accountability.

I studied Kronos's face, twisted with greed and… fear? Of course it was fear. The Titan had eaten his own children out of fear they'd one day destroy him. And one day, they had.

The mosaic baby dangling over Kronos's arm screamed with outrage, his blue eyes bulging… I blinked. One of the eyes really *was* bulging.

Hurriedly, I moved behind the altar and ran my hand across the mosaic. The tile of the baby's eye stuck a bit from the wall. I pushed it. The tile moved smoothly, sliding a quarter inch into the wall.

There was a grinding sound at my feet. An oversized flagstone sank into the floor and slid sideways. A puff of air stirred the dust around the big stone tiles, moving it in lazy, eerie spirals.

Stomach gripping, I knelt to examine the square hole. So, the occultist had built a secret passage to his temple. It *had* to run to the house. Why else go to the trouble? Unless only a cellar lay beneath.

Despite what I'd told Sam, I was not a fan of small spaces. The passages within the house had been narrow, but they'd been human-sized. I turned on my phone's flashlight and shined it inside the small hole. All I saw was more dark.

I reached inside expecting spiderwebs. My shoulders loosened. No spiderwebs—just the rough underside of stones, slick with something unpleasant. I wiped my hand on my jeans.

Slinging my bag crossways over my shoulder, I sat on the edge of the hole and dangled my feet through the opening. There had to be a ladder or steps or something.

I stretched out one leg. The narrowness of the hole limited my reach.

Carefully, I lowered myself through, resting my weight on my elbows. I swung my feet, hoping to touch a ladder. My shoe brushed something jutting from the wall. I wiggled my ankle, and there was a rattle.

Something thunked against the door. CRACK.

I jerked. My elbows slipped, and I was falling.

My shriek cut short when I hit hard ground, knocking the wind from my lungs. The cell phone glanced off a wooden ladder and clattered to the ground beside me. Its light winked out.

I lay in the half-dark and wheezed. Mentally, I explored every ache. Nothing seemed broken, but—

CRACK.

My heart jumped, and I rolled to my side. *What the hell?* It *couldn't* get through that thick door. Could it?

Shadows shrouded the ground where I lay. I fumbled along the cool earth for my phone.

Finally, I made contact with metal and plastic. My trembling fingers touched the screen. It did not light. Frantic, I slid my fingers over the front of my phone. Sharp cracks in the screen threatened to slice my skin.

My chin lowered. The phone was broken. I wasn't a fan of cell phones, but the loss left me feeling even more vulnerable.

Standing, I stumbled to the ladder and grasped its rough wooden sides. Light filtered weakly through the trap door above, illuminating a lever in the wall. So *that* was how the door was operated.

Beside the lever was a small inset door, about one foot wide and tall. I reached for its metal handle and tugged. It didn't budge.

The temple door splintered, and a low growl sounded from above. It was impossible. It *couldn't* have gotten inside. I clapped my hands to my mouth to repress a whimper.

The growl came again, and I recoiled. Grasping the lever, I yanked it downward. The stone slid into place in the ceiling, and the darkness was complete.

I don't know how long I stood there, breath rasping in my ears. It was the scrabbling, faint and echoing, claws on stone, that jolted me into action.

A real cat wouldn't be able to follow me. A real cat wouldn't have been able to get through that thick door. But there was nothing of reality about this cat.

Don't look.

Cold sweat beaded my forehead. Trailing my hand along the wall, I felt until I reached a corner, and I continued on. The wall gave way to emptiness. I stood, heart hammering in my ears.

The occultist wouldn't have put traps in the passage—gaping holes to fall into, spikes... I swayed dizzily in the dark. Reaching into that emptiness with both hands, I touched the walls of another passage.

I stepped inside. Passages had collapsed inside Dragon House. They'd been maintained—somewhat—by Tobin. Had he been taking care of this passage? How heavy was the earth above? The air seemed to thicken, and I gasped for breath.

I walked and walked, arms extended in a T, fingertips scraping against both walls. And then my right hand touched nothing. I edged forward, expecting to run into a wall. But the passage continued.

My breathing grew louder in the dark. The cold deepened, and I shuddered. Go straight or turn right?

Panic welled inside me. I continued straight. The air in the passage grew more oppressive.

My stomach quivered. Had I made the right decision? Would I have to go back? Could I even *find* my way back? What if I'd missed something?

Stop. I was making things worse. *Think of something else.*

Think of Devin's murder.

Any of my suspects could have had the opportunity—anyone who knew about the passages. But the security camera had shown someone coming in from the grounds, not from underground.

Unless the murder wasn't connected to that intruder? I came to another T and continued straight. As to means, Devin had been strangled, at least if the bruises on his neck were anything to go by.

Fortuna had been cheating on her husband and had an odd relationship with Wingate. But there was no way she'd left those thumb-shaped bruises on his neck. Devin had been throttled from the front. A woman hadn't done that.

As for Riga... She'd been taunting me with the cards, and no doubt wanted that scroll as well. But she was out too, and for the same reason.

The wall fell away at my right. Extending my hands forward, I continued on.

Sam, Tobin or Wingate could have strangled the man. They were all powerfully built.

And maybe... August? The tech specialist had motive. He'd had something going with Fortuna—good reason to want Devin out of the way.

But why kill Wingate? Was it as simple as a mob hit? I shook my head. Sparks of light danced in front of my eyes.

No. Devin's murder had to be connected to the scroll. He'd been found outside the library, where the scroll was kept.

According to the security footage, the killer had entered through the library. That pointed to someone outside the house, like Ezra or August, and—

Was that a growl?

I froze, listening. My pulse pounded in my ears. Shaken, I continued on.

Ezra then. He wanted the scroll. He had the strength to kill Devin and some knowledge of boat explosions.

I reached another juncture, hesitated, and went straight.

GRRR...

I froze. The sound had been faint. I could have imagined it. But...

But Tobin could have gone outside to break inside, knowing he'd be caught on camera and knowing that video would point away from him.

I forced myself to move forward. Wingate had treated Tobin badly. Tobin knew this house and its passages. Maybe Tobin was working for an outsider who wanted the scroll too?

But Tobin had saved Wingate last February—*before* he had the complete scroll. And who had put Wingate on that highway?

A great cat howled, the sound echoing. I walked faster through the underworldly passage.

And then there was the dark horse, the X factor, Sam. He was at Dragon House for research. Interested in medieval texts. The scroll definitely fell into that category.

Sam hadn't expressed much interest in the scroll, but he'd always been conveniently nearby when I'd examined it. He'd been in Dragon House when both Devin and Wingate had died, that was opportunity. He looked strong enough to strangle a man, so he had means. And motive...?

The scroll. The murders had to be about the scroll.

I don't know how long I walked that labyrinth. The howl never came again. But a low growl came once, too close, a sound that coiled my insides.

The passage twisted and turned. It sometimes gave me choices and other times did not. Whenever I had a choice, I went straight in the darkness.

My toes bumped a wall—I'd learned the hard way to lead with my feet. I'd cracked my nose twice already. Cautiously, I felt to the wall's sides. I'd reached a dead end.

GRRR...

My stomach spasmed. My hands clumsily felt the wall in front of me. It couldn't just be a dead end. It couldn't—

I touched a metal latch and tugged it upward. There was a snick, and the door opened. I tumbled into a blaze of light.

CHAPTER 27

A MUSCULAR ARM ENCIRCLED me, pulling me against a masculine chest. "Ooof," Sam grunted. We stood in a passage inside Dragon House. I gasped shakily, my muscles loosening. I was out, I was free.

"Shut the door," I shrieked. "Shut it, shut it!"

"*You* shut it."

My arms still captured by his, I back-kicked the door shut. He *could* have just let me go. I glowered at him, my chest heaving like a heroine on the cover of a romance novel.

That cynical thought should have cooled me off. But I couldn't help noticing the hard planes of his chest beneath his soft t-shirt, the whisper of his breath against my cheek. I wriggled, trying to get loose.

Sam shined the flashlight beam into my face, and I winced. He flicked the beam to his own and released me. "What happened? Did you get lost in there?"

"No. Sort of. But there's a—"

An eerie howl echoed through the closed door. Sam swore, his face turning a sickly shade of gray. "What the hell is that?"

"Would you believe a phantom wildcat?" I asked, voice uneven.

His head turned sharply, his gaze intent. "I might. Let's get out of here."

"You might? *Why* might you?" I followed him down the narrow passage. "And what are *you* doing in here?"

"Exploring. Did you really think I could resist returning? My nephews would be furious if I passed up this chance to explore these passages."

I pursed my lips. "You came here on behalf of your nephews?"

"I came here for—" He bit the word off. "Where does it lead?"

"What?"

He turned, and we climbed a dusty staircase. "The passage you were in. Where does it lead?" His voice crackled with impatience.

I followed. "To the temple."

He stopped short, and I nearly stumbled into him. "There's a temple?" he asked.

"It doesn't look like much from the outside. The temple's in that stone outbuilding near the rear gate."

"That makes sense." He rubbed his jaw. "Easy for participants to come and go without being seen." He opened a panel in the wall, and we stepped through a wardrobe into his room.

"Participants?" I asked.

"Participants in Max Sterling's occult rituals. You look like hell."

"Thanks," I said, deadpan. But I walked into his bathroom and peered into the mirror.

My face, clothing and hands were streaked with dirt. At some point I'd acquired a bloody scratch on my cheek. I just hoped I hadn't scraped against a rusty nail. My sister's vest would need dry cleaning...

Hastily, I shrugged free of it and examined its thick fur and satin lining. I released a sigh. It was undamaged.

Sam appeared in the mirror behind me holding a first aid kit. "Here. Let's get you cleaned up."

"I can clean up in my own room."

"And if Tobin sees you looking like this? How will you explain?"

"I can take the passage," I said, uneasy. I had no desire to return inside those passages, and I might run into Tobin there as well. "Is he even home? I was calling and calling—"

"When? I tried calling you and got no response."

I pulled my phone from my pocket and showed him the cracked screen. "Before it got busted."

Sam opened the kit and laid out the contents on the counter. He tossed me a clean, white washcloth. "Here."

The cloth was far from clean when I finished with it, but I felt better. I turned to face Sam. "Thanks— Ow!"

He dabbed my cheek with a cotton ball soaked in something stinging.

"You could have warned me," I grumped.

He brandished the bloodied cotton. "What did you expect I was going to do with it?"

When he finished, he led me into the small sitting area in front of his unmade bed. He dropped into an almond-colored leather chair.

"Tell me about this cat," he said.

And I did. All of it. The cat. My sister's death. Wingate and Tobin's part in it. The luck scroll. And Sam didn't sneer.

I leaned forward in the leather chair. "When Sarah died, her accident was so random. I couldn't stop thinking about luck and fate. I still have no idea what brought her to Tahoe at that hour. And then that anonymous woman called and told me about Wingate's involvement, and I learned about *his* luck obsession, it fueled the fire."

"And the Luck Scroll?"

"Finding the missing piece of the scroll was more than my way into Dragon House. It was a missing piece of the luck puzzle." I shook my head. "I know it sounds crazy—"

"It doesn't."

I smiled briefly. "Doesn't it? I thought the mystery cat might be connected to the mountain lion that photographer brings out every Tuesday," I finished. "But they're not the same cat. What was in the tunnels..."

A remembered chill wracked my body. "It's something else," I said in a low voice.

"So, you're staying on here? Despite everything?"

"I can't stop now," I said quietly. "If I do, I've got nothing. None of it will have mattered."

"Your sister's death won't have mattered, you mean."

"I need to understand what happened." My jaw clenched.

"No, you need to face your grief and let her go. For your sake," he said, cutting across my objection. "This quest for understanding, for meaning, I've seen it before. I've done it. It's part of the bargaining stage of grief."

There was nothing to bargain *for*. "I know she's not coming back," I said, my voice hard.

"Do you?" Sam asked gently.

"And I *am* moving on. My old CEO called. I'm going back to work."

"Is that moving forward or back?"

My chest tightened. "Thanks for the rescue." I motioned to my face and rose. The leather chair made a rude noise against my jeans, and my neck heated. "And for the rubbing alcohol." I strode to his bedroom door.

"You asked for my opinion on the scroll."

I paused, hand on the knob, and turned to face him. "I think Wingate did."

"When it comes to mythology, to understand the meaning, it's useful to break the story down to its simplest components."

Nodding, I strode from the room and nearly smacked into Tobin. I sidestepped him in the ornate hallway.

"What were you doing in there?" His coffee-colored eyes hardened.

"None of your business." I strode down the hallway to my room.

Face my grief. I *had* been facing my grief. That was *all* I'd been doing. I paused outside my bedroom door.

But I hadn't let Sarah go, and my heart squeezed. *Not all ghosts have unfinished business. Sometimes they just have a hard time letting go. Or the people they love have a hard time letting go of them.*

I let myself inside my room. The kitten lay curled on the little sand-colored sofa.

I studied the sleeping kitten, the rise and fall of his sides. His striped tail flicked.

I hadn't let my sister go. I hadn't been moving on.

My obsession with learning why she'd died hadn't helped me process anything. It had been a coping mechanism, like my interest in luck. Like my obsession with work had been a way to cope with not knowing how to have a real relationship with my son.

My throat clenched shut. Joe hadn't only loved my sister because she'd been fun. She'd been *there*.

Paper whispered, and I turned my head in time to see an UnTarot card fall from the desk to the floor. I walked to it and picked up the Courage card. *Weird*. I thought I'd put it in my notebook portfolio.

I pulled my notebook from my satchel and opened its leather cover. The corner of another card stuck from its inside envelope.

I shook my head. Why bother trying to rationalize it? Magic was real. Phantom wildcats were real. Who cared?

Finally, I understood what the Courage card had been telling me. I didn't need courage to face this household. I needed courage to face facts.

Sarah was gone, and my heart cracked. Hot tears welled in the corners of my eyes. I pressed my hand to my chest.

"Yes," I whispered, and the pain enveloped me. I breathed into it. "Yes."

It was all love. Wasn't that what a ghost—*Sarah's ghost?*—had told Riga?

The pain subsided, but it hadn't gone. I knew that loss would never leave, not really. But this time, I truly *wanted* it to go. Maybe I didn't need to hold onto the pain to hold onto Sarah—or to pretend to hold onto her.

Because it was an illusion, wasn't it? The holding on? All I'd really been holding onto was the pain. And maybe I needed to let go of that so I could start feeling gratitude for the memories.

The kitten stirred and sat up. I laid down on the bed and visualized angels cutting the cord to Sarah, to Tobin, to Sam, to Fortuna, to Wingate. And when I opened my eyes again, the pain was gone.

I lay there and thought of Sarah. It hurt, but not as much.

I rolled off the bed and went to the desk, opening the notebook on top of it. *Release and Courage...* I pulled the card from the portfolio's interior envelope.

Was it a coincidence I'd received both those cards, and both built on each other? Sitting at the blond-wood desk, I re-read the emails.

It *had* to be a coincidence that their messages spoke to my life. I knew how Tarot worked. It was vague enough that anyone could apply its messages to their situation.

But...

Biting my bottom lip, I swiped to the electronic pages of my notebook with my sketches and text of the scroll. The simplest components...

Was it that simple?

And Devin's death, the boat explosion... Were they that simple too?

I picked up my electronic notebook and found a new card beneath it—*Time*. My heart stopped, then resumed beating. No one had gotten into the room while I was there.

Magic.

I dropped it to the side of the desk. I was tired of it all, tired of being manipulated. I'd read about Time later.

I didn't know the card was a warning.

A warning I ignored.

TIME

It's a Western habit to ignore death, to pretend it won't happen to us. But ignoring our mortality is a trap. Because the knowledge that we will one day die and be forgotten is freeing.

If two or three generations after we've passed no one will know or care how we lived, then why not live the lives of our dreams? Create the works we want to create? Be the people we know we can be?

Death has a way of focusing us on what matters. In Latin, the phrase *momento mori* means "remember you must die." In the past (and still today), people carried *momento moris* with them. These decorative jewelry or mementos typically portrayed a skull or some other symbol of death to remind them that life was fleeting.

While we live and must function within society, the path of the witch runs at a different level. We play a multi-leveled game, seeing things others may not and acting accordingly.

To take this path, a witch needs to live boldly and honestly. She must follow the lead of Kali, the Hindu goddess of transformation, time, and death, because awareness of time and death is what fuels our transformation so that we can truly live.

The attached chart has 52 columns – one for each week of the year, and 80 rows, representing a lifespan of 80 years. Write the date of your birth at the top of the sheet. Then fill in all the weeks until you reach your current age. E.g., if you're forty years old plus fifteen weeks, then fill in the first forty rows plus fifteen more columns in the forty-first row. At the end of every week, fill in another cell.

We can tell ourselves that yes, one day our lives will come to an end. We can tell ourselves to seize the day. But this simple chart (attached) makes the time you have left more real.

SCAN ME

Time

Seize the moment. Slow down. Appreciate the little things.

This card acts as a *momento mori*, reminding us we came here to live, and we came here to die. Life is ephemeral. This knowledge shouldn't depress us, it should remind us to prioritize, to evaluate how well we're living with the limited time we have.

While technology and modern life seems to make things move faster, we need to resist that tendency. We can only find ourselves and our purpose if we step away, unplug, take our time, bake the cake from scratch, take a walk, play with our children. Otherwise, we'll come to the end, and the past will simply be a meaningless blur.

One way to find the present is to look to the timeless. Read a classic book. Admire ancient art. Live with awareness.

The symbols:

The skulls in the background of this card act as a *momento mori*—a reminder of death and a call to live well. A lion, king of the beasts, wears a wristwatch—the lion is the ruler, and time is his subject. We need to be lions and make the best of the time allotted. The rosebuds are a reminder of the saying, "gather your rosebuds while ye may," urging us to live life to the fullest.

The questions:

Are you ruling your time, or is it ruling you? How can you seize the day?

name:
DOB:

Find joy in the beauty of impermanence

By embracing mortality, you can seize the present moment

CHAPTER 28

I ROLLED MY NOTEBOOK's stylus between my fingers. It was strange how one revelation could unlock other, unrelated ideas. Or maybe the ideas *were* related. Trouble meowed from his spot beneath the desk lamp.

Beneath the kitten's watchful gaze, I worked through my transcription of the scroll and Wingate's notes.

Wingate had been close, but he'd been wrong. The poem and images were more than clues. They were more like an alchemical formula and just as obscure... until you knew the key.

On the writing tablet, I switched between my notes and the UnTarot emails. A knock at the bedroom door made me twitch on the curving, wooden chair.

"It's unlocked," I shouted.

Tobin strode inside. "Maybe it shouldn't be."

"There's no reason for anyone to bother about me. The scroll's gone." I cocked my head. "Isn't it?"

"The cops haven't been able to find it, if that's what you mean."

"Were *you* able to find it?" I pushed back my chair to see him better.

His voice hardened. "No."

"No," I agreed. "It's obvious by now that it's either been stolen or Wingate took the scroll with him on the boat."

The kitten hopped from the desk and butted his head against Tobin's boot. The bodyguard bent to scratch the striped cat's head. "I guess it wasn't lucky after all," Tobin said.

I massaged my forehead. "Did you want something?"

He straightened. "Dinner's in thirty minutes."

"We're still keeping to formal dining hours?"

SHADOW OF THE WITCH

"More casual tonight," he said. "I'm having pizza delivered." He turned and strode from the room. The door banged shut behind him.

Whatever. I turned back to my work. There was a soft thud beside my hand. Trouble had made his way to the nearby sofa and from there had hopped to the desk.

I jotted down another note.

Someone knocked at the door.

I sighed and set my stylus on the desk. "Come in."

Sam walked into the room. "Maybe you shouldn't leave that door un-locked."

"You're not the first person to say that. What's up?"

"I wanted to apologize if I went too far. I'm the guy my family goes to rant to and get advice. Maybe I've gotten a little too used to dishing it out."

I stared down at my electronic notebook. "You weren't wrong. I just didn't like hearing it." My fists clenched. "I was so busy crawling up the ladder, trying to be the best, that I wasn't the best mother. My son Joe... We talk, but we don't really *talk.* I told myself I worked eighty-hour weeks to support him, but that was only partly true."

If Sam really had been neglected, he wouldn't like me for this confes-sion. But I couldn't shade the truth. Sam deserved better.

His expression stilled. "How old is your son?"

"Thirty-two."

"Then it's not too late."

"I can't change the past."

"But you can apologize for it. It's a start. My parents never—" A muscle pulsed in his jaw. He met my gaze. "They both died years ago. My siblings are my family now. We've always been tight, maybe because our parents were so distant." He shrugged. "I can't repair things with my parents."

I looked away. Could I repair things with Joe? I wasn't sure where to start. But an apology, a real one, would be a good place.

"How's your scroll research?" Sam asked.

Grateful for the change of subject, I pointed to my notebook's screen. "I think the scroll is explaining how luck operates and how to bend it toward you through... not rituals, per se, but through a way of being."

"Explain."

"The first image is of Hermes Trismegistus pointing to the above and below—an old alchemical saying. The accompanying text seems to imply that one needs to align oneself with the universal energies."

He scratched his graying beard. "The word *imply* does a lot of heavy lifting."

"No, look. Here, here, and this phrase here."

"Maybe," he said, infuriatingly noncommittal. "Are you sure you spelled everything correctly? This doesn't all look like 15th-century—"

"No," I said, exasperated. "I'm *not* sure. Do you know how hard it was to copy that crabbed writing at speed?"

He raised his hands in a warding gesture. "Gotcha. Sorry."

"I'm not trying to prove the scroll was made by Ripley. I'm trying to understand— I don't understand the hangman's noose in the clouds, but—"

"It's a medieval symbol for good luck."

"How is a *noose* lucky?" It hadn't been lucky for the condemned man.

The orange kitten sniffed my notebook. His whiskers twitched.

Sam shrugged. "The noose was believed to have special powers. Gamblers loved them. Hangmen were known to chop used ropes into pieces and sell them."

Okaaaay. "The next stanza beneath the ouroboros is all about being fortunate to find fortune."

"That sounds circular."

"Like an ouroboros?" I arched a brow.

He shrugged.

"I think... to be fortunate," I said, "or lucky, you have to be the *kind of person* who finds fortune."

"Which is...?" He braced a hand on the back of my chair.

Suddenly, I became aware of his closeness, of the warmth from his body, and I swallowed. "Someone who expects to be lucky. Someone with an open heart. Look, *hence find fortune in every part*—no matter what happens, think of it as lucky. And here, have a humble heart, and this bit about being true to your heart, translates to being true to your values."

"But isn't the whole point of Fortune that it's fickle?" Sam asked. "It shouldn't matter if you're good or not."

"It's not about being good. It's about being *open* to Fortune. And look, there are circles in other images from the scroll too." I swiped through my drawings.

"So that's it? Be open?"

"Of course not. There's more. Here, in the four elements, it mentions gratitude and charity, lightness of spirit and courage." I faltered. The *Courage* card.

"And the red rose is a medieval symbol for charity," I continued. "Generosity meant something else in Ripley's day, but *charity* is awfully close to its meaning today."

"The text," I said, "the images, they're all about being in alignment. These are what the person who wants more luck needs to get into alignment with. And look down the left column of the Four Elements poem," I said, smug. "The first letter of each line."

Sam swore. "Holy hell."

"It's an acrostic." *Thank you, Sarah.* And the acrostic spelled out the four classical Greek virtues—temperance, justice, courage, and prudence. "I suppose one needs to live by those as well."

"It's a working hypothesis," Sam admitted. "But let's face it, this is little more than a self-help scroll."

I laughed. "The alchemists *were* all about personal development."

I sat back in my chair and dropped my stylus to the desk. The UnTarot cards I'd received—*Gratitude, Courage, Generosity...* Was their arrival while I was reading the scroll random coincidence? Was I seeing what I wanted...?

I straightened in the desk chair. No. If I believed in luck, then I had to believe that none of those cards were random. "Besides, it's my scroll. I'll interpret it the way I want to," I said lightly.

"Yours? I thought it was Wingate's."

I tapped the plastic edge of my notebook with the stylus. "Mine."

Sam grinned. "Gotcha. I'll see you at dinner." He ambled from my room.

He closed the door behind him, and I rose, locking it, then returned to my desk. I did a reverse image search online on the symbol I found in the woods. It was an Icelandic sigil called a luck ring and used to protect against evil spirits.

A luck ring... Had Wingate carved it into the tree to protect his temple? I shivered. The cat-thing had hesitated when I'd been near the sigil, but it had gotten inside the temple in the end.

I opened the emails from the mystery school. *Gratitude. Generosity...* I'd been lacking in both since Sarah's death.

Someone pounded on my door. "Pizza's here," Tobin shouted.

I looked up, annoyed by the interruption. My stomach growled.

"I guess I could use a break," I admitted to the kitten.

Trouble shot me a disdainful look.

Pushing back my chair, I stood. "I will not be manipulated by a cat."

I stopped short. But I *had* been manipulated. Chased through the woods, through the passages...

And everything had worked out. If I hadn't been trapped in the temple, I might not have found the secret passage. Was fortune finally working in my favor?

Feeling unaccountably optimistic, I descended the winding stairs and found the others in the chocolate-colored lounge. The picture windows shimmered blackly, the lake behind them obscured by our reflections in the lounge.

Riga, in her Katherine Hepburn trousers and blouse stood by the open firepit with Ezra. The latter, looking like an undertaker, stared at her suspiciously. Tobin stood by a window with a slice in his hand, his back to the others.

At the granite bar, Fortuna flipped open the lid of a pizza box. "Pineapple? Really?" She dropped the lid and opened another. "At least someone had the good sense to order vegetarian."

"None for me. I can't do gluten." August grinned at her from his high seat at the bar.

I snagged a slice of pepperoni and mushroom. "What are you doing here?" I asked the tech specialist. "A problem with the security system?" *Or with Fortuna?*

"That's confidential," Tobin said.

"Not for me." Fortuna slid a slice onto her plate. "We've got a virus."

"Does it look like a cat?" Sam dropped onto an acorn-colored sofa facing the firepit.

"A cat..." Fortuna paled. "You've seen it too?"

"Everyone connected to the internet here has probably seen it," Tobin said roughly. "It's a virus."

"Or a memetic demon." Ezra plucked a piece of pepperoni off his pizza and flicked it onto his plate.

Riga started. "That's—"

"A joke," Ezra said. "It's what I call computer viruses. They replicate memetically, and they're certainly demonic."

I sat in one of the soft chairs by the firepit and took a bite. "Has anyone else seen the cat *off* the screen?" I asked. "In real life?" The flames leapt, the glass baubles in the pit flickering with reflected light.

"Off screen?" Ezra asked. "How would a computer virus go off screen?"

Fortuna swayed and grasped the edge of the bar to steady herself. "That's... Have you seen it too? A big black cat, like a panther?"

"I've heard it," Sam said.

"It's real," I said. "There's something—"

"Forget the virus," Tobin said. "August's handling it. That's not why I invited you here."

"Why *did* you invite us here?" Riga asked him.

Despite my annoyance at the interruption, I was curious too. I relaxed in the comfy chair. Keeping my mouth shut was getting me all sorts of interesting intel. I glanced at Sam, on the couch, and I smiled.

"To finish things." Tobin bit into his slice of pizza.

"You think you know who killed Devon and Wingate?" Riga peered inside an open pizza box.

Tobin scowled at her. "I know."

"And you called us all together to reveal the murderer?" Ezra sneered. "How Agatha Christie."

"Aren't you curious?" Tobin asked.

"Only as to what the police conclude," Ezra said.

"*I've* concluded you had the means, motive, and opportunity to kill both Devin and Wingate." Tobin's fists clenched. He took a step toward Ezra, and the smaller man stepped backward.

I sat up straighter in the brown leather chair.

"Careful," Riga warned. "It may not be as simple—"

Tobin bristled. "Embarrassed you didn't figure it out sooner, *detective?*"

"Ezra makes a good candidate," Riga said smoothly, "but there are still unanswered questions."

"And we'd prefer amateurs don't play detective." The sheriff walked into the lounge. "Ezra. I'd like you to come with us." The bearlike man nodded to Deputy Linnel, at his side.

"Just for a chat," the sheriff said.

Ezra darted a nervous glance at Tobin then hurried to the sheriff. "Yes, yes," Ezra said. "I'm happy to help any way I can."

"I'm coming too," Tobin said, his jaw jutting forward stubbornly.

"I can't stop you from haunting the waiting area," the sheriff said. "But that's all you'll be doing. And you take your own car. Brandy?" He cocked a thick finger at me. "A word, please."

I followed him into the foyer. We watched Deputy Linnel lead Ezra away. Tobin followed.

"I need to talk to you about a call you received about Wingate Weald after your sister's death. I'm afraid a law enforcement officer made that call."

I nodded, but I didn't say Peggy's name. I hadn't told him about the anonymous call all those months ago. If he was fishing, I wouldn't satisfy him. The dispatcher had done the right thing. She shouldn't be punished for it.

"Do you know who called you?"

"It was anonymous."

He gave me a hard stare. "It shouldn't have happened." He turned on his boot heel and strode outside, slamming the door. The flowers on the table trembled in the breeze.

Thoughtful, I returned to the lounge.

"The sheriff's arrival was convenient timing." Sam mumbled through his mouthful of pizza. He set his plate on a nearby low table and met my gaze.

I moved toward Riga. "Can I talk to you privately?"

She nodded, and we moved to a far corner of the room. "Have you seen my sister?" I asked in a low voice.

She exhaled through pursed lips. "Why—?"

"It's all love. *Sarah* said that before she died."

Her brown eyes flickered. "I won't ask how you learned that."

"Did you—?"

"I don't know. The ghost didn't tell me her name. But... it was clear she'd been in an accident. She said she'd been driving early in the morning."

"Why can't I see my sister?" I hugged my elbows. "I've been trying in my dreams. I've seen dead people before, people I loved. Why can't I see *her*?"

Riga angled her head, her auburn hair cascading over the shoulder of her white blouse. "I'm not sure. But it seems that when people are grieving and desperate, the ghosts of their loved ones don't come. It's only when we let them go, that we can see them again."

My chest hardened. *Let go.* Was that what it all came down to?

Riga squeezed my upper arm. "She will come. Excuse me. There's one more thing I have to do here." She returned to the firepit.

I followed. More loudly, I asked her, "What's a memetic demon?"

"I don't know," she said. "I've never heard the term before. But... Ezra might be onto something, even if it was meant as a joke."

"It's only a normal virus." August rubbed his wrist. "Don't worry, I'll take care of it."

Riga shook her head. "I've seen the big cat too, outside the walls of my house. I assumed it was a thought form. Maybe it is one, a new kind, something that can move through the internet *and* the real world."

"What's a thought form?" I asked. *Honestly.* Did I have to ask to get *everything* explained?

"Just what it sounds like," Riga said. "A magician or group of non-magical people build up an idea—a person or creature—in his or their thoughts and gives it enough power to send it into the world."

"For what purpose?" Sam asked.

"For the magician, as a servitor," Riga said. "To gather information, to attack enemies… If it could move through the internet and onto our devices, it could collect all sorts of information."

"You're talking about malware," August said.

"I'm talking about a technomancer." Riga stared at him hard. A draft rippled the flames in the gas firepit.

Her words froze my brain. August was a technomancer? He had access to the security systems at Dragon House. It made sense he might be involved. But a technomancer?

And why *wouldn't* techomancers be real? I'd met a metaphysical detective and encountered a thought form, and… *Was* I a shaman?

"What's a technomancer?" August asked.

"Come off it," Riga said. "That bracelet of yours is a digital talisman. I've seen them before. You're a technomancer. *You* created this thought form. You work for the so-called investors who want that scroll."

"What?" Fortuna asked him. "What is she talking about?"

"I have no idea," August said stiffly.

"Your parents died in a boating accident," I said slowly. Could it have been an explosion, like Wingate's?

"You must have felt powerless on top of all that grief," Riga said. "Tough for a small child. The sort of trauma that would inspire a person to take their power back by any means necessary. Including magic. Including joining a black lodge."

My chest caught. But this time, my reaction was sympathy, not anguish. *Grief.* How could an emotion based in love cause so much harm?

"Black lodge?" Fortuna asked. "What the hell's a black lodge?"

"A group of dark magicians," Riga said, not taking her gaze from August's. "There's a lodge called the Brotherhood that's interested in this scroll."

"You told the Black Lodge about my scroll," I breathed. "You learned I'd reached out to Wingate from your work here at Dragon House, and you told them." Or he'd learned from Fortuna. I shot her a sideways glance.

Fortuna pressed a ringed hand to her chest. "You wanted the scroll... You killed Devin?" She backed away from him. "You killed my husband?"

"No," August said. "I wasn't here. I had nothing against Devin. I'm no murderer."

"No," Riga said. "I don't think you did kill Devin. But you had several hundred thousand reasons to kill Wingate," Riga said.

"No," August said. "I was going to buy the scroll from Wingate outright."

"You sure about that?" I asked. "Wingate would never give up that scroll. He was stringing you along. When did you figure it out?"

August looked toward the windows. "We had an understanding," he muttered.

Riga canted her head toward the door. "Come on. The sheriff needs to hear this."

Sam clapped a hand on August's shoulder. "I'll walk with you. I don't think they've left yet."

He and Riga walked August out the door. At their departure, a tiny ache of loneliness pierced my heart.

"I don't understand," Fortuna whispered. "He said he loved me."

I grimaced. "Maybe he did." Or maybe he'd used Fortuna as an *in* with Wingate, as a way to get closer to the scroll and to Devin. How much *did* Fortuna know? "Tell me more about Wingate's business. Was he any good at it?"

"Not lately," she said. "Devin tried to fix things, but..."

"Does Wingate have a big client list?"

Fortuna stared at the doorway. "Not really. They're all his business associates."

"The mob?"

"I can't stay here any longer. I'm getting a hotel." She wandered out the door.

I looked around the empty lounge, grabbed a pizza box, and went to my room. I wasn't surprised to find the kitten sitting on my desk beside the *Time* card, which had somehow found its way out from beneath my notebook.

I heaved a breath. *Time indeed.* Was it a signal that I should return to Kronos in the temple? Or that time was running out?

No. Fortunate people don't bog themselves down in anxiety. They look forward to the future, no matter what it brings.

First, I'd fuel up with pizza. Then, I'd return to the temple.

AS ABOVE, SO BELOW

⊙ЄΟϹ

Lo, the above, immense and grant
Reflects within concordant hand
The inner man's tyne spark
Brief echoes of the kosmos mark
Align thy soul with woruldlic breath
Surpass the bounds of divine depth
For in the spheres' mirroured sea
Lies the clew to destiny
Seek not Fortuna's fleeting gold
But in the Emerald Tablet's mould

Fortuna arrays with those who see
The firmament in harmony
Sun mone and stars in clarity
Reflect the soule's bryht charity
And when thy spirit unerthes its place
Fortuna smiles with gentile grace
Let not dour shadows dim thy syght
Clasp in thy arms both troth and lyght
For sholde thou walk the vertuous pathe
Fortuna's hande shal turn from wraethe

CHAPTER 29

THE SHERIFF, TOBIN, RIGA, *all* of them were mistaken—about the murders and about the scroll. But I didn't care. I didn't need to prove anything to them, But I did need to prove something to myself.

I opened the wardrobe door. And my sister's husband? Was that how he'd felt about Joe and me? That he didn't need to prove himself to us? Because Joe and I had never been fans of his, and the feeling had been mutual.

My shoulders loosened. I didn't think I'd been too hard on Sarah's husband. But his life going forward was his business, not mine. I needed to release my anger toward him too.

But none of that mattered now. By some stroke of luck or fate, I was finally alone at Dragon House, and I wasn't going to miss this opportunity. I removed my sister's vest from its hanger and slipped it on.

I'd be going into the passage again, and I didn't want to get the precious thing any dirtier. But it needed dry cleaning anyway. And I wanted a part of Sarah with me at the end.

I descended the winding stairs. That night, the portraits on its walls didn't look quite so disapproving. I walked outside, down the front steps, and retrieved my flashlight and work gloves from my SUV.

Clouds obscured the moon. The only lights illuminating the driveway were from the Dragon House windows.

Ambling to the back of the car, I opened the hatch, pulled back the carpet, and opened the compartment where I kept the tire equipment. I withdrew the tire iron, closed the rear door and strode toward the woods.

The temperature had dropped, and the sleeveless vest left too much of me exposed. I'd have to move fast.

"It's a little late for a stroll, isn't it?" Sam asked.

Startled, I spun to face him. "I thought—"

"That I'd gone with the sheriff and August? No."

"Where's Fortuna?" I looked around uneasily.

"I saw her drive off. Sober." He switched on his own flashlight.

"So, we're alone," I said.

He didn't respond. The silence between us lengthened.

But it was a comfortable silence. I could have stood with him for hours, days, years, just being present. Listening to the night sounds. Listening to the scuffling of small animals. Listening to the breeze in the pines.

I smiled. "Want to explore the temple with me?"

"Sure."

We walked together into the woods. Even with my flashlight, I didn't catch the trail right away. It was Sam who spotted it. Manzanita branches snagged his jeans as he passed through.

"What do you expect to find?" he asked.

"Someone's been living in the temple," I said.

He stopped and turned to study me. "I see."

"You've guessed, haven't you?"

"It seemed unlikely Wingate would take his precious scroll on a boat trip," Sam said. "Do you really want it that badly?"

A soft exhalation escaped my lips. "I want to know how this ends."

Sam lowered his head. "I understand that. My whole life..." He looked back toward the lights of Dragon House, glimmering through the verticals of pines. "I found meaning in knowing, in figuring things out. I guess I still do. But the search took me away from family, from forming real connections." He met my gaze, and my heart jumped.

"And now?" I asked, voice low.

"I don't want to live that way anymore. Don't get me wrong, I still enjoy the pursuit. But there's more to life, and I'm halfway through mine. I think it's time to make some changes."

"Can you? Change?" *Could I?*

He grimaced. "I don't expect it will be simple. But the things that matter to me now have shifted. Now that I understand what I really want, change seems easier. What about you?"

I hesitated. "You were right. I can't go back to my old career. I need... time." Time to rebuild my relationship with my son. Time, maybe, to build new relationships. My face heated.

Sam turned and walked on. "You should be a researcher. You've done a helluva job with the scroll. How'd you find that fragment?"

"I paid someone smarter than me."

He barked a laugh. "That'll do."

We made our way to the temple. I stared at the unbroken green door. "I heard the door splinter. I *know* I did."

"What are you talking about?"

My stomach tensed. "The cat thing..." But if it was a thought form, not real, could it have broken a thought-form door? Had it put the sound of the door cracking in my head?

"I heard the door splinter," I said firmly. "That thing got into the temple somehow. It followed me through the passages. You *heard* it."

"Yeah," he said grimly. "I did." He opened the solid green door and walked inside. The beam of his flashlight glittered off the mosaic tiles.

"Kronos eating his children," he said. "Nice."

I smiled faintly. It was strangely comforting being with someone who recognized the old myths.

"Check out the kid's eye." I walked behind the altar and pressed the tile. There was a grinding sound, and the trap door slid backward in the stone floor.

"Cool." Sam squatted and shined his light into the pit. I studied the curls of his salt-and-pepper hair. He looked up at me, and warmth flushed through my veins. "You went down there alone?" he asked. "That took some nerve."

"It beat what was up here."

Bracing his hands on either side of the hole, he swung himself forward and dropped through.

I bit back a surprised curse. "You okay?" I knelt beside the hole and peered inside.

"Fine." His flashlight beam bounced around the small room beneath. "There's a panel in the wall."

"I know. I couldn't get it open." Reaching into the hole, I handed him the tire iron.

"It shouldn't be hard to—Oh. A lock." He grunted. There was a grinding sound, metal on metal, and then a wooden *thwack*. "Got it."

He handed a rucksack up through the trap door, then followed it with his head. He clambered into the temple and sat, one leg dangling through the gap in the floor. "You can do the honors."

I unhitched the ties on the sack and reached in. My fingers touched fabric, and I pulled out an elegant button-up shirt, slacks, men's under-clothes, a tablet computer, a wad of cash—all hundreds—and a scroll case.

"It's here," I whispered.

"Open it to be sure."

I unscrewed the top and peered inside. "It's the scroll—or at least *a* scroll. I don't want to take it out. There's more scroll in here than there was with my piece alone, and the parchment is curled tight. I'm afraid I'll damage it."

"Then leave it. You know what this is?" Sam picked up the canvas sack. "A bug-out bag," he continued before I could respond.

"There's more inside—"

"Leave it," he said. "We need to put this back where we found it."

"Why?"

"For the police. Our prints are on it, but they'll want to see it *in situ*."

"What if he comes back for it?"

"It's his anyway. But we know what we found, and the police will too."

Reluctantly, I replaced the items in the bag. He was right about the police. But the thought of leaving the scroll behind made me a little sick.

Sam climbed down the ladder into the chamber, and I handed him the rucksack. There was a grinding sound, the little door below closing.

Sam handed my tire iron through the hole and climbed up after it. He pulled out an ancient-looking flip phone.

I gave a half laugh. "Those still exist?"

"I hate smart phones." He dialed and pressed it to his ear, took it away, grimaced. "No signal. Call the police."

"I can't. My phone's broken. Remember?"

"Tomorrow, I'm taking you to the phone store." He wiggled the eyeball tile between two fingers, and the trap door closed. "Let's go. I can call the sheriff when we get back to the house."

We trooped through the dark pines toward Dragon House.

"If he returns to the temple tonight," I said, "he'll know someone was in there."

"Yep," Sam said. "And he'll probably run. But that's a problem for the sheriff."

We stepped from the trees and onto the lawn. Snow had begun to fall, fat flakes that took their time melting on my shoulders.

Together, we climbed the steps to Dragon House. Our hands brushed. A spark seemed to leap between them.

He opened the tall door for me, and I stepped into the foyer. The mansion felt almost welcoming now. Sam called the police from the lounge, the firelight from the open pit flickering weirdly across his craggy face.

After a brief conversation, Sam disconnected. "They'll be here tomorrow."

I rubbed the sleeve of my knit top. "Tomorrow? But—"

"There's a big accident on Highway 50."

My heart dropped. *No more roadside crosses, please.* "Oh. Was anyone—?"

"He didn't say."

I swallowed. It wouldn't be right for him to say. Not before informing any relatives. But I hoped he wouldn't have to.

"You okay?" Sam asked.

"Yeah. Yeah. Just... thinking about accidents." And about my sister, who hadn't died alone. Someone had held her hand, someone had looked into her eyes, someone had been a warm, human, loving presence for her.

For the first time since February, I was glad for Sarah. We should all have a loving touch at the end.

I sighed. "Thanks for coming with me. I'm going to hit the hay." I turned to go upstairs.

"I'm sorry," Sam said softly. "I didn't mean to upset you."

"You didn't. I'll see you tomorrow." I jogged up the stairs.

Sam's more measured steps sounded behind me. I hurried inside my bedroom and closed the door, shutting him out.

Trouble raised his head. The kitten looked up sleepily from the foot of the bed.

"We're leaving tomorrow," I said. "This time, I mean it."

We'd leave tomorrow. I could explain things to the sheriff, and then I was done. I didn't have all the answers, but I had faith that someday I would—or at least I'd have the answers I needed. I could move on.

Where I would move on to was another question. I'd thought I could go back to my old job, but that would be a mistake. I could only go forward. For the first time in a long time, I trusted that something better would come.

And maybe someone better too.

"Work-life balance," I told Trouble. "That's the ticket."

He sneezed and rolled onto his side. His tiny striped tail flicked.

It was still too early to go to bed, so I practiced my evening chi gung, then spent another hour or two puzzling over the luck scroll. My sketches weren't as beautiful as the original, but I caught myself smiling.

When I went to bed, I fell asleep easily, thinking of Sam. But I dreamed of someone else.

I awoke to eighteen claws digging into my stomach and an unearthly howl. "Trouble," I mumbled. "What...?"

The kitten howled again.

I coughed, detached the kitten and blinked muzzily. "What is your problem?" I rubbed my throat and reached for the water carafe on the bedside table.

I wasted precious moments lying in bed, not understanding what was burning my nostrils, what stung my eyes. And then I realized what I was scenting.

Smoke.

THE LABYRINTH

Walk the labyrinth, childe of fate
Wyth manner of rites be not too late
Be not gulled by twists and trials
Be not diverted by Fate's cruel wiles
Before the cock crow breaks the morne
The egg shal crack and fortune borne
And in the centre ye shal finde
The treasure of philosopher's minde
In thy soule's truth, Fortuna alines
Wyth he who know to folowe her sygnes
And in the stilnesse of the dawne
Feares and tryalles shal all begon

CHAPTER 30

I THREW OFF MY covers and ran to the door, pressing my hand to the wood. It wasn't warm. Breath quick, I raced back to my bed and lowered the kitten into the pocket of my nightgown. He mewled piteously.

"Sorry." I rushed into the smokey hallway.

My limbs trembled. *Sam.* "Sam?" I shouted and jogged to his bedroom. I pounded on the door, turned the knob. It was locked.

I twisted it back and forth helplessly. Of *course* it was locked. *Damn it.*

Coughing, I ran back to my bedroom. I grabbed my flashlight off the desk and entered the wardrobe. The kitten squirmed in my pocket.

The air in the passage was cool and clear. I don't know how I found my way to Sam's door as quickly as I did. Blind luck? Fate? But seemed to be only a minute or two before I was stepping from his wardrobe and into his room.

"Sam!" I hurried to the bed, where he lay on his side. I shook his bare shoulder. He didn't stir. "Sam," I shouted. "Wake up." I shook him harder. "Wake up!"

What was wrong with him? I grabbed the carafe by his bed, thinking to fling water in his face, but it was empty.

I shoved him onto his back. His eyes didn't open.

Someone pounded on his door. I rushed to it and flung it open with shaking hands.

Fortuna stood in the hallway wearing a t-shirt and sweatpants, her red hair coiled in a bun at the top of her head. Emotions raced across her narrow face—surprise, annoyance, understanding. "Sam—?"

"He won't wake up," I said, voice panicky. "Help me."

Fortuna strode to the bed and looked down for a long moment at the sleeping man. Then she pulled back her hand and slapped him. Hard.

I winced.

Sam's eyes opened. "Ow," he said groggily.

"Get up," Fortuna said. "The house is on fire."

"Okay," he slurred. Sam raised his head. He dropped it back onto the pillow.

Fortuna slapped him again.

"Stop it," he mumbled.

Insides churning, I grabbed the water carafe. I filled it in the sink at the kitchenette.

"What don't you understand about fire?" Fortuna shrieked. "We have to get out of here."

I strode to the bed and dumped the water over Sam's face.

He blinked and shook his head. "Fire? We should leave." He rolled onto his side, the duvet slipping lower on his bare shoulder, beaded with water.

Fortuna swore. The kitten wriggled in my pocket.

"Something's wrong with him," I said.

"No kidding," she snapped. "He's been drugged."

"Who—?" I shook my head. *Never mind.* "Help me get him moving."

Between the two of us, we shouted, pushed, and cajoled Sam to his feet. Thankfully, he was wearing pants—plaid pajama pants to be exact.

He slouched heavily between us, arms around each of our shoulders. We staggered into the hallway.

There was a roar and a burst of heat. Flames shot up the central staircase, and I cried out at the blistering heat. We were trapped.

"The servants' stairway at the back." Fortuna turned.

Her supporting shoulder gone, Sam collapsed, and I tumbled to the parquet floor beside him. At the last moment, I remembered to twist so I didn't crush the kitten in my pocket. There was an indignant mewl.

"Sorry," Fortuna mumbled.

I knelt and reached inside to comfort Trouble. My fingers touched his warm fur. *Fur.* "No, no, no." Sticky heat rose behind my eyes. *My sister's vest.* "Wait." I scrambled to standing and moved toward my bedroom.

"Where are you going?" Fortuna shrieked.

I grimaced. There was no time for me to get her vest. Sarah wouldn't want me to risk it. I drew a slow breath, my insides heavying. "Nowhere."

We got Sam up and moving again toward the back stairs and away from Sarah's vest. I glanced over my shoulder. But my bedroom was so close. I *could* run back.

Smoke and heat billowed up the narrow servant's staircase. Fortuna and I exchanged uneasy glances.

"The hidden passage was clear when I was inside it earlier," I said.

She didn't ask which hidden passage I meant. "Hold him."

We propped Sam against a wall, and she darted around a bend in the hallway. I had to press my full body against his to keep him from folding over.

Eyes closed, he sighed, one muscular arm coming around my waist. It would have been romantic if I hadn't been so damned terrified. My spine bowed beneath his weight.

Sarah's vest... A sick dullness filled my throat. But a vest wasn't worth dying over.

After a minute or two, Fortuna returned. "This way."

We dragged, pushed, and Fortuna slapped him to get Sam to the secret door—an open panel in one of the hallways. It was one I hadn't used before, and I shot Fortuna an interested glance.

"Come *on*," she said.

We tugged Sam into the passage, and she shut the door. I sucked in a lungful of mostly fresh air.

We moved as quickly as we could down the passage, my flashlight lighting the way. I wasn't sure we needed it. Fortuna was unhesitating, turning right down one passage, leading us down a set of stairs and into another twisting labyrinth.

"I'm glad you were here," I told her and coughed. The kitten shifted in my pocket.

"I'm *not* glad." She shot me a glance and adjusted Sam's hand over her shoulder.

He seemed to be walking a little better, not putting quite so much weight on my shoulders. I stepped on something hard and cursed. Why hadn't I put on shoes?

"You should have put shoes on," Fortuna said, as if catching my thoughts. "It's going to be cold outside."

If we ever *got* outside. "I was in a hurry," I snapped. "Why *are* you here? I thought you were getting a hotel tonight."

"I tried," Fortuna said. "But there was an accident blocking the highway. It seemed..." She shook her head. "It seemed like a sign to turn back. It didn't make sense to sit there for who knows how long," she finished quickly.

"How prudent of you," I said with dry humor. *Prudence...* Why did that—?

I stopped short. Prudence was one of the virtues from the scroll. To the ancient Greeks, it meant doing the right thing at the right time. I shook my head. *Not now.*

"What?" Fortuna stumbled, Sam falling heavily against her. "Why'd you stop?"

"Nothing." Sweat trickled down the back of my neck. The passage was growing warmer. I moved forward.

We descended another set of stairs. We were on the first floor now, close to escape—

Fortuna turned down a passage. A set of stairs vanished into the gloom below.

My footsteps heavied. "Where are we going?" I asked.

"We can't get outside from here," she said. "This passage is blocked. We have to go out through the temple."

The temple. I swallowed, my throat dry.

"Move," she urged.

We fumbled our way down the stairs. Sam was definitely improving, his legs taking more weight.

"We go right here," Fortuna said.

The three of us clumsily took the turn. Footsteps echoed behind us, and I slowed, listening.

"What's wrong?" she asked. "Keep going."

"Did you hear anything?" I asked.

"No," she said. "*Move.*"

We shuffled forward. Even though Fortuna knew her way, it took time to maneuver Sam down the narrow turns. My legs quaked from exhaustion. My breath came short and fast. Fortuna huffed too.

"We're almost there," she said.

Sam grunted.

"Not quite," Wingate said from behind us.

I started, and Sam slumped against the stone and dirt wall. I turned.

Wingate looked elegant as ever, even if his face and the collar beneath his navy jacket were darkened by soot. But they weren't as dark as the gun in his hand, partially obscured by his flashlight. The gun and light were aimed at Sam.

CHAPTER 31

"YOU'RE ALIVE," FORTUNA SAID flatly, her voice deadened by the earthen tunnel.

"Disappointed?" Wingate arched a brow. He held the flashlight and gun like a TV detective, wrists crossed. A section of his silvery hair had fallen over his forehead, nearly obscuring one eye.

In the flashlight's beam, Sam slid lower down the rough wall. I didn't move to stop his descent. I was too petrified. Trouble shifted in my pocket.

"Yes, frankly," Fortuna said. "I get why you wanted to run. Your clients can't be happy with you, and they're not the type of people to make unhappy. But what are you doing hanging around here?"

"He thinks I have more of the scroll," I said dully. It was the only reason, the only thing that would keep Wingate here. Ezra had told him a fragment was missing. Ezra had lied, but Wingate didn't know that.

Wingate had been the one following me in the woods—and likely in other places I hadn't noticed. He'd hoped I'd lead him to the "missing" fragment.

"Where are you hiding it?" Wingate aimed the light in my face, and I winced, blinded. "I searched your room. It wasn't there."

"Because it doesn't exist." I raised one hand to shield my eyes. "You have the entire scroll." Was it better if he believed me or not? Which would encourage him to keep us alive longer?

The passage seemed to darken. With smoke? But I didn't smell smoke. All I smelled was the oppressive weight of the dank earth above.

Wingate's lips flattened. "That's not what Ezra told me."

"Ezra was lying. He wanted you to sell him the scroll at a bargain price." I shuddered, the cold intensifying.

"So he could sell it to August and his little group of mad magicians?" Wingate smirked at Fortuna. "That boy thought he could use you, Fortuna, to get in my good graces. The arrogance of the young."

"*You* used August's tech skills," I said, stalling. But what was I stalling for? No one would find us here. If anyone saw the fire, they'd be focused on Dragon House, not on what or who was beneath.

"That security video," I continued. "It was all fake, wasn't it? You got August to create a deep fake of a stranger entering the grounds. But no one came from outside to kill Devin."

Fortuna twitched. "It was you. You killed Devin," she whispered. "You killed your own nephew, my *husband*." Strands of her red hair, fallen from the bun, stuck to the sides of her neck.

"He knew the price." Wingate turned the light on her pale face. "Devon went crying to my clients." The gun wavered. "He betrayed us all. He told them *everything*."

"That you'd lost or stolen their money?" I asked. "Why did you think you could get away with a pyramid scheme? The pool of mafioso for clients has got to be limited. Your pyramid wouldn't stand up for long."

"You know what they say." Wingate shrugged. "Fortune favors the bold."

"What did you do to Sam?" I jerked my head toward the slumped man. Trouble stuck his head from my nightgown's pocket.

"I drugged the water carafes so I could search your rooms," he said. "Alas, you didn't drink from yours."

"And so you decided to burn down the house?" I asked, disbelieving.

"I don't know how the fire started," Wingate said, tone indignant. "I'd never destroy something so old and beautiful."

But the mobster was just fine with destroying real-live humans. My muscles quivered with rage.

"Is the scroll in your car?" he asked. "Never mind. Give me your key fob."

"The fob's in my bedroom." *In the pocket of my sister's vest.* Pain gripped the back of my throat. Her vest wouldn't survive the fire. It was probably already gone. "And I don't have a secret section of scroll. Ezra lied."

Behind Wingate, the shadows in the passage deepened. "He didn't," Wingate said, voice rising. "The scroll makes no sense. Something *must* be missing."

Trouble hissed.

"It makes perfect sense if you're the right kind of person," I said.

"The right kind of person?" Wingate sneered. "Do you know how deeply I've studied luck? No one knows her better than me. There is no better person."

I sighed. "There are millions of better people."

Sam scraped against the rough wall. I shuffled my feet to hide the sound of his movement.

"Don't move," Wingate snapped, the flashlight blinding me.

"You killed Devin," Fortuna said in a low voice. "And then you faked your death to escape the mob. You sack of human garbage."

"Human garbage you've been happy to sponge off," Wingate reminded her. "What do you mean the scroll makes sense?"

"It's about being obedient to Fortune." I turned my head from the flashlight's beam. "It can't be controlled."

Wingate made a short, negating motion with his head. "What New Age nonsense. Obedient? The *point* is to control luck."

"The New Age was based on the old age," I said, and my voice was steady. How I kept it that way, I had no idea. "It's not all nonsense."

An uneven chill guttered from the passage. Wingate's hair didn't stir. The fine fabric of his navy jacket didn't ripple.

I'd felt fear earlier that night. Wingate was a well-dressed thug. He'd have zero compunction about leaving our corpses in the passage below Dragon House. We'd never be found, and that scared me.

But that bitter flow of stagnant air was more terrifying. It came from behind Wingate, tentacles of icy air that reached through my flesh and into my bones. I took a small, involuntary step away from that cold, blacker than the passage behind the mobster.

Wingate raised his gun. "I said don't move." He stepped forward, and I froze.

Fortuna swayed. "What...?" She pointed a shaky finger down the passage. "What's that?"

"If you think you're going to distract me," Wingate said, "you've sadly overestimated your powers of persuasion."

I gasped for air. Behind Wingate, an oily form grew. The shadows deepened into a feline shape.

Trouble howled. A growl behind Wingate answered.

Wingate spun to face the thing in the passage. "What the—?"

Something struck my shoulder, knocking me sideways. Sam jolted past and tackled Wingate at the knees. A gunshot cracked, echoing. Earth drifted from the ceiling, coating the two men. A rumble sounded down the passage.

Fortuna shrieked. "It's collapsing." She bolted in the opposite direction, toward the temple.

Trouble scrambled from my pocket and dropped lithely to the ground. The kitten bounded over the men rolling on the ground and raced into the yawning passage.

"Trouble," I shouted. "Come back!"

Trouble's orange fur glimmered in the darkness. The kitten's shadow expanded, the silhouette of his head scraping the top of the passage wall.

There was a flare of light and a louder rumble. I clapped my hands to my ears. The earth shook, and I staggered. The passage blackened. I couldn't breathe. I was choking, choking, choking on dust and dark and debris. A cat howled.

And then the rumbling stopped, and Sam was gripping Wingate's gun arm in both his hands and pounding Wingate's wrist against the hard earth floor. Wingate punched Sam's torso with his free hand.

I gaped and clutched at the rough stone and earth wall with both my hands. I was alive? I hadn't died? Unless I was a ghost, and—

Sam glared at me. "Will you either get out of here or help?"

I coughed, my ears hot. *Not dead then.* "Fine," I snapped and swung my foot at the back of Wingate's head. He jerked away, and I kicked him in the neck.

The mobster slumped. The gun dropped to the ground, and I snatched it up.

Sam's eyes bulged. "Point it somewhere else."

Embarrassed, I jerked the gun toward the smoke and dust rolling along the ceiling.

Sam staggered to his feet and stood panting. He kicked Wingate in the ribs, and I winced.

"Don't you start feeling sorry for him," Sam warned.

"I'm not. I don't." My heart thudded. "Trouble?" I called, leaning toward the passage.

The little cat emerged from the darkness, his fur dusty, and trotted around Wingate. Trouble sat at my feet and licked his paw. I picked the kitten up with my free hand.

"I guess this means I'm carrying *him*." Sam jerked his head to the unconscious Wingate.

In the end, we dragged Wingate. I couldn't say how we got him up the ladder and into the temple. But when we did, Fortuna was waiting. So were the police.

CHAPTER 32

BECAUSE OF THE KITTEN, I hadn't slept through the fire.

Because Fortuna had been turned back by the accident on the highway, she'd been at Dragon House to help with Sam.

Because August had sent the thought form after Wingate, Wingate had been distracted in the passage.

Because Sam had been there, he'd taken Wingate down and saved us all.

Had it been fate or luck?

Because all along that path there had been human choices. Sam's decision to come to Dragon House to do the drudge work. My decision to save Trouble on the highway. Fortuna's decision to give up on that hotel. August's decision to get his revenge on Wingate.

Had we all been in service to Fortune?

Trouble shifted in his cat carrier on the towing company's laminate floor.

I handed my credit card across the high, black granite counter to the grimy tow-truck driver. In his grimy t-shirt and jeans, the massive man seemed out of place amidst the modern office's faux stone and sleek gray tones.

Dragon House had not been saved, but at least my SUV had survived. The fire department had had it towed so they could better position one of their trucks.

A week had passed since the fire. I'd just gotten my new key fob, so I could finally collect my car. And I'd gotten my answers.

My son slipped an arm over my shoulders. I leaned wearily against Joe's lean frame, and my heart warmed.

Wingate had been shocked the morning of February second to find himself dragged from bed by his suspicious "clients." He'd managed to convince them all was well—or at least partially convince them. They'd left him in the middle of the highway as a warning.

But he'd begun planning his escape to a new life then—and plotting his revenge. He'd known one of his associates had ratted him out to the mob—either Devin or Tobin.

Tobin may have followed Wingate's kidnappers and rescued him from the highway. But Wingate didn't consider that proof of innocence.

It wasn't until August's "memetic demon" had gotten onto Devin's computer and transferred the data off it that Wingate was sure his nephew had betrayed him.

But by that time, I was in the picture with the Luck Scroll fragment. Wingate wanted it and thought my arrival might cause more confusion. So, he waited for me to arrive before he killed his nephew outside the library.

Wingate considered the fact that I—an outsider—had found the body a lucky break. And then after taking the scroll, he'd faked his death in the boating explosion.

The tow-truck driver shot me a suspicious look and ran my card. He grunted. "Looks like you're good for it. This way."

He led us through gently falling snow to my SUV, covered in an inch of white powder. I pointed the fob at it and sighed, relieved, when the car chirped, its parking lights flashing.

"The gate's open." The tow driver strode back to his office.

I opened one of the SUV's passenger doors to wedge the cat carrier between the seats and froze.

My sister's vest lay neatly folded on the back seat.

Hand shaking, I reached out and stroked its soft faux fur.

"You okay?" Joe asked.

I blinked rapidly. "Sarah's vest. I thought I'd left it in the house..." *Had I returned it to the car?*

But I hadn't returned my flashlight to the SUV. I'd brought that upstairs to my bedroom. I wouldn't have left the vest in the car. It had been cold that night, starting to snow...

"I don't understand," I muttered.

Joe shrugged. "I always thought she looked like a guinea pig in that vest."

I glared. "She did not."

He grinned. "Sarah would have approved of your little adventure, I think. And I guess..." He gazed across the lot of towed cars. "I guess I wanted to know the truth about her accident too."

Little adventure? I grimaced. But my son's tone hadn't been *that* patronizing. "At some point, you will realize that older can *occasionally* mean wiser."

Joe rolled his eyes. "Sure, Mom."

All right. I might have deserved that. Nothing I'd done since Sarah's death had been wise. But it had been necessary.

I scraped snow off the windows, and we climbed into the SUV. I started the car and pulled forward, toward the chain-link gate. The burly tow truck driver jogged from his office and waved us down.

I rolled down the window. "Yes?"

"Sorry. I forgot, there's a new discount that started the day of your tow. I'll take ten percent off your charge."

"Thanks," I said. "Do I need to do anything?"

"No. I got it." He stepped away from the car and waved me on.

"Huh," Joe said. "Lucky."

"Mm." I smiled.

We drove to a modest, pet-friendly hotel. I settled Trouble in my room.

Joe gave me a skeptical look. "He could have stayed in the car. It's not like he's wanting for anything." He motioned toward the blanket and water in the carrier.

"Trouble's a special cat." I still wasn't sure how much of what I'd seen in the passage that night had been real. But I'd seen *something.* Trouble's Middle World persona? There was a lot I still had to learn.

Joe shook his head. "If you say so. Who's this guy we're meeting?"

"Sam. I think you'll like him." At least, I hoped he would.

Joe and I drove to a restaurant overlooking the lake and cruised through the packed parking lot. A Lexus backed from a spot beside the restaurant's front door, and I pulled in after it.

"Did you ever find out why Sarah was in Tahoe so early?" Joe asked.

"We may never know," I lied. "And knowing won't change anything."

We crunched through the snow. I stopped at a newspaper box and pulled out a local freebie.

DRAGON HOUSE FIRE ACCIDENTAL

The South Lake Tahoe fire department responded to a fire at Dragon House around 1 AM Saturday morning.

Investigators have determined that the fire was accidental, starting in the first-floor kitchen and sparked by a frayed electrical cord. When the fire reached the grand staircase, the staircase acted as a chimney and the fire spread rapidly throughout the house, which was empty at the time.

Dragon House is considered a total loss.

I grimaced. *That damn coffeepot.* I'd told Tobin to get rid of it.

"You should have invited me along," Joe complained. "I could have helped, you know."

I rolled my eyes right back at him. "Who said I was a crazy lady obsessed with luck?"

"You quit your job and sold your home for a piece of parchment. Why didn't you tell me what you were really doing?"

I touched his wrist. "I should have. I'm sorry."

He blinked. "Oh. Okay."

"But I'm not sorry I quit my job." And I wasn't going back. I'd find something new that had a sensible forty-hour week. I reached for the restaurant door's wooden handle.

"There's something I need to tell you," Joe said.

"What?" I dropped my hand.

He hesitated. "He's got a new girlfriend."

Joe didn't have to say who *he* was. My sister's husband. I sighed. "He's not our business."

"But—"

"He has his own path to follow, and we have ours. Forget him."

"He ruined her life," Joe said hotly. "He probably drove her out onto that road. She was probably running away from *him*."

I shook my head. "All we can do is hope he finds enlightenment."

"Are you kidding me?"

I quirked a smile. "I hear the process is damned painful."

We walked inside the restaurant. The carpet was red, and the wood was dark.

I stopped by the hostess stand, where a young woman and a man with a tag that read MANAGER consulted a reservation book.

I looked around. Sam waved from a table near the window. Behind him, snow frosted the pilings and coated the nearby pier. I pointed and met the hostess's brown-eyed gaze. "We—"

"You're our millionth customer." The hostess smiled broadly. "Congratulations!"

"Wow," I said. "Cool. Congratulations to you on a million customers."

"Do we win a million bucks?" Joe asked.

"No." The manager laughed. He stepped around the hostess stand to shake my hand. "The meal for you and your friend's on us."

"Thanks," I said. "But we're with him." I pointed at Sam.

"Whoever's at your table's included," the manager said. "Mind if I take your picture?"

"Go right ahead." I looped my arm around Joe's waist and posed.

He snapped the photo. "Perfect. Your server will get your email if you like, and we'll send you a copy."

Joe and I needed more photos of us together. "Thanks," I said. "I'd love one." We moved into the restaurant.

"Discounts, magically appearing parking spots, and now a free meal?" Joe said. "What gives?"

"I seem to be on a lucky streak," I said mildly.

We made our way through the red-clothed tables to Sam's. I sat beside Sam. Joe gave me an odd look and sat opposite.

"This is Sam Mägi," I said. "He's a professor of archaeomythology."

Joe blinked. "A what-the-what?"

"Archaeomythology," I said serenely and laid my hand atop Sam's.

My son lifted an eyebrow. "And you're... friends?"

"For now," Sam said.

My cheeks warmed. Sam and I were more than friends. Much more since the fire. But we'd decided to take things slow, if slow meant meeting each other's relatives. I was having dinner with Sam's sister's family next week.

"But you have a real job?" Joe pointed a finger. "Archaeowhatsit is a real thing?"

"I've even got tenure," Sam said and named the university.

"He also saved my life," I said.

"Then I guess I've got no objections." Joe looked at me, at Sam, then back again. "That is what this lunch is about, isn't it?"

"Partly," I admitted. At my age, I didn't need anyone's approval. But after everything we'd come through, I wanted Joe's. My son deserved that.

And I wanted... I wanted what Joe and Sarah had had. I wanted that ease, that closeness. And I wouldn't have it if Joe and Sam were at odds.

Not that I thought they would be. Sam understood the importance of family.

"What... *luck* finding you here." Riga appeared beside Joe's chair. One corner of her mouth lifted. "Or coincidence?"

"I thought you didn't believe in coincidence." I motioned toward the empty chair. "Join us."

"I will." She unbelted her safari jacket. Shrugging out of it, she slung it over the back of the chair beside my son. She sat and adjusted the collar of her white blouse.

"Joe, this is Riga Hayworth. She's a metaphysical detective."

My son's forehead wrinkled. "A metaphysical... What has happened to you? Archaeomythwhatzits and metaphysical detectives? Have you been possessed by Aunt Sarah?"

"Unlikely," Riga said. "I'm fairly certain she's moved on."

I thought so too, and I smiled.

Joe frowned. "I wasn't—"

The manager appeared with menus and took our drink orders. Riga declined, saying she wouldn't be staying for lunch. The manager departed.

"What do you want to tell us?" Sam asked her.

"The sheriff's department has been unable to locate the Luck Scroll," she said. "It appears to have been lost in the fire."

"How odd," I said steadily, "since it wasn't in the fire. As I told the sheriff, it was in the passage beneath the temple." Which meant either the cops had it, or someone had gotten to the bugout bag before them. "Not that it matters to me. I sold my portion. I have no claim on the scroll."

"And there are no copies of your sketches or notes?" Riga asked.

I didn't respond. My electronic notebook had been lost in the fire. Fortunately, it had auto-backed up to the cloud. I had everything I needed. But she didn't need to know that.

Joe looked from Riga to me and pushed back his chair. "This seems like a good time to find the bathroom." He rose and ambled through the tables.

"What did you do with the scroll?" Sam asked her.

She laced her fingers across her blouse. "It's best if the Brotherhood thinks it's gone."

"But it isn't," I said. "What *did* you do with it?"

"It's best if the Brotherhood thinks it's gone," she repeated.

So, she *had* taken the scroll. "And August? If his demon-virus was on my notebook, does he have all my notes?" I fiddled with the fork lying on my folded, red-cloth napkin.

"August is under arrest for interfering with a murder investigation. The police don't like it when videos are faked to cover for a killer. You don't have to worry about that."

I frowned. "But he could have sent everything to his employers before his arrest." It all seemed so unreal. Occultists. Mafioso. A Luck Scroll. My mouth twisted. *Little adventure, indeed.*

"The Brotherhood is more of a membership than employer-employee relationship," Riga said. "But it appears August didn't get a chance to send on your notes."

"Appears?" Sam asked sharply. "Just how dangerous is this group?"

"They have influence," she said. "It's best not to be on their radar."

"That's not what I was asking," he said.

Riga sat up and braced her elbows on the red tablecloth. "You're asking if Brandy's in danger. The answer is, I don't know. I hope she isn't." She met my gaze. "But I think your interest in bending luck should stay private."

"My interest is over," I said.

"Is it?" Riga gazed at me shrewdly. "Because if you started playing the lottery, the Brotherhood might notice."

"I have no plans to buy lottery tickets."

"Why would she?" Sam asked. "The odds of winning are so remote..." His blue eyes narrowed. "A strange thing happened earlier. I didn't have a reservation, but someone had just called and canceled, so I was able to get this table for four."

"How lucky." Shifting the utensils off the crimson cloth, I plucked the napkin from the table and unfurled it in my lap.

Riga's lips flattened. "I don't know how you're doing it—"

I widened my eyes. "Doing what?"

"I read that scroll," she said. "I saw the acrostic. Become obedient to Fortuna, get in the flow, and luck will flow with you. But something else has happened here. You've changed."

I looked down at the empty plate. I *had* changed. I'd let Sarah go, and I'd let go of my anger toward her husband as well.

The thought of Sarah still saddened me. She'd had so much more life to live. But the desperate ache of loss was gone. And the night of the fire she'd come to me in a dream.

We'd talked. I'd told her things I hadn't had a chance to. She'd told me things that had surprised me.

And she *had* fled her house after an argument with her husband. That's why she'd been on that highway.

But she didn't blame her husband, and neither did I. Not anymore.

Like Sarah had said, it was all love.

And I knew now that the people I'd seen in my dreams weren't subconscious wish fulfillment. They were more.

I lowered my voice. "I'm not sure. Ever since that night, my luck has turned. I got an upgrade at my hotel. I got a new key fob in record time. I think..." I looked up and met her gaze. "I don't know what to think. But you're right, I've changed. And it's been a long time coming. I think... I think a big part of it was your emails—the Mystery School's I mean."

Riga muttered a curse. "Those stupid emails."

"Why are they stupid?" I asked, surprised. "They were helpful. Aren't they yours?"

She clawed a hand through her auburn hair. "Not entirely. Look, just... don't abuse your power, and don't be obvious about it."

"I would never abuse it," I said, indignant. "I won't use luck to take advantage of anyone."

"What emails?" Sam asked. "Abuse what?"

"It's a long story, and Joe's returning to the table." Riga stood. "But I'm sure Brandy will explain better than I could."

Joe emerged from a hallway on the other side of the restaurant. How had she known he'd...? I shook my head. *Never mind.* Maybe not every mystery needed explaining or exploring.

Sam captured my hand on my thigh and squeezed lightly. I beamed in response, my heart swelling. Sam and I would have a long time together to explore ours.

It was all love, after all.

***

You can get all the worksheets from the Mystery School in one downloadable PDF HERE.

SCAN ME

NOTE FROM KIRSTEN

THE RIPLEY SCROLL IS real and depicts through symbols the alchemical process of creating the philosopher's stone. All the world has now are 16th and 17th-century copies of it.

The Luck Scroll is wholly of my own invention, though I had to hire an artist, Articult, for the sketches. I have no talent for drawing.

I tried to use medieval images for luck in the scoll images, but explaining them all in the story would have bogged it down. The stylized rose (seen in the Caduceus and Labyrinth images) represented the wheel of fortune in medieval churches.

The labyrinth represents a journey of self-discovery and spiritual transformation. Within the context of the scroll, it symbolizes the process of navigating challenges and uncertainties to reach a state of alignment with luck.

The sun and moon were important alchemical symbols, representing (respectively) masculine and feminine energies, as well as the active and receptive principles. In the scroll, they represent the balance between regular proactive effort and passive receptivity in aligning with luck.

The ouroboros means a lot of things, but for the alchemists, it represented perfection, unity, and balance. It can also represent never ending cycles and repetition (and in its negative aspect, chasing your own tail).

Like the ouroboros, the caduceus symbolizes balance, but it's more about the balance of opposing forces. It also represents the patron of alchemy, Hermes Trismegistus, as well as representing transformation and healing.

I got the idea for Dragon House from Lake Tahoe's Vikingsholm, which I hiked down to every summer as a child with my family. Then, I found the stone castle disappointing. Its exterior seemed so much more magical than the interior. I expanded both in my mind to create Dragon House. I'm fairly certain there are no secret passages in Vikingsholm.

THE FOUR ELEMENTS

THE SPIRIT OF WATER
    Ethereal daughter
    Mercury's restless sea
    Pacified let thou be
    Emancipate thy dewy dros
    Release from myre that which was loste
    And thou shalt find Fortuna's fame
    Never speaking loud her name
    Cease thou now, thy fervent deeds
    Evene measure, fortune heeds
    Judge the nature of the aire
    Under skyes of clouds and faire
    Steadfast in winds' harsh embrace
    The man who wields this hath he grace
    In fortune's eyes and fortune's renne
    Cal the mone and claime the sunne
    Embrace thy fate wyth all thy breth
    Cast off your fear and flee not deth
    Obedient to fortune's charge
    Unerthe now thy ynnermost spark
    Rise as phoenix from the ashe
    And in sacred fyere thy soul must bathe
    God grant ye strength upon the erthe
    Endure the fiery furnace herth
    Prick thou now the green lion bryht
    Restore thyself in fortune's syght

Unerthe the Philosophre's stone
Descend thy airy mountain home
Ere thee succumb to fortune's blyght
Now seek within the inner lyht
Cast aside the shades of nyght
Else lost forever yet thou myght

AS ABOVE, SO BELOW

Lo, the above, immense and grant
   Reflects wythin concordant hand
   The inner man's tyne spark
   Brief echoes of the kosmos mark
   Align thy soul wyth woruldlic breath
   Surpass the bounds of divine depth
   For in the spheres' mirroured sea
   Lies the clew to destiny
   Seek not Fortuna's fleeting gold
   But in the Emerald Tablet's mould
   Fortuna arrays wyth those who see
   The firmament in harmony
   Sun mone and stars in clarity
   Reflect the soule's bryht charity
   And when thy spirit unerthes its place
   Fortuna smiles wyth gentile grace
   Let not dour shadows dim thy syght
   Clasp in thy arms both troth and lyght
   For sholde thou walk the vertuous pathe
   Fortuna's hande shal turn from wraethe

OUROBOROS

Behold thy serpent, wings spread wyde
  A cercle wrought, by every syde
  In its grene coils, Fortuna's flou
  Needs revolve for thine to growe
  In days of wo, in moments bryght
  The serpents turn, both day and nyght
  Seek ye the path of Fortuna's embrace
  If thy heart be opened wyth gentle grace
  Customes simple, rites of the wys
  Come to naught if in thy mynde
  Thou be not in soule and hande
  True to thy heart and to thy lande
  And in thy thoughts thou do refrain
  From ungentile acts, and ye shal gain
  Graynes of erthe and drops of dew
  Blessyngs in their essence trewe
  Thus seek ye Fortuna's tyde
  In ebb and flood, wyth Her abyde
  For if ye walk wyth heart unbarred
  Hennes fynd fortune in every part
  Unto all beneath the firmament
  Fortune favours the fortunate
  So fortunate let thou be
  In lyfe's perfect harmony.
  Embrace the cercle, hold it neer,
  In joy and sorow, love and fer.

For in the serpent's wynged dance,
Lyes the secret of lyfe's chance.

PHILOSOPHER'S STONE

Lo, TAKE YE NOW the quintessence
    And transmute that to its essence
    Elixir of lyfe yet ye distille
    Obedient to Fortuna's wille
    Lest lyke the mage of olden tyme
    Who sought Fortuna's gentler clyme
    Wyth offerings blyssed and customs dere
    Began his quest, released his feare
    And Fortuna's favor he dyd knowe
    Until in arrogance he dyd showe
    His pryde ryvall wyth humylite
    And his gred wrestle wyth charyte
    Losing favor in fortune's syght
    Did he feele ful destiny's blyght
    And lo beneath Fortuna's whele
    Did he receive the losse of wele

SUN AND MOON

OF THE SUNNE AND of the mone
   Take ye both, they both trowe
   Of diligent endeavor be
   And wyth candor thou shal see
   Knightly Sol we humbly begg
   Illumyne this mundane egge
   Wyth bold purpos charge to thy aim
   In dignity to fortune's clayme
   Luna, reflective orb so bryght
   Dancing through dredefull depthes of nyght
   Observe the world through knowing gaze
   Surrender to thy sylver wayes
   For the ballance must be founde
   Between heavens and the grounde
   From the wedding of mone and sunne
   Wyll fortune be in conjunccioun.

CADUCEUS

CLENSE THY VESSELL OF drosse and impurities
   Attune thy spirite wyth supernalle symphonies
   Lest in the divine ballance
   Fickle Hermes, god of chance
   Betwene seene and unseene realms
   Bestowes favoures for the ille
   So aline thyself wyth Holy will
   Ye shal fynd perfecte harmony stylle
   Hold the sacred caduceus hye
   Above the serpentes' wings devine
   Prudence holdes her gentille sway
   To her honoure thee must pray
   For Fortune favoures not the brave
   But to ascende from the darke grave
   Thee mouste make the grevous choice
   Of wysdom and counterpoise

LABYRINTH

WALK THE LABYRINTH, CHILDE of fate
   Wyth manner of rites be not too late
   Be not gulled by erthely twists and trials
   Be not diverted by Fate's cruel wiles
   Before the cock crow breaks the morne
   The egg shal crack and fortune borne
   And in the centre ye shal finde
   The treasure of philosopher's minde
   In thy soule's truth, Fortuna alines
   Wyth he who know to folowe her sygnes
   And in the stilnesse of the dawe
   Feares and tryalles shal all begon

BOOK CLUB QUESTIONS

- For the person who selected the book: What made you want to read *Shadow of the Witch*?

- What did you like about *Shadow of the Witch*?

- What didn't you like about the book?

- Is Brandy hallucinating or seeing something "real" when she sees odd things she can't explain?

- What does the luck scroll reveal about the nature of luck and fate?

- What level of gameplay are you playing at?

- How do you feel meaning is created in our lives?

- Why is gratitude important for April?

- Does Brandy deal with the changes in her life in a healthy way?

- How was the mystery school used to advance the themes in the book?

- Did the worksheets and images in the book add or detract from your enjoyment of the story?

- How did you feel about how the story was told? E.g., was it too fast? Too slow?

- Was there any line or passage that stood out to you?

- Have you read other books by Kirsten? How did they compare to this book?

- Which recurring themes did you notice throughout the book?

- How would this story change if it were told from Mitch's perspective?

- What did you think about the ending?

- How does this book compare to other mystery novels you've read?

- After reading *Legacy of the Witch*, would you read other books by Kirsten Weiss?

MORE KIRSTEN WEISS

THE DOYLE WITCH MYSTERIES

In a mountain town where magic lies hidden in its foundations and forests, three witchy sisters must master their powers and shatter a curse before it destroys them and the home they love.

This thrilling witch mystery series is perfect for fans of Annabel Chase, Adele Abbot, and Amanda Lee. If you love stories rich with packed with magic, mystery, and murder, you'll love the Witches of Doyle. Follow the magic with the Doyle Witch trilogy, starting with book 1, *Bound*.

The Mystery School Series

The Doyle Witches have created a mystery school, and a woman starting over becomes a student of magic and murder...

This metaphysical mystery series is perfect for readers who love a good page-turner as well as the deeper questions that accompany life's transitions. These empowering books come with their own oracle app, the UnTarot, plus downloadable mystery school worksheets. The Doyle Witch magic continues, starting with book 1, *Legacy of the Witch*.

The Perfectly Proper Paranormal Museum Mysteries

When highflying Maddie Kosloski is railroaded into managing her small-town's paranormal museum, she tells herself it's only temporary... until a corpse in the museum embroils her in murders past and present.

If you love quirky characters and cats with attitude, you'll love this laugh-out-loud cozy mystery series with a light paranormal twist. It's perfect for fans of Jana DeLeon, Laura Childs, and Juliet Blackwell. Start with book 1, *The Perfectly Proper Paranormal Museum*, and experience these charming wine-country whodunits today.

The Tea & Tarot Cozy Mysteries

Welcome to Beanblossom's Tea and Tarot, where each and every cozy mystery brews up hilarious trouble.

Abigail Beanblossom's dream of owning a tearoom is about to come true. She's got the lease, the start-up funds, and the recipes. But Abigail's out of a tearoom and into hot water when her realtor turns out to be a conman... and then turns up dead.

Take a whimsical journey with Abigail and her partner Hyperion through the seaside town of San Borromeo (patron saint of heartburn sufferers). And be sure to check out the easy tearoom recipes in the back of each book! Start the adventure with book 1, *Steeped in Murder*.

The Wits' End Cozy Mysteries

Cozy mysteries that are out of this world...

Running the best little UFO-themed B&B in the Sierras takes organization, breakfasting chops, and a talent for turning up trouble.

The truth is out there... Way out there in these hilarious whodunits. Start the series and beam up book 1, *At Wits' End*, today!

Pie Town Cozy Mysteries

When Val followed her fiancé to coastal San Nicholas, she had ambitions of starting a new life and a pie shop. One broken engagement later, at least her dream of opening a pie shop has come true.... Until one of her regulars keels over at the counter.

Welcome to Pie Town, where Val and pie-crust specialist Charlene are baking up hilarious trouble. Start this laugh-out-loud cozy mystery series with book 1, *The Quiche and the Dead*.

A Big Murder Mystery Series

Small Town. Big Murder.

The number one secret to my success as a bodyguard? Staying under the radar. But when a wildly public disaster blew up my career and reputation, it turned my perfect, solitary life upside down.

I thought my tiny hometown of Nowhere would be the ideal out-of-the-way refuge to wait out the media storm.

It wasn't.

My little brother had moved into a treehouse. The obscure mountain town had decided to attract tourists with the world's largest collection of big things... Yes, Nowhere now has the world's largest pizza cutter. And lawn flamingo. And ball of yarn...

And then I stumbled over a dead body.

All the evidence points to my brother being the bad guy. I may have been out of his life for a while—okay, five years—but I know he's no killer. Can I clear my brother before he becomes Nowhere's next Big Fatality?

A fast-paced and funny cozy mystery series, start with Big Shot.

The Riga Hayworth Paranormal Mysteries

Her gargoyle's got an attitude.

Her magic's on the blink.

Alchemy might be the cure... if Riga can survive long enough to puzzle out its mysteries.

All Riga wants is to solve her own personal mystery—how to rebuild her magical life. But her new talent for unearthing murder keeps getting in the way...

If you're looking for a magical page-turner with a complicated, 40-something heroine, read the paranormal mystery series that fans of Patricia Briggs and Ilona Andrews call AMAZING! Start your next adventure with book 1, *The Alchemical Detective*.

Sensibility Grey Steampunk Suspense

California Territory, 1848.

Steam-powered technology is still in its infancy.

Gold has been discovered, emptying the village of San Francisco of its male population.

And newly arrived immigrant, Englishwoman Sensibility Grey, is alone.

The territory may hold more dangers than Sensibility can manage. Pursued by government agents and a secret society, Sensibility must decipher her father's clockwork secrets, before time runs out.

If you love over-the-top characters, twisty mysteries, and complicated heroines, you'll love the Sensibility Grey series of steampunk suspense. Start this steampunk adventure with book 1, *Steam and Sensibility*.

CONNECT WITH KIRSTEN

Sign up for my newsletter and get a special digital prize pack for joining, including an exclusive Tea & Tarot novella, *Fortune Favors the Grave*.

https://kirstenweiss.com

Or maybe you'd like to chat with other whimsical mystery fans? Come join Kirsten's reader page on Facebook:

https://www.facebook.com/kirsten.weiss

Or... sign up for my read and review team on Booksprout:

https://booksprout.co/author/8142/kirsten-weiss

ABOUT THE AUTHOR

I BELIEVE IN FREE-WILL, and that we all can make a difference. I believe that beauty blossoms in the conscious life, particularly with friends, family, and strangers. I believe that genre fiction has become generic, and it doesn't have to be.

My current focus is my new Mystery School series, starting with *Legacy of the Witch*. Traditionally, women's fiction refers to fiction where a woman—usually in her midlife—is going through some sort of dramatic change. A lot of us do go through big transitions in midlife. We get divorced or remarried. The kids leave the nest. Our bodies change. The midlife crisis is real—though it manifests in different ways—as we look back on where we've been, where we're going, and the time we have left.

Now in my mid-fifties, I've spent more time thinking about the big "meaning of life" issues. It seemed like approaching those issues through witch fiction, and through a fictional mystery school, would be a fun and a useful way for me to work out some of these ideas in my own head—about change and letting go, faith and fear, and love and longing.

After growing up on a diet of Nancy Drew, Sherlock Holmes, and Agatha Christie, I've published over 60 mysteries—from cozies to supernatural suspense, as well as an experimental fiction book on Tarot. Spending over 20 years working overseas in international development, I learned that perception is not reality, and things are often not what they seem—for better or worse.

There isn't a winter holiday or a type of chocolate I don't love, and some of my best friends are fictional.

Sign up for my **newsletter** for exclusive stories and book updates. I also have a read-and-review tea via **Booksprout** and I'm looking for honest and thoughtful reviews! If you're interested, download the **Booksprout app**, follow me on Booksprout, and opt-in for email notifications.

BB bookbub.com/profile/kirsten-weiss

g goodreads.com/author/show/5346143.Kirsten_Weiss

f facebook.com/kirsten.weiss

instagram.com/kirstenweissauthor/

youtube.com/@KirstenWeiss-Writer?sub_confirmation=1

OTHER MISTERIO PRESS BOOKS

Please check out these other great *misterio press* series:
Karma's A Bitch: Pet Psychic Mysteries
by Shannon Esposito
Multiple Motives: Kate Huntington Mysteries
by Kassandra Lamb
The Metaphysical Detective: Riga Hayworth Paranormal
Mysteries
by Kirsten Weiss
Dangerous
and Unseemly: Concordia Wells Historical Mysteries
by K.B. Owen
Murder, Honey: Carol Sabala Mysteries
by Vinnie Hansen
Payback: Unintended Consequences Romantic Suspense
by Jessica Dale
Buried in the Dark: Frankie O'Farrell Mysteries
by Shannon Esposito
To Kill A Labrador: Marcia Banks and Buddy Cozy Mysteries
by Kassandra Lamb
Lethal Assumptions: C.o.P. on the Scene Mysteries
by Kassandra Lamb
Never
Sleep: Chronicles of a Lady Detective Historical Mysteries
by K.B. Owen
Bound: Witches of Doyle Cozy Mysteries
by Kirsten Weiss

At Wits' End Doyle Cozy Mysteries
by Kirsten Weiss
Steeped In Murder: Tea and Tarot Mysteries
by Kirsten Weiss
The Perfectly Proper Paranormal Museum Mysteries
by Kirsten Weiss
Big
Shot: The Big Murder Mysteries
by Kirsten Weiss
Steam and Sensibility: Sensibility Grey Steampunk Mysteries
by Kirsten Weiss
Full
Mortality: Nikki Latrelle Mysteries
by Sasscer Hill
ChainLinked: Moccasin Cove Mysteries
by Liz Boeger
Maui Widow Waltz: Islands of Aloha Mysteries
by JoAnn Bassett
Plus even more great mysteries/thrillers in the *misterio press* bookstore

Manufactured by Amazon.ca
Acheson, AB

31425418R00164